A South Star Book

Escaping The Rain

Nick Fletcher was born in Staffordshire, England in 1947, and was raised and educated in Shropshire. He trained as a journalist, working first as a crime reporter, later as a showbusiness writer. He won the Diversey Award for features journalism in 1984. His work has appeared in many national newspapers and in magazines as diverse as Knave and Company. He is also the author of three non-fiction books on antiques.

In 1999, his story Night Of The Seagull was shortlisted for the Phillip Good Memorial Prize and in 2000, another story, Just A Hat And High Heels, won an award from World Wide Writers Magazine. Both stories are included in this volume.

Nick Fletcher is married and lives in Staffordshire.

FOR CASSIE

NICK FLETCHER

ESCAPING THE RAIN

To Simon
best wishes
Nick Fletcher

★

South Star
London

A South Star Book

Published by
South Star Publishing
London W2 1BT

First published by South Star 2000
ISBN 0-9538635-0-6

Printed in England
by Johnsons of Nantwich Ltd
CW5 5AP

Cover photography: GUY HALEY

Author's Note

For advice and/or encouragement I am indebted to:
Malcolm Baylis, Neil Bonner, Jane Hammersley, Jon Harper, Mike Justice, Huw Thomas, David Whittaker and in Hollywood, USA to G.Lynd Bingham and Gary Sears.

For counsel beyond the call of duty I am grateful to Mark Slack and I also wish to acknowledge my deep gratitude to my editor, Miranda Le Croissette.

N.F.

Contents

Just A Hat And High Heels

It was about four in the afternoon when the call came through, and less than an hour later when I knew I'd need a girl who was prepared to take off her clothes in public. The voice on the telephone was, as usual, curiously disembodied, as if resident in the ether.

The tone was businesslike, to the point where you felt that economy of word was regarded as a virtue.

"I have another task for you," said Blickstein. It irritated me when he used that word, as if I was his personal slave rather than a freelance hired because he lacked my inventive skills. But then I couldn't see Blickstein ever admitting to that. We had never met, but I imagined him to be in his forties, fat, balding, and cold enough to be totally friendless.

"I prefer to call it a project," I cut in before he could continue.

"Of course you do," he said with oily condescension. "The details are on the way by courier and should be with you shortly."

"What's the time-frame?"

"One in the afternoon, Thursday."

"Day after tomorrow Thursday?"

"Yes."

"Short notice is expensive."

"Short notice rates will apply."

I knew they would but I wanted to hear him say it, just on the off-chance that it might annoy him. Nothing annoyed him, which annoyed me. He hung up without saying goodbye. That annoyed me too. I hate bad manners.

Twenty minutes later a motorcycle courier delivered the details. Although they amounted to only eleven typewritten lines on unheaded paper and three photographs, they were pompously titled 'Client Briefing', and I prefaced the word Blickstein with one that had six letters less.

It was a straightforward project, just needed a touch of imagination. The idea came to mind immediately, as it was one

I'd had filed away until the right circumstances occurred. Forward planning is the key to business success. Surprising how often people forget that.

In view of the tight deadline I decided I would need a girl to help out. However, locating a girl willing to walk naked across a street in Knightsbridge on a Thursday lunchtime was going to be the problem.

"I know what you mean," said Reuben when I told him. "Thursdays are just so busy."

I had to wait while he finished laughing at his own wit before I could get him to put his vast experience of naked women to the test.

The experience came entirely from spending as much time as he could manage in lap-dancing clubs. That was the only way Reuben was ever going to see a girl naked given that he weighed 280 pounds, had a front tooth missing and didn't use deodorant. But he did have money, and he spent lots of it tucking tenners into sequinned costumes that you could hide under a watch.

Rueben recommended a girl who danced at a new club, called Wholly Angels, in one of those Soho alleys.

"She could trap a Trappist monk," he said. "Or should that be untrap him?"

His whining laughter turned into a coughing fit, and I had to buy him a brandy before he could provide more specific information. His description of her - tall, blonde and very leggy - could have applied to half the lap-dancers in London, but he did add: "She has tits like rocket nose-cones," which I suppose he thought might narrow it down.

Her name, he recalled, was Faye.

As soon as I left Reuben I took a taxi to the club.

A doorman in a smart dark green suit and matching bow-tie - yet unshaven - did his very best to be dislikable.

"You're wasting your time, pal," he said dismissively. "The girls don't see no one."

"I just want you to give a note to Faye," I told him. "And this note," - I gave him £20 - "is for your trouble."

He became almost imperceptibly more friendly, and took the sealed envelope from me.

"I'll see she gets it, but you're wasting your time. She don't see no one."

He shrugged uncaringly and went inside the club, through black-glass doors that revealed just the reflection of a man standing awkwardly and looking lost. It was me.

My note to Faye said I was an agent, that I'd seen her act, that she was right for a project I was casting, and I would be in the Wickham cafe opposite the club at eight, table by the window. Enclosed was £500 in new £50 notes "to cover your time."

It was far too much, so I knew she'd turn up. I knew she would be on time too. When serious money is involved you always get punctuality.

Sure enough, at one minute to eight she walked in and came straight over to where I said I'd be waiting.

Reuben was right. She was a babe. She would have stopped a train if the driver had so much as glimpsed her.

At least six feet six in stilettos, she had layered gold-blonde hair that was almost to her waist and which swayed fetchingly as she walked. She wore a black two-piece suit, the skirt just knee-length, the jacket with a nipped-in waist. It was unfastened, revealing a white silky shirt, which though loose-fitting failed to disguise breasts that were so perfect they had to be implants. You couldn't get that much projection without help from a surgeon .

Her make-up was light and flawless, her eyes clear and pale grey. She wore no jewellery, not even earrings.

Before sliding into the seat opposite, she looked me over in a rather desultory manner. My suit was Armani, and I hoped she would notice. Every sign of credibility counts.

"You must be Whitney," she said, as a statement rather than a question.

"That's right," I said, giving a restrained smile.

"Can I get you a drink?"

"Iced tea, " she said. I passed on the order to the waiter and asked him to bring me a black coffee.

"What's your angle?" she asked, blunt as could be. "Your note said you were an agent. Is that true?"

Her voice reminded me a little of Lauren Bacall. You know, deep and honeyed. But while Bacall's voice had feeling, this girl's was flat and weary.

"It's true," I said.

"True or not, I don't do any personal services, no one-to-ones. Clear?"

The waiter put down the drinks so I paused until he moved away. I was still trying to get a fix on her, discover how receptive she might be.

"I don't want anything personal," I told her. "In fact, quite the opposite. I want something very public. I'm a publicity agent and I need a strikingly beautiful girl for a special project. You have the perfect physical attributes."

"Perfect for what?" she said. I suppose these girls get a little cynical.

"Perfect for creating a lot of publicity," I said. "I'll level with you. The job requires you to walk across a busy street completely naked. "

No immediate reaction. She was looking at me hard, still treating every word with the suspicion of experience.

"If I didn't know you weren't kidding I'd ask if you were kidding," she said, starting to get up. "The answer is no. Showing my attributes, as you call them, in a club is one thing, but naked in a street? No way. Thanks for the tea."

"It pays exceptionally well," I said. "You'd be surprised how exceptionally well. In fact, you'd need to be sitting down when you hear how well it pays."

That got to her.

"Try me," she said, settling back in her seat.

"It pays three thousand pounds in cash, in advance, and that's on top of the £500 fee you got to meet me here."

"Let me get this absolutely straight," she said. Suddenly, she was focussed. She edged forward in her seat, elbows on the table, fingers twirling in discernible nervous excitement. "You give me all that money to walk naked across a street. That's it - the whole thing?"

"Not completely naked. I want you to wear just a hat and high heels."

"This time you must be kidding!"

I grinned and shook my head. "It has to look classy, elegant. The hat and shoes are just the right finishing touch."

"What colour is the hat?"

"Does it matter?"

She sighed so nicely, but it was in exasperation.

"Of course it matters! How else will I choose my shoes?"

It's surprising what is important to some people. I'm asking her to walk naked in public and she wants to ensure she's colour co-ordinated! With dyed blonde hair she should worry! I give her another £100 and tell her to buy her own hat.

The deal was done. I knew it would be. I find it an invariable rule of life that too much money is never refused. I slipped the envelope containing three grand across the table, and after glancing at the contents she slipped it inside her coat.

"There could be other benefits too," I added. "This is going at attract sensational publicity. You'll be in the newspapers, magazines, probably the TV talk shows. It is going to be the biggest publicity stunt of the year."

"TV?" she said. "Really?"

"Guaranteed," I said.

In ten minutes I gave her a precise briefing, vagued my way around a few questions she threw at me, including exactly what it was we were publicising, and we parted.

I watched her walk away. You have to watch a girl like that.

It was Thursday. At a quarter to one I was at the location. At five to one she arrived, and stood under the coppery canopy of the Montport Hotel. I was across the street, near Luigi's Restaurant. She wasn't expecting to meet me - I'd told her it was going to be a hidden camera shoot and I'd be with the crew.

Even dressed she was attracting a little attention.

Her black satiny coat was calf-length and belted tight at the waist. The broad-brimmed hat was a muted red, which the milliner probably described as crushed strawberry.

Her stilletos were black. Red hat, red shoes?

Obviously not.

Men nearby were giving her the eye, and doubtless undressing her. I found it darkly amusing that, in minutes, they would really see her naked.

I saw her glance at her watch. It was two minutes to one.

At one precisely, she stepped forward from the shade of the awning above the entrance to the Montport and into the bright, bouncing sunlight. In a swift fluent movement she slipped the belt, opened the coat and let it fall from her shoulders. Head up, eyes fixed, she stepped to the edge of the pavement.

A taxi rear-ended a stretch Mercedes that had jerked to a stop to let her pass. The street was busy and shouts and whistles were being triggered and then car horns started blaring. There was more crunching of metal and shattered glass, and around Luigi's diners were getting to their feet, shouting, pointing, elbowing, climbing on chairs. "She's naked," I heard someone cry. "Christ, she's naked."

There was much jostling as guys vied for a better view, and

even I found it difficult to look away. She walked with that dancers' walk, short strides, lots of hip swing and those computer-designed breasts moving up and down in perfect unison. Her languid pace, as instructed, and tall stature gave her a certain haughty appearance, enhanced by that magnificent hat.

A big, whooping crowd had quickly formed on both sides of the street. By now she was halfway across, and the cars had parted like a metal version of the Red Sea to let her pass. The rising swell of excitement was verging on mayhem. It had all gone to plan, and I turned away to carry out my part of the project, my route open and unhindered behind the crowd.

At 4.30 I got the city edition, and sure enough on the front page there was a picture of the girl crossing the street, back view, snapped by some enterprising tourist who had sold the print. The caption said the girl had been arrested.

But it was not that story I was looking for. Splashed big though it was, there were bigger headlines above it.

It seemed that a man named as Gabriel Mancini, finance director at the London headquarters of the global Nataku Mura Corporation, had been shot once in the head at close range with a silenced gun as he lunched at Luigi's Restaurant.

The killing had taken place just one day before he was due to give evidence for the prosecution in a fraud trial involving several of the firm's senior executives alleged to have embezzled £40 million.

No one, it seemed, had seen the assassin.

A Date To Remember

September 10th, 1967. It is a date I have never forgotten because it is the date Russell stole Patricia from me. It was very deftly done, and he didn't even have to try too hard but merely take advantage of a situation which presented itself.

The day had started well enough, cloudless and warm, and with so much for me to look forward to. It was to be my first date with Patricia. We were 14, school friends for years, but now both at that compelling transitional stage when the forming of a relationship with someone of the opposite sex became monumentally important.

So, finally, I gathered together enough confidence to ask Patricia if she would go with me to the Saturday matinee at the cinema. It was a significant move. In those days we all knew that a date at the cinema was a prelude to a special, mutually exclusive relationship which had various benefits, such as kissing.

The film was Double Trouble, starring Elvis Presley, and I thought Patricia liked Elvis. At least I'd heard her mention him. She said yes right away when I mumbled the invitation, and my heart began pounding in a way it had never done before.

Patricia was tall and leggy and had short-cut blonde hair, and a few freckles which gave her a mischievous, tomboyish look. She had large blue eyes and a wide flashing white smile, and I had only recently realised I adored her.

For years I had taken her for granted. Our parents were friends and so we saw a lot of each other as we were growing up, but she was always just someone to play games with. It wasn't until the last couple of months that I had started to notice her. I mean really notice her. As a girl.

She was well known in our neighbourhood, whizzing around on a bright candy-pink bicycle, a cheery yell to everyone she met. Other boys were beginning to notice her too and I knew it wouldn't be long before they started asking her out, and I suppose that's what pushed me into making the move. And she had accepted! I thought she might not. Even at 14 I was aware that wavy red hair and black-framed glasses were not visual assets, though not as aware as I would be a few years later.

The film was due to start at 2.15 on that Saturday afternoon and we had agreed to meet outside the Grosvenor Cinema at 2pm. By noon I was ready, my wayward hair heavily slicked down with water and the collar of my new suede coat turned up to emulate the tough look older boys created in their leather jackets. Every couple of minutes I re-combed my hair, or checked for spots.

I had brushed my teeth seven times.

For me, it was just a five-minute walk to the cinema. Patricia lived on the other side of town, which is why we had agreed to meet outside the Grosvenor. It was a small, single-level cinema with a cream-painted Roman-style facade. More importantly, it had double seats on the back two rows, with no dividing arm-rest.

At 1.45 I was walking around the living-room in circles, so keyed-up that my mother - who had guessed the significance of the occasion - told me to calm down. "You're like a coiled spring," she said, trying to sound severe, but smiling at me.

Then the telephone rang. My father answered. "What!" I heard him say. "How serious?" There was more one-sided staccato conversation and my father put down the telephone.

"Ruth has been taken ill," he told mother, who had rushed in from the kitchen. "They think it's a stroke. It's bad. She may not pull through. We must go to the hospital right away."

"Give her my love," I said, but I could tell from my father's warning face that there was no escape.

"But I'm meeting Patricia," I protested.

"You can see her another time," he said. "Your aunt's in hospital and you'd rather see a film than visit her? Don't be so selfish."

"But I said I'd meet Patricia there," I insisted. I can't let her know."

My mother intervened. "The Grosvenor is only a couple of minutes away. We're leaving now so we'll stop off and you can tell her what's happened."

I felt immediately better, less panic-stricken, though far from happy. It wasn't fair. I'd never much liked aunt Ruth anyway. She always kissed me when I visited and left lipstick on my face. And her breath smelled.

Father stopped our new two-tone cream and blue Triumph

Herald outside the cinema and told me to be quick. I could see Patricia with a cluster of other people on the wide flecked-marble steps. She was wearing a sleeveless cornflower blue dress and white slip-on shoes. Her arms and legs were a deep even brown from a long summer of bike-riding and tennis. She was beautiful. I just wanted to be sitting next to her on a double seat in the darkness, holding hands and whispering.

"I can't come," I blurted. "My aunt's been taken to hospital. We have to go see her. I'm sorry. I'm sorry."

"It's all right," she said, touching my arm in reassurance. "Of course you must go."

Then Russell stepped forward. He was another school friend, not close, but someone I often played cricket with. He had been standing near enough to hear what I'd said and he quickly volunteered himself as stand-in. "I'll keep you company if you like," he said to Patricia. He spoke to her as if I wasn't there.

"Oh. Well, yes. All right," she said, glancing at me. "You don't mind, do you?"

Her wide eyes stared questioningly at me and there was no way I could say that I minded very much indeed.

"No, I don't mind," I heard myself saying.

"That's settled then," said Russell, taking her arm. "We'd better go in. It'll be starting soon."

I don't know what happened on that late-summer afternoon almost thirty years ago, in the dim and covert atmosphere of the Grosvenor cinema, but the next week, when I asked Patricia out, she smiled only briefly and said she had a busy few days ahead and wouldn't have any spare time. The following week it was another excuse and when, desperate, I persisted a third time she told me she couldn't, honestly, because she was now seeing Russell and it wouldn't be fair, would it?

I nodded my understanding as if it was all of no consequence and walked away. You can't show yourself up, can you? And in any case, what had happened had happened and was irreversible.

Over the next few years I heard a lot about Patricia, though when we met by chance we never did more than wave or just say hello. Patricia really blossomed, as I knew she would. She won several local beauty pageants and then the regional heat of some Miss Britain contest. Her photograph was often in the newspapers. Usually, she was bikini-clad, full-breasted and with a pouting smile. Yet despite the provocative poses, her eyes still seemed to hold the same innocence as that breathless day when she said she would meet me at the cinema. It was September 10th, 1967.

Russell went out with her for just three or four years, then they split up, so I heard. I don't know why, but the reason didn't matter. He'd been with her, held her, kissed her. Seen her naked. Had sex with her.

It should have been me doing all those things. I hated Russell and I hated aunt Ruth, who, against the odds, had made a near-complete recovery.

When she was about 20 Patricia left the area. According to the local newspaper, she was "pursuing her modelling career in London." She never became famous and I never heard of her again. I suppose she met someone, married, had children. I lost touch with Russell too. He submerged into suburbia, I suppose.

My life went much the way I expected after the loss of Patricia. I became more withdrawn, and a strange sense of hopelessness seemed to pervade. What small confidence I had as a schoolboy had faded. I came to realise that my ungainly appearance and that loathsome red hair were socially unacceptable to the female population, or at least all the girls I encountered. There were a few awkward attempts with other girls, but nothing lasted. None of them came even close to Patricia, anyway. By my early thirties, with receding hair, dumpy physique and pebble-thick glasses I knew inescapably that I was destined for eternal bachelor status. Youthful hopes of a blissful life with a pretty wife and kids and dogs had been dashed, right from the very day Russell took Patricia from me.

I was certain, unshakably certain, that had Patricia and I been able to fulfil our date, my life would have turned out so differently. Hardly a day passed without some little thing reminding me of what might have been.

A young girl flashing by on a bicycle, a short blonde haircut bobbing in a crowd of shoppers. The memories of Patricia never faded.

Yet, in other ways, things did go well. After school I took a job at an estate agency, and eventually became a partner. Then old aunt Ruth finally died and - big surprise - left me not only her large old rectory but lots of stocks and shares and almost a whole street of terraced houses which she rented out. A couple of years later I sold them to a development company, and did well enough to semi-retire while still in my forties.

It meant I could indulge in gardening and watching sport.

Sport was the reason that, today, I was having a satellite TV system installed. With the BBC gradually losing most of the major sports, satellite was the only way to go if you wanted to see the big events.

The retailer who supplied the equipment was sending someone round to install it and fit the aerial, or dish, as he called it. He was due at 10am, and at about ten past a white van came up the drive. It stopped outside the widow and I knew immediately it was Russell.

On the side of the van in bold letters was the name Russell Q. Gibbs, and one glance at the driver confirmed it. There could be only one Russell Q. Gibbs. The Q was for Quentin. He was very proud of that Q, even at school. The rest of us had middle names like Mark and Robert and Paul, and thus mundane initials. But Russell had to have a Q, and he emblazoned it on his books, essays, even on his satchel.

At school he was tall for his age, had jet-black hair combed directly back, and bold bushy eyebrows which seemed to emphasise his customary indolent stare. All these years later he was much the same. He hadn't put on weight, hadn't lost his hair and it was still as dark as ever. I reminded myself that he would be arrogant enough to dye it.

He showed no sign of recognition when I opened the door, but then why should he? I bore no resemblance to my teenage appearance.

"Mr Williams?" His voice hadn't changed either. It was as if I had last heard it only yesterday. The perfunctory tone and disinterested expression rolled back the years to the very moment outside the cinema when he effectively dismissed me and took Patricia.

"I'll get my ladders and make a start," he said, and walked back to his van.

I stood in the hallway, quite still, quite calm, yet with just one single thought surging through my mind.

Coincidence was not an acceptable explanation for this remarkable reunion. No. Fate had clearly delivered Russell to me, three decades on, for a purpose.

I was in no doubt about it and I knew exactly what that

purpose was. I had no need to debate its wisdom, no need for even the briefest hesitancy. I was being presented with an opportunity to even the score, to pay Russell back for snatching away my golden dream. But what price the lonely years, the ruined life?

I strode outside and looked up towards the roof. Aunt Ruth's old house was a three-storey Georgian rectory set in two acres, shrouded by trees and not overlooked by neighbours. Russell was near the top of a three-section aluminium extending ladder about 20 feet up, a length of cable dangling from his left hand and a tool of some kind in his right. He was leaning inward against the ladder for support and balance.

I grabbed the ladder with both hands and jerked it violently, twisting it to the side. There was a short surprised cry, and I saw Russell falling headlong.

I looked away as he hit the flagstones. It was enough to hear the impact, though the thud was much more muted than I anticipated.

Russell was lying on his side, in almost a foetal position, facing me. His head was partly crushed, and dark-red blood was spreading around it. His eyes were wide open and staring at me. I walked over and knelt beside him. If he wasn't dead, he was close to it, and either way it didn't matter because I wouldn't be calling an ambulance for quite a while.

After all, I would tell them when they came, I'd left him to get on with the job, telling him to give me a shout when he'd finished. I'd been over in the greenhouse, doing some repotting. It was almost an hour later that I began to think the job seemed to be taking a long time, and went to see how he was getting on. And there I found him, at the bottom of the ladder. Obviously, I'd no idea how it happened. He must have just slipped or perhaps overbalanced.

I studied Russell. Though he was absolutely still, and didn't seem to be breathing, I thought I saw just a flicker of movement in his eyes. I fancied I could detect just a trace of complete bewilderment though, of course, it was hard to be certain.

I don't know whether or not he could hear me in those final seconds of his dying, but I told him anyway.

"September 10th, 1967," I said softly, and then went back into the house to make a cup of coffee.

Losing Lysette

It was early Friday afternoon, and I was putting some clothes into an overnight bag ready for a trip up to Malibu. I'd reserved my usual room at a small motel I knew, just off the highway, with views out towards Zuma Beach. Tough week, and I needed the break.

The phone rang and it was Warren. It sounded like he was sobbing. I'm not mistaken. He's crying so much that he's gasping for breath. Eventually, he manages to tell me that Lysette has left him. I can't say I was surprised. I knew they were wrong for each other the moment he introduced me to her. She was a scatty underweight graphic artist who had lived for a while in a commune in Westwood village. Warren was third assistant accountant at a freight company. It was no match, yet they really seemed taken with each other when they met at Vincent's party.

I remember Warren cleaving through the jostle of drinkers and dancers, towing her behind in his haste to show her off to me. She was tall and thin, virtually flat-chested, and wearing a short orange dress with a diamante sprinkle on the shoulders and bright orange lipstick. Her hair looked hard and bleachy. It seemed to have been cut too short and was now growing out. But she had flashing indigo eyes, and the kind of facial bone structure you see on billboard models.

"This is Lysette," he told me triumphantly, rather as if he's won her as a prize. "Isn't she wonderful?"

"Jeff Bruce," I said, introducing myself and shaking her bony hand. I noticed her fingernails were also bright orange. She said nothing, just twitched the corners of her mouth in a half-smile. Then he whisked her away, giving her a grand tour of all his friends. I'd never seen him so taken with a girl so much or so quickly.

I could see it was a disaster looming. It had been a year or so since he and Donna had split, only a month before their wedding. I was never sure why. They didn't fight, they seemed happy enough. But one day he got home to find all her clothes gone and his Alfa Spider missing. There was the usual I-need-some-space note, and the car was found a couple of days later in an alley in Echo Park. My guess is she met up with someone and took off. It happens.

Warren took it bad, but not as bad as he was taking it now. He was still crying in that peculiar way men cry, loud and whoopy. He kept repeating: "She's gone, she's gone." I decided I'd best get over there.

"I'm on my way," I told him. "Just hang in there. I'm leaving right now."

The drive over to his apartment in West Hollywood took about thirty minutes. It was a hot sullen afternoon, airless and hazy. I knew I'd rather be heading out of LA on the Pacific Coast Highway to the fresh, feathery breeze of Malibu, not threading through a slow-flowing contamination of cars and trucks to wet-nurse Warren. I guess that's what friends are for.

I was worried about Warren. I knew he was stuck on Lysette but, even so, I was more shocked than surprised when they got married a couple of months back. I'd seen it coming. His eyes had become cloudy with the vitiate of love. He had become doting and sickeningly attentive to her. Sometimes I could tell it irritated her, but mostly she gave the impression she liked being worshipped.

From what I could gather she had been burned by a few bad experiences in the past, and so while Warren may not have been her ideal type I guess she appreciated him being a genuine guy. "He's given me real stability," I heard her tell someone.

She had become clingy, clutching his arm a lot when they were out. Her favourite phrase was "Isn't Warren just great." She used it so often I once challenged her about it, when he was out of earshot of course.

"Exactly what is it that's so great about Warren?" I asked innocently. Her hesitancy was damning. She stumbled uncertainly from one cliche to another, until her voice tailed off embarrassingly, and she knew I'd caught her out.

Once I went out with them to a trendy diner, down along the Santa Monica beach front, on a late summers night. It was supposed to be a foursome but Kelly, a girl I was seeing at the time, was called in to work at the last minute. Rather than call the night off we went as a threesome. It was revealing to see them together.

No matter how much they pawed at each other, or kissed as

often as high school sweethearts, to me they just looked a wrong couple. She was too shockwave for him.

Warren was the conventional type, if you know what I mean. Neat short hair, clothes from a discount store. He dressed exactly like the third assistant accountant would do, even away from the office. And it wasn't just the way he dressed. He was too regular, too routine. Each morning he went running for exactly 20 minutes. He always took his lunch at 12.30 precisely, was back at his desk at 1.30 precisely. He even wore his neckties in pre-arranged rotation. Can you believe that?

Lysette dressed as if she walked into a closet blindfold and took a random choice. Extreme colour clashes were frequent. Clothes at opposite ends of the price scale were put together with so little regard that I began to think it was intentional, just to grab more attention. One day I saw her with a black satiny Versace jacket, 20-doller Levis and old scuffed shoes. She carried it off though. I thought she looked pretty good.

The night we were in Santa Monica was the first night I got to know much about her. She was 22, had an arts degree from UCLA, and worked in a studio in Century City designing movie posters.

"Did you see the billboards for Alligator Valley?" she asked. "That one was mine." I hadn't seen it, but I told her it was sensational. She seemed pleased.

I found her really difficult to get to know. She was so scatterbrained she couldn't stay on any topic long enough for it to develop. But there was an edgy quality to her character, a ricocheting unpredictability that kept you attentive. I thought she was everything Warren didn't need, and couldn't appreciate. I figured he was rebounding from Donna. In the year since she left he had not started up any serious relationship, not even tried.

I'd dragged him out enough times to cruise the bars on the Strip. "This just isn't me," he kept complaining. "I don't like the kind of girl you go for. They all look like wannabe actresses."

He said he wanted someone just like Donna, but Lysette was nothing like Donna. No way. In fact, she was more like a wannabe actress. She was already half in the movie business anyway.

It was that night in Santa Monica that he asked her to marry him. I was there. I heard the whole thing. We were wandering along the beach, and the waves were slapping in with a lazy muffled rhythm. It was a warm and clear night with a full moon in the east, making the sand look like a fresh fall of snow. I was a pace or two behind them as they skipped hand in hand, whispering and laughing. I saw Warren give her a half-turn spin and kiss her full on the lips. He glanced back towards me and said: "I love this girl. I really love her."

Then, to my astonishment - and I think Lysette was pretty shocked too - he dropped to one knee and, with measured seriousness that verged on absurdity, he said: "Lysette, you're all a man could ever want. I'm so lucky to have found you. Please will you do me the honour of marrying me."

I remember the words exactly. It was so corny he must have stolen the lines from an old movie. I was watching Lysette's face, and I think at first she was going to laugh. Then I guess she saw him, pale in the moonlight, looking up at her like some whimpering begging puppy you couldn't kick away. I was wondering how she was going to get around to saying no without hurting him, but then she said quietly: "Yes. Yes I will."

Even her voice sounded surprised that she had said it.

Warren leapt to his feet, threw his arms around her and swung her in a circle three or four times. He tried to do the same to me, but I wasn't as easy to pick up and we collapsed on the sand, hollering and hugging and back-slapping.

"You have to be best man," he said, and I was. They married just three weeks later in a small white-washed Art Deco-style church down in Pacific Palisades.

Lysette had chosen it. She had a lot of arty friends down there. It was just as well. She had been orphaned when only six years old, and no relatives attended. She said she had lost touch. Instead, the church was packed with artists, actors, designers and writers, many eclectically dressed. I was expecting Lysette to be wearing something wild and way out, but she was quite demure in a short simple lacy white dress, and white camellias pinned in her hair. I had to admit she looked terrific.

Warren was as excited as a third assistant accountant allows himself to be at a public event. He fawned around Lysette, and in his speech praised her so much that the guests were shifting uncomfortably in their seats, unsure where to look. Lysette just fixed her smile.

None of this idolising behaviour from Warren was surprising. He was like that with Donna. Everything she wanted she got without effort. Maybe it became boring for her. Certainly when Warren bonded, he bonded big. He used friends - and especially women - as monuments to his emotional needs. I'd known him three or four years, and he hooked into me real fast when it became evident we got along. Some people kept him at a distance, a little uneasy with his cloying ways. I didn't much mind. I'd never had many close friends myself.

Since I moved to LA I'd drifted around from one copywriting agency to another, while working on my screenplay at night. Everyone is working on a screenplay in LA. Ask any waitress in a diner, any guy working the valet parking, even the grocery delivery boy. They've all got a screenplay. You just hope that one day you get an opportunity to pitch it. Even then, it's a long shot. A guy I know in Pasedena has pitched seven screenplays - good ones, I've read them - and come up with nothing. I'm still trying to hustle my first ten-minute slot with a producer. It'll come to nothing when it happens, but I need it to happen to get it out of the way. Then I feel I've started for real.

Warren lived on Holloway Drive, in a small Spanish-style stucco-fronted three-storey apartment building, well-covered with fast growing ivy and a couple of sentry palms out front.

I pulled up behind his black BMW convertible.

Funny. That was how we met, at a gas station, both of us in identical black BMWs. We started joking, then got some beers. Sure, he wasn't strictly on my level, but an OK guy. He was even a little in awe that I was a writer, even just a copywriter. I liked having him around. He made me feel I was somebody.

When Warren opened the door he had a bottle of Jack Daniels in his hand, though he hadn't consumed much of it. Still weepy, with red-watery eyes and down-mouth expression, he was still in his suit, though he had taken off his tie. He'd left early for the weekend and come back to find the same kind of note Donna had left. He had no idea where Lysette was. What girlfriends she had were scattered all over town, and the few whose numbers he knew claimed they hadn't seen her all week.

Slumping heavily into a chrome and leather armchair, he ran his hands through his short cropped hair as if it were long and untidy. "We were so happy, " he said, his voice low and strangely detached. "We were so, so happy. Why has she done this to me?"

"Who knows why women do anything," I said. "That's the reason we're crazy about them. If we understood them, all the fun would be gone."

I was trying to sound optimistic. "I bet she'll be back in a day or so. Maybe you had a fight and she's just trying to teach you a lesson."

"We never fight," he said, angry in his defensiveness. "We've never even raised our voices the whole time we've been together."

Bad sign, I thought. I couldn't see Lysette liking that level of tranquillity. There was an underlying feisty streak in her, and once or twice I had seen it skim perilously close to the surface, times when Warren's sheer ordinariness rasped. I didn't think she liked to always have to hold back on everything. Maybe she had come to realise that opting for safety, security and a genuine nice guy was stifling her natural spirit. Still, it had been her choice.

I made some coffee in the big oversize blue and white cups they bought from an antique shop up in Carmel on honeymoon. It wasn't until after I poured the coffee that I realised the cups were an inappropriate choice, but Warren didn't seem to notice. He was calmer now. My presence had helped settle him, though I felt I was of little use. He kept repeating: "I've lost her," between sips of coffee, dazed like a small child baffled by a turn of events beyond its undeveloped comprehension.

His hands were shaking as he put down the cup, slopping coffee onto the glass-topped table. "I must find her, I must explain," he insisted.

"Explain what? You haven't done anything from what you say."

"I want to tell her I love her, tell her I'll do anything she wants."

"You did whatever she wanted anyway. You couldn't have given her any more."

Warren seemed to have stopped listening, lost to his own thoughts. Then he leapt from the chair.

"Let's go look for her!" There was uncontrollable excitement in his voice and a sudden shine to his eyes.

"Where do we start?" I asked scathingly. "There's a city of four million out there, and that assumes she's still in the city. I suppose you tried her office?" It was so obvious he might have overlooked it.

"That's the strange thing. They said she quit her job a week ago. Said she was going back East. No forwarding address. Why would she say that? She wasn't from the East."

"How do you know? You hardly know anything about her."

His excitement had evaporated faster than it came. Now he was sky-diving into black self-pity. He began to cry again, this time low and whimpery. I felt awkward. A girl cries, you put your arm around her. A guy cries, you stand by the window and pretend you haven't noticed.

"I can't go on without her," he moaned between gulping sobs. "She was my whole life. Now it's finished."

Okay, the guy is hurting and I'm doing what I can. But this pathetic mewing is beginning to get to me. Maybe I should try to snap him out of it.

"For Christ's sake, Warren, have you heard yourself!"

I raised my voice in feigned exasperation. "You sound like someone in a shitty TV movie. So she's gone. Well, maybe she'll be back, but if not there are a million other girls. Start over."

Warren swept his cup from the table in a burst of unfettered rage, sending it spinning across the bleached teak floor. The coffee splashes hovered on the polished surface like thick black oil.

"I don't want anyone else! There can never be anyone else!" He slammed his fist onto the table. He was mad, and I backed off the snap-out-of-it plan.

"Okay, okay," I said, waving him back to his chair. "I shouldn't have said that. I'm sorry. I know what she means to you."

"I don't think you do!" His tone still had a spasm of anger, and a need to convince me of the depth of his feelings for Lysette.

"Right from the start, she was the one," he said. "You were there, at Vincent's party. You saw it. Next day I took her to lunch at The Ivy on Robertson Boulevard. Know why I chose that place? I chose it because it was so romantic, all those adobe walls and open fires and lots of antiques. You need just the right atmosphere when you're dating someone so special. And boy, was she special!"

He was looking at me as if expecting some kind of reassurance, so I nodded dutifully like a good friend does in such a situation, and said: "Sure. She was great, just great."

Warren almost smiled. The nostalgia trip was easing the pain, at least for the moment. "We'd agreed to meet there, and I was at the table when she arrived. When she sat down, I saw her hands were trembling. She was nervous! Can you believe that? Nervous of meeting me. I'm dating a goddess and she's the one who's nervous!"

She was no goddess but I let it pass. They say talking through a problem is therapy, and Warren was much less frenetic now. I sat back and let him continue to reminisce. He began to relate other incidents from their apparently idyllic life together. The picnics at Topanga Park, the people-watching afternoons at Venice Beach. Meeting for cappuccino and donuts at Alfredo's. Browsing the bookstores on Applewood Drive.

Picnics? Bookstores? Lysette? None of this undemanding, sugar-frosted lifestyle was Lysette. I hadn't had too many deep conversations with her. None in fact. But I knew from discarded clues that this wasn't what she wanted. Sometimes I'd seen her squeeze a bored expression into a sweet fraudulent smile. Often, especially of late, I'd noticed her about to speak, perhaps challenge whatever Warren might be saying, then change her mind and remain silent, or seamlessly acquiesce. The signs were marshalling. Warren was too ... well, I suppose ordinary is the word... too ordinary for her. I knew that from the start. In the early days I almost got around to telling him that over a beer at the Ranchwood bar, where we sometimes hung out. He was so enraptured by her, talking about her incessantly, that in the end there seemed no point. Maybe it wasn't up to me to tell him. It's the kind of thing that you have to find out for yourself.

For what it was worth my assessment was that below her shiny unrippled surface she was wild, but had had a few bad experiences and was now trying tame for a while. Sooner or later, she would realise tame was a state which didn't suit her, but meantime she was resting up.

Warren wasn't her kind of guy, but I knew the kind who were. I saw them in bars all over town. Lean, steel-muscled, and with that hard ruthless charm that women always say they found out about too late. I don't think so. They see it right away, but feel they can deal with it. Women just go for that type of guy, believe me. They just can't stop themselves.

One night I recall Lysette sitting on the window seat in their apartment. I'd been invited to dinner and Warren was cooking pasta, calling to us now and then from the kitchen. Lysette was perched on some large Aztec-weave cushions, arms circled around her knees and staring out across the speckled tangle of city lights towards the last defiant remnant of the setting sun.

There was just a pink-washed gash along the edge of the darkening sky. Her hair was pulled away from her face, tied in bunches. She reminded me of a wistful little girl, yearning for something lost, something precious.

"You're looking thoughtful," I said gently, but she didn't hear. I repeated it louder and she was startled, reacting to just the sound, not hearing what I'd said.

She clicked on the instant smile and said: "Sorry. I'm ignoring you. Whatever must you think."

"Forget it," I said easily. "I often get lost in my own thoughts. Sometimes, it's the only thing that keeps you sane in this town. Want to know my daydream?"

Her washed-out face showed a mere flicker of casual interest, but her eyes were lit with unnatural intensity.

I lowered my voice, not because I didn't want Warren to hear, but because it added an edge of drama to the moment. "Promise you won't tell? Not even Warren."

"I promise." She came over and sat on the floor in front of me, tucking her bare feet under her.

"Well, I dream I'm up at my favourite spot at Malibu. It's late at night, it's warm, and the waves are charging in like a stampede of big white horses. The beach is empty, totally deserted. I'm running along the sand, straight and fast. My hair's streaming back, my fists are pounding the air, my heart is bursting. I feel good, kind of spiritual. I've never ever felt so free. And you know what? I'm completely naked."

She hadn't expected that last part, and she cupped her hand over her mouth in exaggerated astonishment.

She smiled, but her eyes were becoming distant. I knew then with unshakable certainty that she understood what I'd been saying.

This was one of those times I guess she knew she was being caged by normality. Sure, the cage was nice, and she had helped build it herself. But every day with Warren added another bar, another lock. I saw it was all closing in on her, maybe clearer than she did.

Then Warren came in to ask about the wine and she got to her feet to get glasses. I guess that was the nearest I ever got to real communication with her, and even then she'd said hardly a word. I remember thinking that within her some sort of suppressed struggle was taking place, with jagged instincts tearing her in opposite directions. Part of me wished I could help, but I knew it was best to leave it alone. She had to choose her own path, and when to take it.

Now, just weeks later, it seemed that time had come.

I found Warren was at my side, hauling me from my chair, insisting we go to a bar he knew on Sunset where he recalled some of Lysette's artist friends often gathered. "They may know something," he said. "It's all I've got."

He clearly needed a straw to clutch at, and this one was as good as any. And I thought a few beers might help too. I drove him down to Rondo's. Lysette wasn't there of course, nor any of her friends. At least none Warren could recognise, and as I knew hardly any of her friends I couldn't help much either. We sat on tall chrome-legged stools with cold Millers, and hoped the world would soon start to look better.

Every beacon of bleached blonde flashing through the fusing colours in the swirling crowd started Warren on a soaring arc of hope that seconds later ended in a plummet of despair.

"Do you know what it's like to lose someone, I mean really lose someone?" he said. "It's like bereavement, like they've died. Then you feel you're dying. All the feeling starts to drain from you. You get numb. Your stomach twists into a knot and then locks up."

"Have another beer," I insisted. Sooner he was drunk, sooner he'd stop this morose self-analysis.

"I feel my whole future has been wiped out. Its all blank, nowhere to go. She was it. She was my future."

"Lighten up," I told him. "OK, its a bad day, the worst. But you'll deal with it, believe me. I've been there. Hurts like hell for a few days, then you start over. And who knows, maybe tomorrow the heartless bitch will be back."

"Don't you go calling her a bitch." He lunged at me, a limp half-meant punch which slipped by me, cannoning a bottle across the bar top and smashing the glass of a big tall guy drinking alone, the macho kind, mean look, narrow eyes, less brain than a Louisiana hillbilly.

Was this guy riled? He was up on his feet and reaching for Warren, but I stepped between them and thrust a 20-dollar bill in his face. "Let it go, buddy," I said. "He's had too much. We're outa here."

The big guy snatched the bill, gave Warren a warning glare and hauled his 230 lbs back on his stool. I caught hold of Warren and dragged him towards the door. He'd started to protest, and tried heading back until he realised his legs were giving up on him. I guess he'd had eight or ten beers, and I figured he'd be getting sleepy pretty soon. Warren never could take his liquor. Some guys got belligerent, Warren got drowsy. I was cool. I'd just sipped at mine, leaving mostly full bottles on the bar.

Outside, I eased Warren into the car and fastened his seat belt. As I closed the door, he slumped onto it, his face distorting against the glass, lip curled higher than Elvis. The freeway was quiet. It started to rain, light misty stuff which silvered the surface and gave the tyres a soft hum like a lover's murmur. I gunned the car hard, the needle on a hundred. I knew the speed cops didn't like to get wet.

Warren's legs just about held out long enough for me to get him into the apartment. Half-supporting him I lowered him onto his bed, the big double bed with a frieze of zoo animals carved across the oak top rail. I recall he and Lysette buying it a while back from one of those junky antique shops down on Beverly Boulevard. He was sliding into sleep by the second, his arm flopping limply over the edge. He was murmuring again. "I've lost her.. lost her."

"It's OK Buddy, its OK," I said. "You'll feel better tomorrow. I gotta go now."

I looked at my watch. It was already nine and I still had the long drive to Malibu ahead of me. I had the promise of the hot wind feathering the sand, the pounding crash of galloping white horses. And Lysette waiting for me with a careless smile framed by bright orange lipstick.

Black Confetti

I should have told her right at the start. The opportunity was there as soon as the invitation arrived. But I just couldn't do it, not right then. I needed time to think. Right there, right then, it seemed too big a thing to tell, too big for someone not under obligation to understand.

That was the problem. The obligation. Without it I could have said no. But it was there, and I couldn't ignore it. For a while afterwards I thought of ways to side-step it. But, if all those years ago Robbie McLaren had side-stepped, I wouldn't be here now, and Alison would be married to someone else.

I should have told her at the time. Looking back, it was the right thing to do, to have trusted her to understand. If you can't trust a wife of 25 years to understand, maybe she's not who you think is she is.

Perhaps I'm not who she thinks I am. Either way I didn't tell her. I just felt there was a risk she wouldn't comprehend it. She could be like that sometimes, not on such big issues, mind you. But then we hadn't had to face any big issues really, and that was what concerned me. She had come close to not understanding one or two minor matters - that bit of horseplay with Marion, for instance, or spending more on a new car than I promised - and this was something much, much bigger. There was no way of predicting how she might react. I wanted to tell her, of course I did. We hadn't had any secrets throughout our marriage, well, any to speak of. We'd been very happy. Yet I'd always felt that even the happiest relationship is always teetering on the brink, just waiting for the slightest push to send it over the edge. How often do you hear of an idyllic marriage being wrecked because of a some minor infidelity, for instance. In my case, infidelity wasn't the problem. I wish it were, really, because at least something like that can be explained, if not excused. You can say you were stupid, or lead on, or drunk. But obligation is hard to explain to someone not there when it was bonded, when the seal is set for a lifetime whatever happens afterwards. It was an inescapable fact that I owed Robbie

McLaren.

Robbie's invitation had lain on the breakfast table for some minutes, leaning against the marmalade jar, facing me, its gold script containing barely thirty words yet plunging me headlong down a chasm to my past.

"That looks like an invitation."

Alison's voice pulled me back to the moment, and to the lie. Well, not the lie, just the absence of truth.

"It's a wedding invitation," I said. There was no point in hiding it. I would have to go, because Robbie was calling in his debt.

"Oh good," she said. "It's been ages since we've been to a wedding. Someone from the office?"

That's when I should have told her. Yes, she would have been shocked. Incredulous perhaps. But the damage-limitation would have been easier. I can see that now. But now, of course, the damage has been done, though to what extent is uncertain.

"No," I said, perhaps too lightly. "Someone you don't know. An old friend who I haven't seen for years. Can't think how he even found our address."

How had Robbie tracked me down? I knew what had happened to him, obviously. But how did he know about me? And about Alison? For the invitation card bore her name too.

I put those queries aside, concentrating on finding exactly the right words to avoid a lie yet erase a part of the truth. She reached forward and picked up the invitation. "It's only three weeks away," she said. "I shall have to start to think what to wear, and whether to get a new hat."

"No need for you to come, really," I said. "You don't him. You won't know anyone there." It was worth a try, but I knew the reply before it came.

"Of course I shall come. It will be nice to meet one of your old friends. In any case, you know how I love weddings."

So it was settled. Less than three weeks to break it to her. It was just a question of when. It needed the right moment, the right phrases. It needed presenting in the best possible light. Except there wasn't a best possible light. How could there be?

"When did you last see this Robbie?"

"It must be thirty years or more." I knew exactly how long it was. Thirty two years and seven months. You don't forget the date that something like that happens. "He's also enclosed a letter. Doesn't say much, but he does ask me to be his best man."

"How nice. But why would he ask someone he hasn't seen for 30 years to be best man."

"I don't think he has many friends," I said. That would certainly be true. "Besides, I think he's asked me because I owe him a favour."

Alison's quizzical expression over the top of her glasses told me she wanted more.

"Robbie and I were at school together, best friends. He was an only child, so was I. We were almost like brothers. One day, when I was 12, we were on our way home from from school. It was winter and very cold. There had been a hard frost for several days. The lane passed by a lake, or perhaps it was just a very big pond. Anyway, it seemed vast to us at that age. It was frozen - frozen solid, we believed.

"I was sliding on the ice when I heard a crack, like a muted gunshot, and in a second I went through. There was no one else around at the time, just me and Robbie.

The cold was incredible. I was virtually paralysed with shock and fear, and all I could do was cling to the edge of the ice, my head barely above the water. My hands were numb in seconds and I kept slipping off. Robbie slid out to me, flat on his stomach, spreading his weight, and got hold of my collar. He couldn't lift me out, but he did keep me from going under. All the time he was yelling for help. He held me up for 20 minutes, shouting himself hoarse. His fingers were freezing to me, but he wouldn't give up. He was crying with the pain in his hands. All the time, he kept saying: "Don't worry, I won't let you go. I won't let you go.

"Eventually, some passing workmen heard his shouts and pulled me out. Robbie saved my life. Simple as that. It's something you never forget."

Alison had been watching me with fascination, listening like a child, imagining that bleak winter landscape and the terror of two small boys.

"What a wonderful story," she said, almost reverently when I'd concluded. That's when I should have told her.

I can see that now.

It was a difficult journey to plan, not much motorway and a crisscross of B-roads cutting through to the Welsh border. Even so, the drive had taken much less time than we had allowed, and we arrived almost an hour early. It was too late by then, of course. Several times I tried to build myself up to telling her, just as I had done during the past three weeks. But the more the days passed, the harder it became. She would have been upset, and angry. She would have demanded to know why I hadn't told her right at the beginning, when the invitation came, so that she could have refused. Then I would have reminded her that I had suggested that she shouldn't come, that it was my way of trying to protect her, save her from all the upset. Then she would ...what's it matter? I didn't tell her. And even if I had told her, she would have never sanctioned me going, anyway. She would have forbid it, cried incessantly. I never could bear seeing her crying. I learned it was always easier to avoid the difficult situations, not make waves. That's why we'd been so happy for so many years.

The church was tiny, barely able to hold 50 people. It was greyish-stone, irregularly constructed as if put up a century before by amateur builders. The pitched slate roof was topped by a spire, if you could call it that, just three or four feet high, housing a single bell. There was a centre door slightly sheltered by an open-fronted timber porch, and down each side of the rough stone walls were three plain-glass sash-type windows, obviously meant for use in a house. In the back wall there was one tall thin stained glass panel perhaps six feet by two, giving an immediate symbolic presence to a building which otherwise could have been mistaken for a cow shed. Indeed, there was an adjoining farmyard, with rusting machinery and a muddy red tractor and trailer visible over the low wall that fringed the church. It was an odd, misplaced structure, lost in nowhere. The windows were streaked and dirty, a piece of iron guttering hung loose from its bracket. The grass was neglected, shrubs were encroaching. The sense of abandonment was stark.

Alison was certain we were at the wrong venue, but the directions had been clear, and the location confirmed by a man cutting a hedge at the bottom of the lane.

I opened the bleached oak door and saw immediately this was not a derelict church. The whitewashed walls were vivid with the yellow, mauve and lilac shades of summer flowers, hung in bunches down both sides. More flowers decorated the ends of the plain pine pews, tied in delicate posies. The rough-plaster walls, exposed splintery beams and worn board-floor spoke silently of simple basic faith. This little, forgotten church comprised just one single room, and it was completely empty.

"What a lovely setting," breathed Alison, hardly daring to hear her own voice in the stillness. "I feel quite humble."

We went outside again to see if anyone else had arrived, but the lane was still deserted. Alison started to wander among the leaning, lichened gravestones scattered randomly around the church, and I followed. From behind one tall stone monument, smoke was drifting.

We both seemed to notice it at the same moment, and walked around the front of it to find a man sitting on the gravestone, smoking a cigarette.

It was the vicar, his white collar almost gleaming above a cheap, creased grey suit. He was middle-aged, balding with wispy bits of uncombed white hair. His cheeks were flushed red, possibly because he was embarrassed at being found using a grave as a seat. He leapt up, throwing the cigarette to the ground and stamping on it.

"You've caught me out and no mistake," he said, glancing at his watch. "I didn't think you'd be here yet."

"We had a long journey and allowed too much time," explained Alison, shaking his hand. "I don't suppose it will be long before other guests start arriving."

The vicar appeared oddly perplexed, narrowing his eyes and squinting hard at Alison. "Other guests? There are no other guests. Just you."

For just a moment he had a slight doubt, for he quickly added: "You are Mr and Mrs Mannering?"

"Yes," said Alision, before I could say anything. "What do you mean, we're the only guests? You can't have a wedding with just two guests!"

The vicar was uncomfortable, uncertain. He had expected her to know, and he was looking at me trying to gauge if I knew. I think he could tell from my unease, and silence, that I did.

"You must know the background," he told her. "Otherwise, why else would you be here?"

She stared at me, bewilderment shading her face. She knew I'd held something back, something significant. Her anger was developing the way it always did, with stealth and a cold heart.

She turned back to the vicar, her voice razored with over-emphasis. "No, I am not aware of the background, so please tell me. It is obvious my husband has no intention of enlightening me."

I nodded to the vicar. He seemed relieved to get my prompt,

and sat down again on the edge of the gravestone, this time uncaring about whether or not it was inappropriate. I stood by, wishing I had told her. Wishing I wasn't there.

"It's hard to know where to start," said the vicar. "I suppose if there were any other guests they would have come just to throw black confetti. After what Robbie and Pauline did, such hatred is quite understandable. I've known Robbie for many, many years and even I, as a man of God, cannot begin to explain it."

"Explain what?" shrilled Alison. "Explain what?"

Lighting up another cigarette, the vicar took two or three long pulls and slowly let the blue smoke drift from his mouth.

"Just over thirty years ago, when Robbie and Pauline were both fifteen and still at school, they were very much in love with each other. At first, no one paid much attention. Teenage love comes and goes. It's part of adolescence. But when it became clear to Pauline's parents that the relationship was serious, obsessively serious, they intervened. For one thing, her parents were very wealthy - her father was a surgeon, I believe - and frankly, they felt their only daughter could do better. Robbie's parents were also opposed to the relationship, though for different reasons. They thought Pauline's parents were, as I think they put it, "too stuck up and above themselves." From their point of view it was Robbie who could do better.

"Both sets of parents tried gentle, then more intense, persuasion to break the relationship, but Robbie and Pauline not only defied the warning but flaunted their love, even saying they intended to elope when they were sixteen, in a few months time. This threat alarmed Pauline's parents in particular. They forbade the girl to ever see Robbie again. She was kept virtually a prisoner in her room, and arrangements were put in hand for her to move to a boarding school outside the area. Yet somehow the two youngsters met in secret and, from what came out later, made a pact. A truly dreadful pact."

At this point, the vicar needed another cigarette. He fumbled in his jacket for the packet, then for his matches. Alison never once looked at me.

"That night - the night of the pact - they embarked upon the most extraordinary mission, one which appears to have had a double purpose. It was meant to demonstrate the depth of their love and, at the same time, remove the obstacles to its development.

"Each gave the other a key to their respective homes. At a pre-arranged time, around 2am it turned out, each left their home to go to the others. They lived about a mile apart. Halfway, they met and, from what they said later, exchanged one single kiss but not a single word.

"Robbie let himself into Pauline's home. He walked into her parent's bedroom and, taking a hammer from his coat, smashed their skulls while they slept. At virtually the same time, over at Robbie's house, Pauline was killing his parents in precisely the same manner."

I was watching Alison intently. Her eyes were wide, her lips slightly parted, spellbound in horror. "Oh my God," she whispered. "Oh my God."

Although she had turned to look towards me, she seemed to be staring past me into the distance. "I remember it now. I was still at school but it was in all the papers and on the TV news. The love-struck killers, they were called."

It seemed she was just saying her thoughts rather than speaking to me.

"They were called many other names too," said the vicar. "Believe me, that was one of the more polite. The media was all over the case once they were caught. They didn't get far. They were picked up the next day on a ferry to Ireland. At the trial the judge said that in view of their ages they should be detained indefinitely. For the past thirty years they've been in prison. Pauline was released a few months ago, Robbie quite recently. The first thing they wanted to do was get married. They truly believe they are destined for each other. And their love has certainly endured.

"I met Robbie in prison. I was the chaplain at Winson Green. I suggested they marry while still serving their sentences, but they refused. Their love demanded a proper church wedding, they insisted. And so here we are."

Standing up, he dusted down his suit and checked his watch. "They'll be here in a few minutes. They've been staying at a local hotel."

"How did Robbie find me? I never visited or wrote to him." Despite everything else on my mind, it was one of those idiosyncratic things I just had to know.

"Private investigator. Robbie said it was important for them to have someone at the ceremony who knew them, who would witness the fulfilment of their love. They knew no relatives would attend - the killings had split both families - and they didn't want anyone from prison. They felt it would taint the occasion. But Robbie said he knew if he could find you, you would come. He said there was a special bond between you, that you were the only person he knew would come. I know he will be delighted you're here, and delighted to meet your wife, too."

"Then he's in for a disappointment." Alison's tone was alien, harsh with revulsion and condemnation. She hit me hard in the face, not a slap, a full punch, slamming knuckle-hard into my cheekbone. "How could you," she said flatly. "How could you bring me to the wedding of two murderers?"

I was about to say something, probably beginning with: "I meant to tell you...", but she was holding out her hand.

"Give me the keys," she demanded. "I shall wait in the car."

There was no point in trying to dissuade her. There were no words for what I wanted to say. Truly, I hadn't meant for her to be there under false pretences. I had intended to tell her before we arrived. Truly? Was I really being truthful with myself? My inability to reveal the malignant background horror may have been a sign that I realised it was something that would come between us, cast too dark a shadow.

The vicar had been watching with keen interest, though choosing not to intervene. I had the feeling this was not the only blow he had seen struck at a wedding. As I handed Alison the keys, he merely shrugged.

"Understandable," he said affably. "Quite understandable."

Alison walked away, an upright figure seeming to be fading from a fervid and fragmenting landscape. A certain fidgeting tension remained and, perhaps to ease it, the vicar started to tell me how he had become a friend to Robbie while being the prison chaplain.

"Let's face it. I'm probably the only clergyman in the country who would officiate today. Why do you think we are at such a remote location? If the media knew, they would be like a pack of wolves. The public outrage would be immense. While this event is scarcely at the Hyndley and Brady level of frenzy, it would still generate national hysteria, and the media would help it all they could."

At the gateway to the church an immaculate ivory Daimler pulled up, its fluted chromium grille glinting like a yawning smile. A tall, stone-faced chauffeur got out and walked around to open the passenger door with elaborate dignity. Robbie stepped out first, looking older than I imagined, and with cropped receding grey hair. His dark blue double breasted suit looked expensive, probably hired.

Pauline, who I remembered as a slim, quiet girl with straight dark hair was still slim and still dark haired, though it was now cut in a short rather manly style.

Her eyes were steady and uncurious as she looked directly at me. Her dress was dazzling white, long-sleeved and quite low-cut. There was no veil, no train, just a hoop of tiny flowers in her hair.

They each thanked me for coming, making no comment about the bizarre circumstances. I explained Alison was unwell and staying in the car. They knew what I really meant, but expressed concern anyway.

The ceremony took 25 minutes. In his address the vicar made no mention of past events but made a number of references to repentance and the forgiveness of sins. There were two hymns, and with just the four of us singing unaccompanied the atmosphere was discomforting and forced. There was a Bible reading, and the vicar recited an extract from a love poem by Elizabeth Barrett Browning, chosen by the bride.

During the ceremony the sun broke through and streamed into the church, creating parallelograms of radiant light which picked out the vivid colours of the flower clusters lined along the aisle. Robbie and Pauline had a rim-lit aura as they exchanged vows in firm, positive voices. On cue, I handed over the plain gold band Robbie had given me earlier and the chauffeur was called in to sign as a witness. Then it was all over.

Yet I knew at that moment that, really, it would never be over. It's repercussions had already started to ripple.

Outside, Pauline lightly kissed my cheek. For the first time I saw her eyes up close. They were fired with unnatural energy and unrestrained delight. Robbie shook hands, firmly and longer than I liked. "Someone who knew us had to be here," he said. "Someone had to see how nothing has changed, how our love has survived the separation, how we are still the couple we always were."

While my presence clearly had some unfathomable symbolism to him, made some statement, significant only to their distorted perspective, I did nothing to prolong the event. I uttered a few stilted pleasantries, my eyes pebble-dead. The Daimler moved off, tyres whisking up clouds of fine brown earthy dust as if intending to obscure their departure.

The vicar had already lit another cigarette. I think he was glad it was over too. He was drawing in the smoke in rapid, staccato gulps, needing to get to the nicotine fast.

I got in the car and drove off down the narrow lane, waiting for Alison to speak first so that I could tailor my explanations. But she never said a word. And once the silence set in, I just couldn't bring myself to start the conversation. Frequently on the way home I glanced across at her, but her face was always turned away, as if there was something compelling to see out of the side-window. I noticed she was sitting awkwardly, on the furthest edge of her seat, shoulder hard against the door. She wanted to be as far away from me as possible.

Night Of The Seagull

27 August 1994

She had been crying, and crying a lot. There were still bursts of sobbing every couple of minutes, and her eyes were so wet I could see them glisten in the street lights even though I was across the road from where she stood. Two friends fussed around her, touching, hugging and murmuring what I imagined were reassurances.

It was none of my business. They were just kids on holiday, and from the occasional half-sentence I could hear it seemed the one who was crying had earlier in the evening been dumped by her boyfriend. I say kids, though I suppose they were all about sixteen or seventeen. At that age, it's all end of the world stuff. The scars of teenage love cut right down to the soul.

I sat on the edge of the low wall in front of the cafe. St. Ives was always the same at this time of year, jammed tight with a heaving mass of sun-burned flesh and offensively-coloured clothes. It had acquired a cultish reputation as a paradise for the young, stemming maybe from the surfing boom of the Sixties, and thus attracted thousands of teenagers, many of them on their first holiday away from their parents. I preferred the town out of season when, though seldom quiet, it had a less frenetic air about it. Of course, the tourist factor was something I took into account when deciding to come to live in St. Ives, but I loved the addictive ambiance so much I went against the misgivings of friends and came anyway. Besides, I wanted to spend my life in a place that Isabelle and I used to visit so often. Friends told me it was not a good thing to do, that it would be a constant reminder. They felt I was still grieving her death, but I felt it would bring back just as many warm memories.

The young girl continued to cry, sometimes gentle sobs, sometimes uncontrollable retching spasms. Her two friends circled dutifully as if trying to protect her from further hurt. They took it in turns to comfort her, but nothing they said seemed to make much difference. They were now leaning on the rail that skirted the harbour edge, directly opposite me. Behind them was the gentle slap of the incoming tide. That, the noise of passing traffic and the talk and laughter from the crowded pavement outside the Sloop Inn muffled any further fragments of conversation I might pick up.

Summer night was sliding in. I finished my coffee and walked away, leaving them to their consuming angst.

My cottage was on the hill, on the east side of the town, hung high above the tight-packed rooftops which fronted Porthminster beach. Looking out to sea each morning was still a fresh, inspiring joy. In fact, it was a constant distraction as I worked mainly from home. That in itself was another reason I could come to live in Cornwall: I was a copy editor and proof-reader for a London publishing house. After Isabelle's death I wanted to leave, but Marcus suggested the perfect solution.

"Go freelance," he told me over an unnecessarily opulent lunch at Carey's. "So you take a pay cut and lose a few perks. But you'll have time for yourself, and you'll still be earning. You know what the business is like these days, like a damned madhouse. We can keep you busy for years."

Daytime, in the summer anyway, I pottered around, read, kept the garden from getting too wild. I preferred to work during the evenings. For one thing, it occupied my mind. Nights can get to you sometimes, especially when you're on your own. Usually, I'd spend a couple of hours proof-reading, then take the five-minute walk down to the seafront, sit at the cafe, watch the passers-by.

It was coming up to midnight, I was tired of jumbling words yet still sharply awake. From the window I could see a twinkling straggle of lights along the harbour front, mirrored in a flat, unshifting sea.

Pulling on a sweatshirt, not bothering to switch off the lights or even lock the door, I walked down the dark, narrow lane, a warm breeze on my face and the sound of crickets rippling along the verges as if they were following me.

St. Ives is an old fishing village, almost as far south-west in Cornwall as you can go. Land's End is about 20 miles further on. Back in the mid-19th century it was a busy bustling community, with as many as 400 boats using the harbour. There was a major fishing fleet, mostly catching pilchards, and scores of big sailing ships exporting tin, copper and stone. Any time I closed my eyes I could picture the flurry of activity around the wharf and in the narrow, crowded, noisy streets. Now, the streets were still packed and noisy, but with holidaymakers lugging beach bags and oddly recalcitrant children. Yet I still loved the town, especially late on warm summer nights.

As usual I followed the curve of the harbour and rounded onto Smeatons jetty, a long projecting finger of stone and concrete backed by a high wall, a small lookout tower and little else. Sometimes, in the embers of the evening, before all the light had faded, I saw what seemed to be a very old seal sneak around the edge of the jetty, paddling gently along looking for scraps left by the fishing boats, his scuffed and scarred nose breaking the dappled water.

I was making a half turn by the small lighthouse tower when I saw someone high up on the wide stone wall that backed the jetty. It was a girl, dressed in black and a stark silhouette against the dark, mellow blue of the night sky. There was still the trace of a prowling breeze and her long hair was lifting from her shoulders, trailing back as she faced out to sea. It seemed to me she was about to jump.

She was on the edge of the outer wall, her stance slightly crouched as if about to launch herself into the water. There was a chance I was mistaken, but it was too risky to ask her. My rubber-soled deck shoes made no discernible sound as I took the few paces to her, reached up and grabbed her wrist from behind. She gave a short startled yelp and I pulled her down onto the lower step. It was then, close up, that I recognised her as the girl I had seen earlier, opposite the cafe, the one who was crying.

"What do you think you're doing?" I said, deliberately sharp.

"Let me go."

"I will, as soon as we get lower down, away from the edge."

She tugged and pulled from me as I dragged her back a few paces, yet I thought her degree of resistance could have been stronger.

Before releasing her wrist, I said: "If, when I let go, you run away and jump off the edge, be assured I'll come in after you and pull you out again. But I hope you don't because this shirt is new and I'd hate to see it ruined."

I let go and she didn't run away. She stood there head bowed and uncertain, and then started to cry. I wanted to put my arm around her shoulders, comfort her. Instead, I started talking.

"I saw you earlier, by the cafe, with a couple of friends. Where are they?"

"I told them to leave me alone," she said, the short sentence staccato as she gasped for air between convulsive sobs. "I want to be on my own."

"It didn't do Greta Garbo much good."

"Who?"

"Never mind. I don't think you should be on your own. Where are staying? I'll walk you back."

"I don't want you to." Her voice was vehement in her rejection.

"Maybe not, but I'm not leaving until you do."

She backed away from me slightly. "Leave me alone. I'll scream. I'll say you attacked me."

Screaming was not something she was going to do. I knew it, and so did she. Looking uneasy and confused she sat down on a bench, still crying in subdued erratic whimpers.

I suppose she would have been quite pretty had it not been for the circumstances. Her face was red and puffy, and half-dried smears of black mascara gave her eyes a haunted, sunken look. Her hair, long, dark and naturally straight, didn't seem professionally cut. She had a slim face, and its paleness and the dark eyes heightened the perfect cheek bones that, on a kinder day, might have caught my attention.

I reminded myself that at nearly forty I should stop looking at girls of this age, though in St.Ives, in summer, it was difficult. They were everywhere.

"What next?" I said.

"I'm staying here."

"Fine. I'm staying here too."

Standing with shoulders slumped, her hands twirling a pull-cord on her track-suit top, she said nothing. She looked a mess. Only those exquisite cheekbones and the poignancy of her eyes shone. But at least her sobbing had subsided.

"I'm all right. You can go." Her voice was calmer, firmer, but I felt it was still too soon to leave.

"I'm not going anywhere until you come as well. I'm going to walk you back at least until we reach the lights over there." I pointed across the harbour. "After that, you can do what you like."

As she made no effort to move, I sat down beside her on a wooden-slatted bench.

"Let me guess. You had a row with your boyfriend. He's given you the push."

Unaware, of course, that I had heard snatches of conversation a few hours before, she appeared surprised.

"I hate him. He's a bastard."

"Sadly, most men are," I said. "It's just that at your age it seems more important than it is. It gets magnified, out of proportion. Hurts for a while but, believe me, it passes."

"And you'd know, would you?"

"Yes, I would. The memory of hurt never fades. It can sneak out and bite you even years later."

I could tell she didn't much care what I said, and part of me wanted to walk away. It was still too soon, her mood might change, so I had to keep talking.

"Look, I don't suppose it matters how much I or anyone else tells you this, but all this really isn't that important at your time of life. Adolescence is always traumatic. You grow out of it. You get older, wiser. You'll meet another boy, one who will treat you with more consideration."

"You said all men are like him."

"They are at some time or another, but mostly they grow out if it too."

"Did you?"

"Eventually."

"Did you ever dump anyone?"

"No - usually it was me who got dumped. Well, used too. It doesn't happen anymore."

"I suppose that's because you're married."

"I'm not married, not anymore. My wife was killed in an accident."

"Oh ... sorry."

"Doesn't matter. It was a long time ago."

"How long?"

"Nearly five years. Anyway, this isn't about me. It wasn't me who was going to throw myself off the jetty. "

Her head came up sharply, eyes angry. "Neither was I! I've told you - I just wanted to be on my own, to think."

"Odd place to think, on the edge of a sheer drop! It seemed to me you were going to jump."

"I was not!" Scanning my face for acceptance, she decided I was still sceptical.

"All right, when I first went up there it had crossed my mind, but I'd already decided it was stupid. So I didn't need you interfering. You needn't have bothered."

The anger seemed authentic enough, and I suppose by now she was feeling foolish about the whole thing.

"Come on, let's walk back," I suggested.

"You needn't think I'm coming back to your hotel!"

"I'm not asking you to - for one thing, I'm not at a hotel, I live here. I was just planning to walk you back to wherever you're staying."

A little dubious but I think mostly convinced, she walked with me, but not too close.

"Where do you live then?" I was surprised she asked, and a little concerned. If she had changed her mind, I wanted none of it! Taking home a young emotionally unstable girl would be asking for far more trouble than I wanted to deal with.

Waving a hand in the direction of Porthminster beach, I said: "I have a cottage on the hillside over there. But we're not going."

"I just told you that," she said, sharply enough for me to realise I had misread her intent. "I was just interested, that's all."

Now I felt foolish. We had turned left off the jetty and were walking along the harbour front. There were still a few people around, but she gave no sign of wanting to part.

"What's it like then, this cottage?"

"Small, but a nice big garden overlooking the sea."

"Point to it."

"It's dark - you can't see it!"

"Is it over by those lights?" She indicated a thread of orange dots extending west along the hillside.

I nodded. "It's at the end of that lane, the last cottage."

"Must be great getting up everyday and seeing the sea. Some people think it always looks the same, but it never does. It's always changing, minute by minute. I could watch it forever."

Little by little, normal conversation was gentling in, and I continued to encourage it.

"I know what you mean - I often find myself just staring at it when I should really be working. A couple of hours can slip by without my noticing. And sometimes, in the early morning when there's just me walking on the beach, I like to think that for those first few minutes of the day I own the ocean, that it's all mine as far as the eye can see. Silly, really."

We were still walking unhurriedly towards the Sloop Inn. She glanced across at me rather oddly for a moment, then looked away.

"In fact, I can just about recall a rhyme I used to recite..." I was going to say 'to Isabelle', but stopped myself in time. "Can't remember who wrote it but it goes: 'The fair breeze blew, the white foam flew, the furrow followed free - we were the first to ever burst into that silent sea.'"

"It's by Samuel Taylor Coleridge," she said quickly. "It's from the Ancient Mariner - I read it as a school project a couple of years ago."

My face must have shown my surprise, for she added acidly: "We don't just read trashy magazines, you know."

By now, we had reached the junction with Fore Street, and I asked where she was staying. It was a small hotel at the top of Barnoon Hill. We turned off and started up a steep narrow street towards the hotel.

We were just about halfway up when we heard a scuffling in a darkened recess where two cottage walls abutted. It turned out to be a seagull, a youngish one judging by its size. As it walked forward to the feeble outer reaches of light from a street lamp further down I could see why it wasn't flying. There was a large tangle of thick wire around one of its legs, trailing back four or five feet. The bird again attempted to get off the ground but flopped down again, exhausted.

"Don't touch it", I warned, as she stepped forward to help it. "They can be vicious."

Taking off my sweatshirt I advanced towards the bird, driving it back into the corner. It was too tired to put up much resistance and I threw the shirt over it, pinning down its wings, and then lifting it up, cradling it like a baby. In a couple of minutes, as I held it, the girl was able to untwist the wire.

"Its leg is quite raw where the wire has rubbed." Her concern was as undisguised as that of a child.

I looked at the wound. "Doesn't matter. That will soon heal up. Seagulls are very hardy birds."

"Do you really think he'll be all right," she said doubtfully.

"Sure, he'll be all right."

"I'm going to call him Gulliver," she declared.

"Why Gulliver?" I said, trying to make a connection with the Lilliput of Swift's novel.

"Because he's a gull, stupid!" For just a moment she smiled.

The bird had calmed. It was time to get him airborne, and I was preparing to pitch him upwards when she said: "No, not yet. Wait a minute."

Ignoring my warning, she reached forward and stroked the

gull's head with her forefinger. "Good luck," she said, nodding for me to release him. It soared away in curving ascendancy, its underside lit by the upglow of the street lamps.

"He'll be all right," I reassured her as we watched the gull glide from sight. "By the way - what's your name?"

"Rachel."

"I'm Jack."

For the next few minutes we walked without words, her mood subduing and me unable to think of anything to say that wasn't trite. When we reached the hotel she stood by the steps as if waiting for me to say something, so I felt forced to have another attempt.

"Go in now. You'll feel better after some sleep. Put tonight behind you. Believe me, he isn't worth it. Your life will move on." It all sounded desperately false and her disbelief was evident.

"It will," I insisted, wishing I was home, away from the situation, away from the awful helplessness of words.

"You're a very pretty girl. You'll have no shortage of boyfriends..." The sentence trailed away as I struggled to leave her on a note of hope.

"Look, if you were five years older and I was ten years younger even I wouldn't be walking away from you now." It sounded stupid as I said it, and I could tell she was uncomfortable, embarrassed. She was looking steadfastly at the ground. Then she turned away and without a word, went inside.

The walk back to my cottage seemed longer. The breeze had taken on a chilly edge, and by now the crickets had sung themselves into unnerving silence.

27 August, one year later:

Gary the postman woke me, hammering the door. I asked him why he hadn't left the mail in the box by the gate as usual. He handed me a postcard, asking if it might be meant for me.

"Daftest address I've ever seen," he said.

The postcard showed seagulls silhouetted on a sunset beach. On the other side it was addressed to: "Jack - last cottage at end of long lane above Porthminster Beach, St. Ives, Cornwall."

It was postmarked Cambridge, and said: "I'm still OK!!! Thanks always. Rachel. P.S. Hope this finds you!"

Yes, I told Gary. It's for me.

27 August, two years later:

Postcard arrives. This time, a picture of a solitary seagull standing on top of a post. Postmarked Marbella. It reads: "Do you think this might be Gulliver on his holidays? Still keeping away from jetties!"

It was signed with the single letter R.

27 August, three years later:

Postcard arrives, showing seagull soaring against indigo sky. Postmarked London, SW7. It says: "Will always remember this date. Forever grateful. Met wonderful man (called Jason) who really loves me - just like you said I would! R."

27 August, four years later:

No postcard.

Not, I suppose, a surprise, though I was faintly disappointed. At least she was getting on with her life, which was more than I was doing. I started to do some editing work, but by early afternoon I found the absence of the postcard beginning to increasingly prey on my mind. Heavy cloud had started to roll in, helping darken my mood. Finally, I could work no more.

"You're being Eyorish," Isabelle used to tell me when I was a bit down about something, likening me to that rather dismal donkey in the Winnie-the-Pooh stories.

I was just making coffee when there was a knock at the door. I opened it, and there was a girl. No, it was THE girl. It was Rachel. She was a little taller, her hair was cut shorter, but there was no mistaking those cheekbones. She was wearing jeans, walking boots, dark green corded jacket, and slung over her shoulder was a small rucksack.

"Hi," she said brightly. "Remember me?"

I didn't know what to say. I just stood there.

"Is this a bad moment?" she said, suddenly concerned.

"Is there someone with you?"

"No. No. Come in. I'm just a bit surprised to see you."

Slipping off the rucksack, she looked around the cottage as she stood in the centre of the room, first undoing her jacket, then running her hands through her hair and shaking it .

"Would you like some coffee? I've just made some."

I didn't quite know what to say. I felt I should be full of questions, but I felt oddly uneasy. I busied myself pouring coffee.

She had taken off her jacket and was prowling the room, picking up books, looking at photographs, absorbing the detail.

"Did you get my postcards?"

"Yes. Yes I did, thanks. Seems you've moved around a little."

Nodding rather absently, she took the mug of coffee.

"What about you," she asked. "How's your life been?"

"Much the same. Just work and more work."

"Do you live here on your own?" It was an undisguised direct question.

"Yes."

"I thought you might have moved. I'm glad the cards found you."

"Seems a long time ago, that night on the jetty. How old were you then, sixteen?"

"Seventeen."

"Like I told you, it all works out in the end. You just have to let the time pass. You get older and wiser."

"Are you any wiser?"

"I doubt it. At my age you don't change much. You make your mistakes early on, hopefully learn something along the way."

"And what have you learned?"

"Hard to put into words. Tolerance, I suppose. And perhaps, more than anything, to love while you can. You never know what's around the corner."

"You mean what happened with your wife?"

"In a way. But I feel I knew that by then anyway. Maybe that's why it worked out so well for us. We just knew we were right as soon as we met. You can sense it."

"Not always. I didn't with Paul Jarvis."

"Who?"

"The boy I almost threw myself off the jetty for. You were right. After a few days I began to see him for what he was, especially as he started going out with my best friend."

"There you are then. Lesson learned."

"With him, maybe, but not the rest."

"The rest?"

"Long story. If you want to hear it I'll need more coffee."

I started to get up but she waved me back. Through the open kitchen door I watched her searching cupboards, finding fresh cups. It was strange seeing someone in the kitchen. There were often times, even after the years alone, when I wanted someone to be there, be part of the cottage, part of my existence. When I worked it didn't matter, so mostly I worked longer hours.

She found some biscuits and took a couple without asking. Then she curled up on the old Queen Anne-style wing armchair, hugging a cushion and nibbling around the edge of a chocolate biscuit.

"You were telling me about the rest," I prompted.

"You won't want to know the details," she said, as if changing her mind about telling me. "But you were right. All men are bastards, at least all the ones I've met."

"A lot of them, were there?"

"Well, four or five. Five if you count Alastair, and really," - her expression was enigmatically scornful - "you wouldn't count him."

"What about - what was his name on the postcard - Jason? Last year you were in love."

Her face flushed with contempt.

"He was just the kind of man I always wanted. He was funny, generous, really caring. After all the silly boys, he was ... well, just everything. We were talking of getting married this year. Then he was offered a job in the States. I didn't want to go, I love to travel but I couldn't live abroad."

"So what happened?"

"Can't you guess? I said I couldn't move to America. He says okay, not to worry. Then without telling me he just gets on a plane and goes!. He sent a letter a few days later, saying it was over. Predictable stuff - he was too young to settle down, he had to consider his career. Another deceiving bastard!"

"When was all this?"

"About two weeks ago."

"What have you been doing since?"

"Walking around the Lizard coastal path, sorting myself out and coming to the big decision."

"What big decision?"

There was a pause while she took a sip of what by now was cold coffee. Over the top of the mug her eyes were bright with a sudden constrained excitement.

"You really don't know why I'm here, do you?"

"Haven't you just called in to say hello?"

"I've come back to be with you!"

The single shocking sentence was spoken with something approaching messianic fervour. In my mind I repeated her words to see if there was any possible interpretation that could be put on them other than the one that was obvious.

"What do you mean - to be with me?"

She sat upright, staring at me with intense earnestness, and said: "I should have come back long ago. It's like you said. You know at the time. No matter how often I put you out of my mind, it was always you that came back when I was miserable. When some guy used me, lied to me, treated me like shit. When I was awake all night crying. I never forgot that night we met. It wasn't so much what you said to me, just how you were. You were concerned about me. I mattered. You cared, even though you didn't know me."

"I would have cared about anyone in that situation," I cut in, worried at this crazy rambling.

"I know - that's just the point, you would. That's what makes you what you are."

"And what's that?"

"Someone who is truly genuine."

"The world is full of genuine guys!" I was so tense I found myself gripping the arm of the chair.

`"You just haven't met one yet. It's still too soon. You're only 21, for God's sake! Take your time with your life, wait for it to happen. You'll meet someone special, really. You'll fall in love. You'll know it when it happens."

Deep inside I knew my words weren't reaching her.

"It has happened! Don't you see! I've never forgotten you. It's been hard not to come back sooner. Even when I was with someone else I kept thinking of you."

"This is nonsense. How come you were in love and planning to marry Jason until just a couple of weeks ago? You weren't thinking of me then."

"That's just the point," she said triumphantly. "That was the test. I knew I had to make the big effort. For a year I devoted myself to that relationship, convinced myself it was the one. All the signs were there. Initially it felt right. But it wasn't - it failed the test. Fate was telling me my first instincts were right."

"First instincts?"

"For you! You're the one! I've know it since that night. I tried to convince myself it was stupid, I've even spent the last two weeks sitting in deserted coves gazing at the sea and telling myself it was stupid."

"You're right, it is stupid!"

"No it's not!" She jumped from the chair and knelt in front of me.

"Of course it's stupid. Regardless of how you think you feel about me, doesn't love have to come from both people? Or doesn't that fit your theory?"

"But you do love me, you just haven't realised it yet! Our meeting was meant to be."

"Be serious!"

"I am being serious!" Although her voice was rapid and insistent, she appeared calm and quite unexasperated. Still kneeling on the old arabesque-pattern Turkish rug in front of the empty fireplace, she leaned forward and placed both her hands over one of mine, imploring with the soft cool touch of her fingertips.

`"Even though I knew it was meant to be I gave it another test, just be absolutely sure."

"Really." My disdain for her theory was undiluted, and there was no reason for me to hide it. "How?"

"I knew that if I came back and you were still alone, even after five years, then it was an omen."

"What makes you think I'm alone? I might be seeing someone."

"But you're not - I can tell."

There was such unshakable conviction, it seemed pointless to try to invent. But I couldn't give in, she had to be persuaded this was infatuation, and totally one-sided.

"All right, maybe something I said back on the jetty did strike a chord with you. But be realistic. I'm almost 20 years older than you, I've lived alone for the past eight years. I'm almost a recluse, for God's sake. What makes you think a relationship between us would work? We don't know a thing about each other. We're as close to strangers as you can be!"

"We're not strangers!" Her voice rose in contradiction. "I knew all I needed to know about you that night you walked me back up Barnoon Hill. I was vulnerable then, yet you didn't try anything, you just really cared about what might happen to me. And when you bothered to help that seagull, I saw something else I wanted in a man. Back then, I suppose I thought I might find those qualities in someone else. But now I know I won't."

There was something rather childlike and trusting about her certainty, but her armoured persistence was making me angry. Had she become hysterical - or hateful - then I could have concluded that she was unstable, an emotional runway fleeing to a refuge of perceived reassurance. Yet she was more composed than I was, so serene, so unshakably sure.

"Okay, I'm flattered, I admit that. But what makes you think I want anyone else? I loved my wife. She died, and I live with her memory."

"I know. And I know I'll never replace her in your memory. I wouldn't want to. But you have to acquire fresh memories too, your life has to move on. It was you who told me: "You'll meet someone, and you'll know it."

"It has to work both ways!" I almost shouted with the frustration of not being able to break down her wild, untenable belief.

"It will. It will. You just have to give us a chance. It's fate."

"But I don't believe in fate, or omens!" I leapt out of my chair, forcing her aside, needing to be away from her. With a few feet between us the claustrophobic sensation that had irrationally swept over me abated, and I turned again to face her.

"We make our own decisions, they're not made for us ..."

Until then I was sure of what I was saying, but when I heard that last sentence I realised in a bitter, desolate instant I was wrong. We did not make our own decisions, otherwise Isabelle would never have died. For neither I nor she would have decided she should skid off the road in a rainstorm and hit an oncoming lorry.

The realisation robbed me of further words. I walked over and sat in the bay window seat, looking across Porthminster beach and out to sea. It was darkening now, the flat sheet-steel water beginning to merge with the horizon. Pale grey wisps of mist drifted in like a crowd of ghosts and vengeful rain was splattering on the patio tiles, the final cruel act of a bleak and broken day.

She came and sat opposite, again reaching forward holding my hand, but this time saying not a word. Some minutes passed, I don't recall how long, and I just stared out into the night, my thoughts random, incoherent. Without my realising it she had moved around the curved window seat and was leaning against me. I had never felt so bewildered. Even if I dared to contemplate the situation it seemed ridiculous. Even if she was genuinely serious, and not just emotionally disturbed, it was still too big a leap for me. Yet when I saw her earlier in the kitchen, making coffee, it did, for just a second, seem ... seem so right.

Then there was the obvious and - when I thought about it - compelling temptation of a beautiful and apparently compliant young woman. Just thinking like that made me the sort of man I had tried to tell her to avoid.

Swooping out of the rain a large white seagull suddenly clattered onto the stone window sill and settled, shaking the water from its wings and looking into the room with sharp curiosity, its bright orange beak banging on the glass. I had never seen a seagull land there before, usually they always perched on the outer garden wall.

Rachel saw the seagull and was smiling. Her eyes shone with a righteous zeal that held me, stilled and strangely certain.

"Look," she said. "It's Gulliver. He's home too..."

Bar Stool Hero

She walked into Dino's bar with the flowing grace of a woman who knows the effect she has on men, but couldn't care less. A tray-laden waiter neatly side-stepped a man who had stopped dead to ogle her, and all along the brass and mahogany counter heads turned with robotic precision in her wake.

Even old Dino himself, who claimed he'd given up looking at women 20 years ago, and given up sex years before that, paused from polishing a glass to watch her grand entrance.

Yet, surprisingly, she seemed unaware that she had made a grand entrance. Without looking to either side she walked across to a table against the far wall and joined another woman, already seated, who was a little younger but less impressive.

The companion was attractive enough, in a didn't-quite-make-enough-effort kind of a way, and in her mid-twenties, whereas the woman who had sent ripples of lust lapping to the very edges of Dino's bar was probably in her early thirties. It wasn't that she looked it, just that her effortless casual manner pointed to a certain worldliness.

I happened to be looking at the doorway when she came in, and I have to concede that I thought she had made a mistake and walked into the wrong bar. Don't get me wrong - Dino's place was quite chic but she just out-chic-ed it. The plain simple short crimson dress hung and moved in a way that showed why a thousand dollar dress costs a thousand dollars. It was part of her. It was an off-the-shoulder number that fitted tight. Her waist, already small, looked even smaller in the shadow of her frontal attributes, which my expert and much practised judgment estimated at 38 inches.

She was tall, maybe five feet ten, but that did include her shoes which were high-heeled and also almost invisible. There was a minimalist representation of slender straps vaguely holding the shoes on. From across the bar, at first glance, she appeared to be barefoot and walking on tip toes. Her hair was dark, but not quite black, and neck length, sweeping slightly under at the edges. It just brushed the top edge of her shoulders, which were beautifully tanned. I immediately decided that you could only get that kind of tan by lying completely naked in the sun.

There was George and Huxley and me, all in the bar doing what we did every Friday night, sitting on tall stools drinking Buds. Of course we were talking too, sometimes about baseball, but mostly about girls. It was more than just a Friday night habit. I guess you could say it was some form of ritual.

Strictly speaking we shouldn't have been in Dino's because he didn't encourage entry by anyone under about 25. He was frequently known to refuse service to those who he decided did not have the emotional maturity to populate his establishment and provide the somewhat philosophical ambiance, cosy camaraderie and often bizarre conversational twists that he so appreciated.

"It's my bar and I can do what the hell I like with it," he snarled at anyone who protested. We all thought he had just seen too many episodes of Cheers.

We were tolerated because Huxley's older brother was a great friend of Dino's youngest son, and that gave us a connection which we were not slow to exploit.

Even then, it hadn't been easy. Dino had made it clear from the start that we would be allowed in only if we kept our distance. We had to stay at the extreme end of the bar, not talk too loudly, not... well, the list of rules was extensive.

We didn't mind because Dino's bar had a certain clientele, built up over years of careful selection and undisguised discrimination. The big plus for us was that it was close to several large office blocks, and so attracted some truly fantastic women. Admittedly, they were the kind who were cool, elegant, unapproachable, and utterly unattainable. But we didn't mind. We just liked to look at them.

Many of them were women who ran their own lives, maybe had their own businesses. We didn't know because we never got to talk to a single one of them. We imagined they stopped off for a chilled Chardonnay or maybe, if it had been a tough day, a Jack Daniels on the rocks on their way home from the office. Those that came later usually came in twos or threes for serious gossip or maybe to fill in time before a movie or a show.

It has to be said that not one of them would have glanced in our direction, even if we had stripped naked and danced on the bar. Still it was nice to look, to speculate, even though we were three total losers.

We were all too young to have had much serious experience, and certainly not with women like that. At nineteen Huxley was the oldest, by a year.

I got along with them okay, we had been friends since school, and we all lived on the same street. But the big difference was that while I knew I was a loser, they hadn't come to the same conclusion about themselves. Of course, I could see it in them; they just couldn't see it in themselves. However, they were absolutely certain I was a loser and said so. Often.

I didn't mind much. Despite their constant put-downs and regular acid sarcasm we had a lot of fun together and, anyhow, it made me feel better hanging out with a couple of guys who always felt they could make it, even if I knew they couldn't. Mind you, in their favour both George and Huxley had had some experience with women, though with women their own age. Each had notched up a couple of ultra-short liaisons with local girls and once, for almost two weeks, Huxley had gone out with Amanda Zeitz, who had since been signed up by a model agency. She dumped him but he maintained he dumped her, as if you would.

My sister heard the truth from a friend of Amanda's, and it confirmed my view that Huxley was, like me, a loser when it came to women.

The big problem was that both George and Huxley knew that my experience - and you know what I mean by experience - of girls was less than minimal. They had known me since school and knew the only girl I dated, Marilyn Allen, had told me I was history after two dates, and that I hadn't got very far in that time. I hadn't even kissed her.

"It's all about confidence," Huxley would tell me almost every week at the bar room session. "You just have to go up to them and get things started."

That was a problem, getting things started. I could no more walk up to a girl and start a conversation than become President of China. That's if China had a president - I wasn't certain.

George took another view of the reason for my terminal shyness, and resultant lack of success. He put it down to just getting off to a bad start. He theorised that at the time when what he called "natural developments" in my body should have been telling me it was time my collection of stamps and Star Wars stickers should have been abandoned so I could refocus attention on girls, I just carried on with my collecting.

"I mean, you didn't even collect copies of Playboy," said George, and no matter how many times he told me the incredulity in his tone never diminished. "You just hung around too long at that schoolboy stage. It's like any kind of race, if you miss the start you never catch up."

Oddly, this incisive understanding of male behaviour seemed to desert them when we were in Dino's bar. For while I conceded that both were quite capable of dating girls our age - though being dumped right away - they knew that the women at Dino's were in a different league, light years away from our tightly confined and stunningly unadventurous world.

Still, it was safe to merely browse, and our Friday nights were something we looked forward to. Some of the women we saw often, and there was one particularly aloof blonde that Huxley idolised with a fervour that bordered on the religious.

We knew nothing about her, though Dino, in a rare unguarded moment, had let it slip that her name was Celestine. That excited Huxley to almost warp-speed.

"Exactly the sort of name I knew she'd have," he said, actually panting.

I had to listen to hours of Huxley, aided by George, salivating in low tones precisely what they would like to do to her, and then, when they'd exhausted all options, have her do to them. It was an interesting speculation and sometimes I too indulged, but not often because before long Huxley and George would turn on me, making it clear that I would probably find myself incapable of doing anything to her. "And the chances of her wanting to do anything to you would have more zeros on the end than the Wall Street phone bill."

I wasn't sure that they knew how many zeros there might be on the Wall Street phone bill, and was dumb enough to start arguing.

Then the goddess in the crimson dress drifted in and she stopped George and Huxley in mid-sentence. They just gaped like everyone else.

Maybe half a minute passed while the woman sat down with her friend, who had obviously been waiting for her. Then

Huxley got his mouth working again and gave his verdict.

"She's just incredible."

George must have opened his concise mental dictionary on the same page.

"Incredible," he breathed softly. "Just incredible."

Huxley was nodding like an android in malfunction mode.

"What I'd give to walk right up to her and ask her out," he murmured.

"What I'd give to lay her," said George, getting straight to the point.

"Just talk to her," repeated Huxley, still in some kind of trance. "It would be enough just to talk to her."

"I'll go over and talk to her," said another voice.

Then I realised it wasn't another voice. It was my voice.

It had somehow sneaked out from the back of my head, dodged round the side and spoken without me having any knowledge of it. Huxley and George were looking at me with the level of amazement you would normally reserve for the sight of a herd of giraffes riding unicycles.

"What?" said Huxley.

"He's only joking," said George, feeling he was pointing out the obvious. And that really riled me. They knew I couldn't do it. They were certain I couldn't do it. They would bet every damned thing they owned that I couldn't do it.

So I had to do it.

"No, I'm not joking," said my voice, again taking the initiative. "I said I'll go over and talk to her."

The sickening enormity of what I'd said was fast hitting me. My face was burning, my body felt frozen and my stomach had been stretched out, tied in barbed-wire knots and then stamped on. The pain was so acute I was having to breathe in half-second gulps.

Almost in unison we looked across to where the two women were sitting. They were engrossed in an intense feminine communion, leaning forward almost conspiratorially.

"Do it," said Huxley. "Let's see you do it."

"I have to pick the moment," I said, desperately stalling for time. "I can't just interrupt."

Huxley and George groaned derisively.

"He's backing out," said George with extreme elation.

"I knew he would - he always does."

I knew I was going to have to do it, but at that very moment the two women stood up and the younger one was picking up her bag.

"He's off the hook," said Huxley, his disappointment evident. "They're going."

In fact, only one of them was going, the younger one. She said her goodbyes and left, and the vision in the crimson dress sat down again and took a delicate sip from a drink only half finished.

"Now's your chance," said George, but before I could find some reason for delay the same uncontrollable force that had borrowed my voice took possession of my legs.

I found myself climbing off the bar stool and walking towards her. I had maybe ten strides to construct an opening line. I ran through my mental files of neat opening lines, carefully stored from movies, TV shows and books, so that when I reached her table I'd be able to utter something that wouldn't make me appear totally stupid.

The file-search didn't take long. It had somehow been erased. My mind was suddenly as empty as a southwest sky.

Only my legs were working, and by now they had reached her table.

"You must help me, please," I heard myself saying. "My friends back there have bet me that I don't have the courage to come up and speak to you. And they're right, I don't. I should never have come over. If you'll just talk to me for a couple of minutes it will save my life. Well, not my life, my reputation. Well, maybe not my reputation, I haven't got a reputation. It'll just save me making a fool of myself. Please..."

It was a speech totally bereft of any finesse, and as foolish as it could get. I could hear myself ricocheting through the words and sentences, bleating like the college nerd.

She stared up at me and tilted her head slightly sideways so that she could see past me towards George and Huxley. Though I couldn't see them, and dared not turn round, I was convinced they were gleefully watching my wincing humiliation.

"I thought I'd heard just about every opening line there is but I guess that's a new one," she said.

In my mesmerised state, even the sound of her voice started nervous tremors.

Her wide grey eyes seemed to hold a certain restrained amusement. I could hold her gaze only for a couple of seconds before my eyes were relentlessly dragged down to the smooth touchability of those tanned shoulders, and then inevitably, and shamelessly, to where the tight-fitting dress squeezed her breasts together in a smooth sculpture of almost unimaginable pleasure.

"It's not an opening line," I protested needlessly. "I had to come over because they knew I couldn't. They know I never know what to say. They're always telling me I'm a loser. I suppose tonight I just couldn't take any more."

She looked thoughtful and took another glance past me towards the bar.

"I guess this is serious," she said. "You'd better sit down."

Had she said that? I couldn't believe it. I managed to pull out a chair and sit opposite her, still not able to look back towards the bar. My heart was racing, pounding with exhilaration.

"So if they hadn't forced you to come over and talk to me, you wouldn't have?"

"No. No, I wouldn't."

"So you don't find me attractive then?"

"No. Yes. Yes, of course I do."

It was a neat little verbal trap and I'd walked right into it. I shook my head at my incompetence and stumbled on. "You must know you look sensational, fantastic, like a dream."

Please God, I prayed, let me come up with at least one phrase that wasn't a cliche.

"Then why did it take a bet to get you here?"

"You wouldn't have the least interest in me."

"You're right, honey. I wouldn't."

She sipped her drink very slowly, watching my face over the rim of the glass.

"But hey - why let that put you off? Believe in yourself. Okay, I'm a lost cause for you, but don't be scared to try."

I must have looked as if I wasn't grasping all this because she felt the need to explain further.

"This is how I see it. I'm a beautiful woman. Know how I know? Because guys have been telling me everyday since I was twelve years old. I guess I have to believe them. But beautiful women have a problem. Every guy they meet wants to try his luck."

She shrugged her shoulders, the sudden movement lifting

her breasts like a twin sunrise.

"Sure, some guy will get lucky, if he happens to be the right guy at the right time. But let me tell you something. The guys who get lucky aren't always the ones who look like they should be in the movies. Understand? It takes more than that. Sure, it helps if he looks like he should be co-starring in a Bruce Willis movie, but its not everything. What really counts is everything else."

I felt I should say something, but couldn't come up with anything even remotely intelligent. She carried on anyway.

"I turn a lot of guys down. Have to - I have a lot of choice. Sure, being hassled is tough sometimes, but if it didn't happen I guess I'd miss it. We all need our ego boosting. But most guys can't deal with rejection, they take it hard. What they don't get is that it's not personal, it's just numbers. Those that make an impression might progress. Those that don't..." She let the sentence hang for a couple of seconds to then fall as a guillotine of emphasis..."just don't."

Her eyes became attentive, losing their lazy, laid-back look.

"I hope you're taking this in, honey. I don't usually give lessons."

Every word I ever knew had slipped out of my head. All I could do was nod.

"I guess the bottom line is this. If you're too scared or too dumb to try, you don't have a chance. You're never going to be that lucky guy. So what have you going to do in the future?"

"Try," I said quickly, reacting to the prompt.

"Right," she said, flashing a sudden teasing smile. "Because if you don't, you'll never again be sitting in a bar with someone like me."

Easing forward in her seat she caught Dino's attention with a small wave of her hand. She could have caught the attention of anyone in the bar - I just knew they were all looking at us.

"What are you drinking?" she asked.

"Bud."

Dino came over. His face was usually impassive, but I could see from a few adjustments to his wrinkles that he too was registering a certain amazement.

She ordered a Bud and a mineral water, and I took the opportunity to make a half turn back towards the bar, where I was rewarded with the glorious, heart-surging sight of George and Huxley transfixed and staring.

"Never stop trying," she stated again as if giving me a phrase to commit to memory, a homework exercise. "Always believe in yourself, and remember the odds are never as bad as you think."

Leaning back, she studied me for a moment, a sharp appraisal at the speed of a snapshot.

"You're not bad looking - nice hair but too long - and when you learn to lighten up a little you might even be interesting to talk to."

She anticipated my smile before I'd realised I was going to smile.

"Don't get your hopes up, honey. You know I'm not for you, but somebody somewhere sure is."

Reaching over, she squeezed my forearm, and I prayed George and Huxley saw the gesture. I knew I'd remember it forever. Her long slim fingers with neat unpainted nails pressed into my flesh and triggered volcanic shock waves.

It was her right hand and she wore no rings just a fine chain of wispy gold, so delicate it looked like it had been cut from a spider's web.

"Don't let them," - she inclined her head towards George and Huxley - "get to you, or anyone else. I guess it took some nerve to come over here - to me that says a lot about you. Was it worth it? Do you feel good now?"

"I feel this is the greatest moment of my life."

"If it's that good you'll remember it the next time, when there's nobody making a bet."

Glancing at her watch, she said: "There's a cab due to pick me up in a couple of minutes. I've got to go."

She looked briefly pensive, then smiled.

"Say, why don't you come with me? We can leave together, you can even get in the cab with me. But don't get excited - I'll be dropping you at the next block. Your friends will see us leave, so it's going to look real good to them."

"You'd do that for me?"

"You, but not for everyone," she said wryly.

We finished our drinks, got up and walked side by side to the door. I never looked back. The cab was waiting and I opened the door for her, rewarded with one fragmented second of stunning thighs as her dress rode up. I got in beside her, and the cab moved off with a brutal tyre squeal as the driver stabbed the gas-pedal to veer in to the traffic.

A minute later it was all over. She told the driver to pull over when we turned onto Century Boulevard, and then nodded for me to get out.

"Make yourself scarce for a while," she advised. "What you say when you next see them is up to you. But be understated - it's more convincing!"

The cab moved off, it's tail-lights quickly melting into the speeding swirl, and I realised I never even asked her name. But one thing I did know. Next Friday night in Dino's Bar it wouldn't be George and Huxley doing all the talking.

I was the new bar stool hero.

Miranda's Letters

I suppose it was about five years ago that Henry mentioned the existence of the letters. Had he not been so drunk, I doubt I would ever have found out.

We hardly knew each other then. We'd met quite by chance, both viewing a flat above an antiques warehouse in Bermondsey. Our appointments should have been half an hour apart, but the agent was stuck in traffic and by the time he arrived we'd introduced ourselves.

"Grid-locked all the way back to Blackfriars Bridge," the agent said, fumbling to find the right key. "I'm really running late - I'm going to have to ask you to view at the same time. First one with the deposit and two references on my desk will get it. And there are others interested. Okay?"

We looked around, trying to view separate rooms, but the place was not that big, and we kept meeting up and making jokey comments. By the time the agent locked up and left us on the pavement we felt we knew each other.

Then, it came out that we were actually both on the same six-month training course. The coincidence got us into a pub for a longer chat, and before an hour had passed we agreed that we could share the flat.

"It's got two bedrooms," I said. "If we bring any girls back, at least we won't have to watch each other at it."

"Pity," said Henry, looking rather regretful. "Mind you, I won't be bringing any girls back. I'm engaged."

"Engaged! How old are you? Twenty two, twenty three?"

"Twenty two. We were childhood sweethearts."

Inevitably that got us onto the subject of first loves. That, and a couple of bottles of cheap French red we'd picked up to celebrate moving in.

I told him how a haughty blonde called Elizabeth had shredded my heart when I was seventeen, ending an intense six-week relationship for no obvious reason, and frostily refusing any sort of explanation.

"Hits you hard," I said. "I thought my life was over. You

think it's the only girl you'll ever meet."

Henry was nodding and trying to pour wine at the same time. It was splashing all around the glass and onto the table.

"I know the feeling," he said. "I was near to topping myself when I split with Miranda. She was half Portuguese, you know."

"What was the other half?"

"English, of course," he snapped, as if there could be no other possibility. "Lasted six weeks. But what a six weeks."

"I don't think that's grammatical," I interrupted. I can get a bit pedantic when drunk. "You can't say: 'What a six weeks.' Doesn't make sense."

"Did you understand it?"

"Well, yes..."

"Then for fuck's sake shut up. Do you want to hear about my broken heart or not?"

"Sorry," I said. "You'll have to get used to me. I can be a bit of a bastard at times."

"No way," he said in that thickly assertive voice that alcohol always provides. "You're a nice guy. I can tell."

I shook my head. "Believe me, I can be a real bastard at times." The wine was beginning to hit me too. I don't know how we got onto this track, but it wasn't the way I wanted the conversation to go.

"Tell me about Miranda," I prompted, switching subjects.

His expression brightened. "Oh yes, the lovely Miranda. Did I tell you she was half Portuguese?"

"Yes - but you didn't say which half."

He threw a handful of peanuts at me, and got into what turned out to be a rather interesting little tale.

"I met her in a cafe in Kensington High Street. She was waitressing and spilled some of my coffee when she put the cup down. I made a joke of it, and asked her out on the spot. She was just fantastic. You know how these Mediterranean girls can look. Superb. Dark hair and eyes. Slim. Lovely smile. She lived in a flat over Earls Court way. We spent every night there. We were hardly ever out of bed."

He paused at the memory of it, and it was obviously pretty memorable.

"Strange thing was, she fell for me too. Absolutely hooked. Even though we saw each other every day she would write me long letters. Very erotic they were. Mixture of undying love and descriptions of our sex-play. Quite a turn-on - I think she knew that too."

"Sounds like the perfect girl to me. So what happened?"

"She found out about Louise."

"Louise?"

"My fiancee."

"Another fiancee?"

"No. No. The same one. Childhood sweetheart, remember."

"Got you. Go on then."

"I'd been engaged to Louise for two years. Our parents had been friends for ages. They were delighted for us. Still are, of course. We're getting married next June."

A sudden thought struck him. "You must come to the wedding," he said. "You'll like her. Everybody does."

"So what happened to the lovely Miranda ?"

"Walked out. One night she heard Louise leave a message on my answer phone. I couldn't get to the phone - we were having sex at the time. It was awful. Not the sex, the message. As Louise started rambling on about something to do with our wedding, Miranda's rhythm started to slow. She was on top, and I could see her face changing. Nothing I could do. I was too far gone. Then Miranda just got off me, dressed and left. Never listened to anything I said. Never said a word.

"I tried to see her next day, of course. Thought she might have calmed down. But she had left her job, wouldn't answer the door at her flat, even changed her phone number.

"After a few days I decided it was probably the best result in the end. Everything was set with Louise, families were swapping ideas about the wedding. Besides which, I loved her. Really. I really did. Okay, great sex is one thing, and Miranda certainly gave that, but, well, love is love."

There was one of those pondering pauses that comes when a certain line of conversation has reached its natural end.

"You must come to the wedding," he said again and I nodded agreeably.

"I kept the letters," he added abruptly. "Had to. You couldn't throw letters like that away. Absolute pornography. Women so rarely write that sort of stuff."

That was all Henry said about the letters at the time, and there was no reason to pay it any particular attention.

I went to the wedding, up in Staffordshire where they were living. Henry had done well. Louise's parents were rich. I mean rich. Father had a Ferrari Testarossa, mother a Mercedes SLK.

They'd bought the happy couple a massive thirties-built Tudor-style house with a three-acre garden on the outskirts of Stoke-on-Trent.

Henry had a management job with his father-in-law's firm, a big electrical retail group. Nice move if you can make it.

A few months later I got an excited phone call to say Louise was pregnant. They called the kid Carlton. Don't know why, but you'd need a reason, wouldn't you?

I visited now and then, long weekends, a whole week one summer. Mistake. It would be hard to find a city with less sense of identity than Stoke-on-Trent. The place appeared to have been planned by people who had been kept in isolation and never allowed to meet each other. It was a sprawling monument to unfettered urban mess. But at least the countryside around was pleasant enough.

Had it not been for his job Henry would doubtless have chosen to live somewhere more pleasant, and I found I was rather pleased that there was this less than idyllic aspect to his life. Increasingly, I wanted there to be something wrong with his perfect existance. I had started to dislike him.

Slivers of resentment needled into me. His life was just too good. He had it all, and without the effort. It had all fallen to him, undeserved.

All right, you could say it was jealousy too. Every time I stayed in that lifestyle magazine mansion my own unremarkable semi seemed that bit more uninhabitable. When we went to lunch in his new Porsche, the repayments on my five-year old BMW seemed too punitive. And then there was his neatly dovetailed marriage to Louise, the adorable childhood sweetheart, while I was struggling to hold on to a bitchy fourth girlfriend in less than three years. Kathy says I lack ambition. "We can never move to Hounslow if you stay merely the assistant sales manager."

Merely. It's the way she says the word. Stretched out and sardonic.

But then I didn't have a father-in-law with a business empire and a fucking Ferrari, did I? I nearly told her that, but what's the point.

I suppose things might have carried on in much the same way for a while until my resentment of Henry become so intolerable that I would have to come up with reasons not to visit. But then one weekend, everything changed.

I'd been asked up there for Carlton's birthday. I'd gone alone as usual. I avoided taking girlfriends. Seeing that kind of lifestyle, they would expect much more of me. Maybe even a kid. Especially Kathy.

Carlton was four, a nice enough kid but with one of those over-cute floppy American haircuts that made him look girlish.

The kid seemed to have bonded Henry and Louise in a way I suppose kids do. They played the perfect parents, he was the perfect offspring. It was all so nice it sometimes made my teeth hurt.

That evening, while Louise was preparing dinner, Henry was giving me a tour of his latest acquisitions.

The highlight was a late-Georgian walnut bureau, beautifully original and with a nicely fitted interior comprising more than a dozen small compartments and miniature drawers.

It had, he told me unnecessarily, cost five thousand pounds. I was irked by the dismissive way he had mentioned spending such a sum. Five grand would have paid off the loan on my car, and left a bit over for a nice weekend in Brighton with Kathy.

Louise called to him from the kitchen and I was left alone at the bureau.

Only half-interestedly, I looked to see if it had a secret drawer. Such bureaux often did - my father used to be in the antiques trade and when I was a kid he would hide sweets in secret drawers, encouraging me to find them.

Secret drawers were originally intended to hide away gold coins or important documents. Most were located behind a slim panel which looked solid and immovable, but which could be sprung open by a hidden switch.

Idly, I pulled out the lower left-hand drawer of the fitted interior and slipped my finger into the space. It was the most common location for the switch, and there it was. A push, and the panel came open. Behind was a slim drawer, a foot wide and little more than an inch deep. Now I could impress Henry with my antiques expertise!

I pulled open the drawer and inside saw a dozen or so letters. I had only to see the name Miranda and lots of kisses on the bottom of one page for it all to come back to me. The drunken night in Bermondsey. The sex-crazed Miranda, the pornographic letters.

No thought. No indecision. I closed the drawer, replaced the panel. And kept the letters.

The plan was already forming, yet instantly, it began to go wrong. Footfall. I look around and Carlton scampers in. Henry, I imagine will be close behind. The bundle of letters was too bulky to fit in my trouser pocket - I wasn't wearing a jacket - so as I backed away from the bureau I slipped the bundle under my sweater, trying to hold it in place with my forearm.

Henry came in, and as I tried to appear to be moving casually I felt the letters drop to the floor. Henry didn't notice, the sofa was in his line of vision, and I moved away trying to distract him. Then Louise called again.

"Back in a minute," he said, throwing up his hands.

I turned to scoop up the letters but they had vanished.

Dropping to my knees to see if they had slipped under the edge of the sofa, I looked up to see Carlton just in the act of throwing them onto the blazing log fire.

"Rubbish," he said proudly. "I burn rubbish."

I grabbed a poker and tried to flick them from the flames, but the intense heat at the heart of the fire had already incinerated them to crumbling fragments .

It didn't matter! Suddenly it hit me that it didn't matter. Henry wouldn't know they had been destroyed, just that they were missing. It could still work.

The following week I rang Henry to say I was coming up to Staffordshire on business and could we get together for lunch.

We met in one of those nice old pubs which had been refurbished by stripping out everything original and replacing it from a catalogue of replica Victorian pub fittings. As usual Henry was so affable you wanted to punch him. He even insisted on paying the bill.

Once the waitress had bought us the coffee I got directly to the point, in a sort of indirect manner.

"You know how everybody pays these days by credit card or cheque," I said. "Well, if you had to come up with a load of actual cash how much could you raise?"

He looked mildly interested at the turn in the conversation. "Hard to say - a couple of thousand, I suppose."

"Not five grand - or ten?"

"If I had to. It would have to be a bloody good reason though."

"It is," I said. "I have the letters."

"Letters?"

"The letters from Miranda."

He was still looking perplexed. He hadn't made the connection because it was just too improbable.

When it did connect, he said "You can't have."

"Believe me," I said. "I have. I found the secret drawer of your bureau. They're on lilac notepaper - right?"

Henry said nothing. His eyes were so distant, he just wasn't with me. When he finally spoke he had worked it all out, and didn't need an explanation.

"I was going to say I can't believe you'd blackmail me, but it seems you are." He was pretty calm, I thought.

His voice was terse, but no louder than it had been during lunch. "You think I'll pay?"

"I know you'll pay. Remember, the letters are from after you met Louise. It was an affair. And remember the detail. All that juicy detail."

"I had you down as a good friend." He sounded bitter, but so would I in his position.

I shrugged. "Nothing's forever. It was a chance opportunity and I took it."

"I won't pay."

My smile was confident, a sign to indicate serious intent. "You may say you won't pay, but you will. Think about it. Louise. The kid. The house, the cars. Even the job. All gone. You were fucking Miranda while planning your wedding. No woman could forgive that."

He was silent for only a couple of seconds. I had already thought through what he was thinking through. He saw it was a no-option option.

"You're right, of course," he said, as composed as if it was just a routine business decision. "How much do you want."

"Ten grand, cash. A one-off payment. No photocopies taken. You have my word."

"That is so reassuring," he said. This time, an acid trace of distaste, maybe even contempt was evident.

I didn't mind. He was entitled to feel pissed off.

Two days later I drove in to a wind-blown hotel car park off the M6. He was already there, and I parked opposite his silver 911.

It was the right sort of day to collect blackmail cash. The sky looked like a bad watercolour, heavy drags of sullen blackish clouds, and the circling threat of rain.

Henry got out as I did, and we faced each other. It might have been the way he was standing, leaning against the car door, but he seemed smaller. There was just somehow less physical presence. Strange how you notice detail without looking for it. I saw his shirt had a Boss logo and almost laughed, because Henry wasn't the boss right now. It seemed really funny for just a moment, then it didn't. I suppose I was just nervous.

He was the first to speak.

"You could have asked for more, and got it," he said.

I nodded. "I know. I'm not greedy. I just want enough to even things up a little. I didn't get your breaks."

"Envy can be a terrible thing."

"Let's not get philosophical. Have you got the money?"

He reached into the car and took out a white envelope.

Funny, but I expected it to be brown. He held it tight to his chest. "Have you got the letters?"

"Money first," I said, taking an envelope packed with newspaper from my pocket. It wouldn't matter once I had the cash in my hands.

"Ten thousand seems a lot of money for an envelope full of ashes," he said quietly.

"What?" I was trying not to let the shock show.

"You don't have the letters," he said. "Carlton told me what happened. He told me what he did with them. He tells me everything he does. He leads a small life. Everything that happens is significant to a child."

"I salvaged a few," I said. What else could I say.

"Not according to Carlton. His account was very specific. 'All gone,' is what he told me. 'Letters all gone.' I believe my son."

"When did you find out?" I was glad it was all over. I was, really. There was a sort of inner release. It seemed even my spine relaxed.

"The day after it happened. He just came out with it when I was putting him to bed. I went to check straight away. Couldn't believe it. I just couldn't understand how you found them. A secret drawer is supposed to be secret."

"I'd seen one before," I said, wondering why I was bothering to explain. "I found the switch."

Henry wasn't looking at me. He was watching the clouds as if the threat of rain was more important than this hollow, tainted confrontation.

"In view of what happened to the letters I'd put it down to pure accident, that you were too embarrassed to tell me," he said. "I never expected blackmail."

"I told you I was a bastard, when we were Bermondsey, " I said, as if it was some kind of justification. "You just didn't believe me."

"I do now."

It should have ended there. I expected him to turn away.

He wasn't the sort to get angry, to want to hit me. Or even to insult me. The time for that had already passed.

Yet I knew he wanted to say something else. It was evident from his uncertainty, his cloud-gazing. And the fact that he was still there at all.

"Thing is, I really have liked you all these years," he told me, at last finding the words. There was still a little affection there, though stifled.

"Louise does too. And if you'd asked us for ten thousand we'd have given it to you. And I don't mean as a loan but as a gift. If it would have helped you out - business opportunity perhaps, or settling a debt - you could have had it."

He realised he was still clutching the white envelope.

"In fact, you can still have it," he said. "I drew it from the bank even though I'd rumbled you. You're right - it's such a small sum to me, I won't even notice its gone."

Taking a pace forward he placed the envelope on the bonnet of my car. I stared at it as he got into the Porsche and drove off in a wide, sweeping arc.

The envelope lay there, a white rectangle of promise, stark against the metallic black paintwork. My name was on it, hand-written in light blue ink. I picked up the envelope and tore it open, hard and swift, down one edge.

Clusters of disintegrating black flakes billowed out, the wind throwing them up into my face like a scatter of dead leaves.

The envelope was packed full of papery ash.

I saw that a few unburnt fragments had a colour and texture which made them unmistakable.

They had once been banknotes.

Playing The Ace

I am rarely stuck for words but I have to admit the question really threw me.

After all, it's not often someone asks you how much money you want to get beaten up. And I mean beaten up. Not just cuts and bruises but loose teeth and maybe a couple of cracked ribs. The first instinct is to not seriously consider the proposition because nobody offers to pay to do that sort of thing. Either they want to beat you up to settle some score or they don't. Nobody offers money to do it. Well, I suppose there could be somebody with a really weird perversion, but I think I'm a pretty good judge of people and the man making this bizarre offer didn't strike me as being any kind of deviant. He also didn't come over as a loony, though the fact that he was a member of the Peerage did not entirely preclude him from the possibility.

He spoke very quietly, yet I knew he was aware of the impact of his question. You didn't need loudness for that kind of question. You just said it softly and let it beat its own drum. Despite his outward calmness, I could see signs he was edgy. He was glancing all over the room instead of at me. His hands scrabbled around the desk, realigning the ashtray, herding errant paper clips. For a man worth a reported twenty million pounds he was tense. You don't expect to be tense when you have that kind of money, unless just having it makes you tense.

"It's an interesting question, is it not?" he said. "You may need a minute or two to think about it."

I was thinking about it. Oh, yes. I was thinking about it. I knew he was serious and I knew he had serious money. And it is knowing the money exists which makes the difference. It's one thing to say you'd never accept money to be beaten up if you don't believe the money will be forthcoming. But when you are certain the money is there it concentrates the mind. You start to ask yourself how much the pain will be worth.

Now, don't get the idea I'm one of those tough-guy types you see in the movies. The last fight I got involved in was in the schoolyard when I was eleven years old. No, I could just use the money. As long as there was enough of it, of course.

This was how I saw the cash for pain situation: I was a moderately successful private detective. Note I didn't say I was a private eye. I don't like the phrase. It's too American, even though I love those Philip Marlowe stories. But I digress. We were talking money. Last year I earned about £25,000, which just about paid the rent and got me a modest car.

It's well short of the good life. Cracked ribs and reconstructive dentistry would probably lay me off for three or four months, so we would be talking ten grand just for starters. And that's without any compensation for the pain.

"I am pleased to see you are giving the proposition a degree of consideration," he said, walking around the old mahogany desk and sitting down on a green leather swivel chair. Whatever his problem was, I wasn't sure I wanted anything to do with it. But I at least had to find out what it was about. After all, he was an Earl. He just rang me up, told me he got my number out of the directory, and wanted to see me right away. He wouldn't discuss why on the telephone, but made a point of telling me he would pay a consultation fee even if I decided not to take the case. You just can't refuse that kind of offer, so that afternoon saw me making a twenty-mile drive out to the Shropshire countryside. The tall arched and very ornate ironwork gates of Carthleven Hall were open but there was a prominent notice on the stone pillar warning off unauthorised visitors. At first I couldn't see the hall as the single track tarmaç driveway curved gently through a spinney. Then a large stream, or perhaps it was a small river, snaked in from the right and ran parallel before making a turn over a small humpbacked bridge of mellow creamy stone work. Then I saw it, a truly magnificent building, which I later learned was a 14th century country house. It's simple elegant lines were topped by a flurry of spires and groups of tall chimneys, and there was much decorative stonework running around clusters of majestic stone-framed windows. The central part of the building had vivid green ivy climbing right up to the apex of the pitched roof. There was a backdrop of towering tall trees and in the foreground were a few well-placed giant oaks. It put me in mind of my own house. I had an oak tree in my garden too.

There were acres of lawns, and where the driveway curved through and ended there was a huge turning area around a circular Italian-style fountain. From a distance the centrepiece appeared to be a goddess stretching her arms towards the heavens and cascading water from a large urn which she held aloft.

It was such a stunning scene that I actually stopped the car for a few minutes, got out and stood just taking it all in. It seemed to me to be the epitome of pure Englishness. The perfection of the scene was almost savage in the way it hit me, and it heightened my curiosity about what problems the Earl might have to cloud this peaceful setting.

The entrance to Carthleven Hall was an iron-studded oak door. Set in the wall alongside was a highly polished brass bell handle, boldly inscribed with the word 'pull'. Suddenly I'm reminded of that Philip Marlowe story - The Big Sleep - which starts with Marlowe visiting a rich old general at a Hollywood mansion. "I was everything a well dressed private detective ought to be," says Marlow. "I was calling on four million dollars."

I felt much the same way. Except that twenty million pounds makes you want to be better dressed.

My progress down the driveway had clearly been observed. Before I could reach for the bell pull one half of the double door opened and a smiling man greeted me, slim to the point of thinness and with charcoal grey hair combed straight back and sleeked down. The pin-striped trousers told me he was a butler. "You would be Mr Max Slater, sir." He said it as a fact. "I will inform his Lordship that you have arrived. Please be seated." He indicated a fine carved high-back chair in a hallway best described as a foyer. It was as big as any foyer in a hotel, and at the centre was a wide staircase which went up to a deep spacious landing before splitting off both left and right and then out of sight. Scattered around was much oak and walnut furniture, some pieces decked with fresh flowers and the walls were closely packed with oil paintings in heavy gilt frames. The butler returned and asked me to follow him. We went down a corridor with doors off on both sides and then turned into a large room, which I took to be the Earl's study judging by the desk and the walls of books. It was a typical country house private library, with tightly packed ranks of leather spines and a distinct impression that no one had ever pulled out a single book in years.

The Earl stood alongside his desk, one of those large double-sided partners desks with drawers on both sides. He walked forward, hand outstretched, saying: "Mr Slater. How kind of you to come."

He was quite a tall man and he would have been taller were it not for a rather pronounced stoop, and he was a big man in other respects too. He was heavily built and had a paunchy stomach effectively held in by a stretched green velvet waistcoat. He was wearing a sort of greenish-grey tweed suit, brogue shoes, and his tie had some sort of badge on it which suggested an old regiment or maybe an old school. His manner was entirely affable, but it's one of my rules in life to never take things at face value. I looked for some of the signs and found them. There were slight shadows under the eyes, which suggested lack of sleep, and there was an intensity burning within them that put me just a little on edge. But it was his right hand that gave him away. It was resting on the tooled leather surface of the desk, angled towards me as I sat opposite. In his hand was a fine gold fountain pen, a Parker judging from the distinctive arrow clip. He had not been writing, merely toying with the pen as we spoke. But it was how he was holding the pen that put the first crack in the veneer of affability. He was gripping it vertically, rather like a dagger, with four fingers around its stem and his thumb more upright, applying unwitting pressure. It was the amount of pressure that surprised me for I could see now that this superbly engineered pen was beginning to bend. I would have to have been less bright than a TV weather girl not to conclude that some rather nasty problem was seriously troubling the ninth Earl of Carthleven.

The pen snapped, so did the ink container, like a tiny silent bomb. The blue ink splattered across the Earl's fingers and dripped messily onto the leather-topped desk. It looked as though he had a savage gash across his hand and it was spurting blue blood. Despite the tension of the moment I thought of how appropriate that was for a member of the aristocracy.

"Damn!." The Earl was shocked at what had happened. He stared almost uncomprehendingly at the oozing stain on his hand, and at the blue spots on his shirt cuff. "I must apologise," he said, beginning to assert himself again. "I don't know what I was thinking about."

I sat down, uninvited, in the chair opposite the desk. "I think you'd better tell me what's on your mind," I told him.

The Earl wasn't looking at me, he was using a blotter to soak up the excess ink, and I think stalling for time to perhaps gather his thoughts. At length he looked up and held me with a steady direct stare. "The reason that I asked you how much you would require to suffer some physical hurt is because there is a substantial risk of you incurring some injuries if you choose to assist me with what I can best describe as a family difficulty."

He paused, I think to see if I wanted to make any comment or ask any question, but I find it's best in most circumstances to let people just talk. Given a free run they often say more than they intend to, and sometimes there's a lot you can pick up from what they don't say. I nodded for him to continue.

"I freely admit Mr Slater that you are the fourth private detective that I have consulted, and the previous three all declined the case, despite my offering what I considered were very generous terms."

This was more serious and more intriguing than I anticipated. Private detectives are on the whole a hard-nosed bunch, often ex-policemen, and always characters who realise that somewhere along the line somebody is going to take a punch at them, so for three to refuse suggested that there was a lot more to this case than the kind of routine stuff that private detectives spend most of their time dealing with. I just knew this wasn't going to be an unfaithful wife, some family larceny or a missing person enquiry. My guess was blackmail, but I had had enough by now of the Earl creeping up to the subject.

"Let's get right down to it," I said bluntly. "I might turn you down too but I'm going to at least know what it's all about, so just tell me, the way I like it, which is short and straight."

"You're right of course," he said almost apologetically. "The truth of the matter is that my daughter, Destry, has left to live with a man of whom I do not approve. It is imperative the relationship ends."

"You say your daughter is called Destry?" He just had to be kidding.

The Earl nodded, and I thought there was just a hint of a wry smile.

"Her late mother had seen a certain Marlene Deitrich film shortly before the christening. Until then she was going to be called Victoria."

"How old is Destry?"

"Thirty-four."

"Forgive me if I look amazed," I said, doing my best to look amazed. "A woman of thirty-four is entitled to do exactly what she wants. She is hardly likely to come back just because I ask her nicely."

"I don't expect you to ask her to come back. I want you to ask, or rather persuade, the man she's with to give her up."

"Why don't you just pay him off?"

"Because he is probably as wealthy as I am."

"Ah."

"Ah, indeed," said the Earl. "Now you see the nature of the problem. You can see why it needs specialised handling."

"You want me to appeal to his better side then?"

"Therein lies another difficulty," he said. "I very much doubt this man has a better side."

"Who is he?"

There was a long pause, and I actually felt the Earl was building himself up to utter the name. Perhaps she had eloped with Mike Tyson.

"His name is Barratt. Lonsdale Barratt."

Barratt is a common name. But there could be only one Lonsdale Barratt and now seemed a good time to get up from my chair, politely thank the Earl for his time, and tell him I would send my consultation bill in the post, and make a dignified exit.

"That would be the one and only Lonsdale Barratt?"

"I believe so."

Barratt was in his early fifties and had already served two separate life sentences for murder. He had various other convictions for causing grievous bodily harm, and he once broke the arm of his own lawyer who he thought wasn't doing a good enough job defending him. Barratt had been a successful armed robber for some years, laundering the money and investing it in legitimate businesses, mainly property and clubs.

His first murder victim was a member of his own gang, who stepped out of line and was shot dead, apparently to emphasise that Barratt didn't tolerate indiscipline. He served twelve years for what the trial judge described as 'a clinical execution'. The second victim was a young man who foolishly decided to have a go when Barratt was sprinting for the getaway car after a bank blag. Barratt claimed his shotgun went off accidentally but the jury didn't believe him. He got a life-sentence, but was out after another twelve years. Well-paid lawyers and tame psychiatrists did their job.

Barratt had been out for a while now. Trusted friends had run his business affairs while he was inside, and had built up a huge property empire which spread right across Birmingham. In the big property boom of the mid-1980s Barratt had reportedly made millions selling out to developers, prime sites he had picked up cheap years earlier.

I had never met him personally, but I knew a few who had. They could search through a dictionary all day long and never find one good word for him.

"Asking Lonsdale Barratt to stop seeing your daughter would put me in intensive care for weeks," I said. "And that's if I survive at all."

He was undeterred. "My original question still remains," he said. "How much will it take for you to get hurt?"

"Fifty grand," I said, off the top of my head. A stupid sum which I knew no one would pay. It gave me the out.

"Agreed," he said immediately.

"What?"

"Agreed. A fair sum in the circumstances. Is it the usual arrangement for you detectives. Half now, half later?"

"Why not?" I said. I still could not believe he was going along with it.

He was off his head for offering, I was off my head for taking. Whoever said money erodes the soul had it right.

We made the necessary arrangements, the Earl wrote me a cheque, and I told him not to worry if he didn't hear from me for a few days. Finding Barratt would be easy. Getting to him and talking to him was going to be the problem.

I was just leaving the study when I remembered it might be useful to see what the daughter looked like. The Earl said he would fetch a photograph and even before I saw it I had this feeling she would be a babe, just like they were in the Marlowe stories.

Was I disappointed? A little, I suppose. I have a weakness for blondes and Destry was a rather stern-looking brunette. She had a passing resemblance to Charlotte Rampling, but appeared an aloof and frosty character. Very hands-off, I'd say. No fun at all. Maybe Marlowe did get all the luck.

Back in my office I switched on the coffee percolator and settled down by the telephone. I put a call through to an old pal, Terry Clarke, who was a freelance crime reporter feeding the tabloids. I had to be careful what I told him for these tabloid guys forget all about friendship when it comes to a good story. If he'd known that I'd connected an Earl's daughter to Lonsdale Barratt it would be all over the front page, if not a ten-page picture spread on the inside. I just told Terry someone had asked me to locate Barratt. If anything turned up that was worth a news piece he would be the first to know.

"Watch your step," he warned. "If Barratt gets even a sniff that you are enquiring about him you can expect at least both legs broken, and you can bet that while it's being done there would be ten people to swear they saw him eating lobster in St Tropez."

He said as far as he knew Barratt operated at an office suite above a night-club called Romanski's on the north side of Birmingham. That was all I needed. Not only was I going to get both legs broken but I was going to go deaf from the noise.

Terry faxed me a batch of background cuttings on Lonsdale Barratt, going back right to the start of his criminal career as a juvenile. It wasn't my idea of fun reading, but I had to scour every line because I was looking for an ace. Let me explain: if you go into any situation involving confrontation or even negotiation you need an ace card. Timing is everything. You play it only when all seems lost. The surprise, sometimes even shock, element of a good ace card can often turn the situation on its head, and put you in control.

There was no point in my confronting Barratt with reasoned tone, logical argument and polite use of please and thank you. He would probably respond by breaking my fingers one by one. The only way to get his attention would be to get something on him, something unexpected. Something personal.

After half an hour among the cuttings I came across a possibility. Tucked away in a background feature was the revelation that Barratt's mother Marjorie was still alive. Now in her eighties, she was tucked away in a nursing home in Southport.

I called Terry again for any unpublished snippets he might have about the mother-and-son relationship and it was certainly worth the call. He told me that Marjorie had suffered recurring nervous breakdowns during Barratt's murder trials and had never really recovered. Barratt had put her in a private nursing home and took care of the bills. "Now comes the interesting part," said Terry. "Barratt never goes to see her."

Now that was a surprise.

"He just can't bring himself to visit anymore," Terry continued. "It upsets him too much. From what I can gather, he worships her yet hasn't seen her for ten years. He eases his conscience by paying for her to have the best of everything. I suppose he knows it's down to him that she's in there, and he just can't handle it."

My cynicism was bursting to get out. "You mean he has emotions? He could handle killing a couple of people without getting too upset!"

"Different thing altogether," said Terry. "Even psychopaths can get emotional about their old mum."

He was probably right, and I had to take a chance on it anyway.

That afternoon I drove up the M6 to Southport with a large food hamper on the back seat. Except that I didn't see it as a hamper. To me, it looked like an ace card.

The nursing home was a big white-painted Victorian house set back from the road but still within sight of the sea. Well, with binoculars perhaps. The tide goes out so far at Southport that your lilo would be washed up in Nova Scotia.

The receptionist could have been quite pretty but the makeup was too heavy and she should have sued her hairdresser. Her fingernails were painted neon blue and were at least an inch long. How she ever used her computer keyboard was a mystery. Putting the hamper down on her desk, and giving her my best smile, I went straight into my well-rehearsed story, so slick and credible I began to believe it myself.

I told her I was Marjorie Barratt's great-nephew. Hadn't seen her for years but I was in the town on business and thought I'd surprise her. "She probably won't recognise me," I said. "I was only a kid when we last met. I used to go round to her house for tea. She made a fantastic lemon drizzle cake. So I've bought her a nice food hamper to share with her friends."

"What a lovely gesture," said Miss Fingernails, and took me through to meet Marjorie. She turned out to be a sweet old lady, thin and bent, wearing a pink floral dress and a cardigan several sizes too big. When I was introduced, she looked puzzled but then said: "You're not Alfie's boy, are you?"

I had no idea who Alfie was but I readily agreed I was his boy, and her puckered cheeks refolded the creases into a smile. "Well, I never," she chuckled. "You have grown up into a big boy."

Miss Fingernails arranged for some tea to be sent in and I spent half an hour listening to the old dear rambling on about people I was supposed to know. Some of it made sense, much of it was from ga-ga land. I kept agreeing with everything she said. Oddly enough, she never once mentioned Lonsdale. I think she had blanked out her only son, and who could blame her?

Time to go, and time to do what I had really come up to Southport to accomplish. I took out my camera, called an attendant, and asked her to take a snap of me with Marjorie for the family album. She took several. I had my arm around Marjorie and she gave me a gummy smile right on cue.

On the way back to Birmingham there was only one question on my mind. How could such a nice old lady have ever given birth to a monster like Lonsdale Barratt?

The next day I waited until around 10 pm before heading for Romanski's. No point in rushing to get at the hospital food. Actually, I guessed that it would be quite late before Barratt put in an appearance. These clubs were open until 2 a.m., so right now the action was only just beginning.

The club had taken some finding. It was on the fringe of a industrial estate, and I suppose it had been bought because it had all the space that a warehouse could offer. Scores of kids were drifting towards the place, the guys with greased hair and earrings and looking like Colombian drug pushers and all the girls minimally-dressed and smoking. They were all heading to a club with their eyes open and a smile on their faces despite the fact that they were going to be ripped off by the admission charge, the drinks and the drugs. And they say today's generation is bright.

The place may have been a warehouse but they had spent some money on the frontage. Las Vegas style. Lots of neon lights, Roman pillars, fake stone statues. It was architectural mix that would have frightened Sir Norman Foster. You could hear the music from fifty yards away, that insistent underlying tinny downbeat that kneaded the brain. All the records sounded like that these days. I just hoped that Barratt's office was soundproof. That's if I ever got in to see him.

The first problem came as I walked up the steps. Two bouncers in tuxedos stepped forward, their hair cropped and their eyes black and glinty.

"You sure you're in the right place, sir?" It was the sir I

didn't like. It was tacked on with sarcasm. I suppose a thirty-something guy with receding hair, no body piercing, and a suit that didn't look like it had been made by a sports company was going to stand out a bit.

"I'd like to see Mr Barratt," I said.

"Mr Barratt doesn't see anyone without an appointment."

"How would I get an appointment?"

The bouncer on the left grinned and said: "Mr Barratt doesn't give appointments."

"It's very important I see him," I insisted. "It's a personal matter."

"What kind of personal matter?"

"That's the problem," I said. "If I were to discuss such a personal matter involving Mr Barratt with two of his employees, at their insistence, I know that Mr Barratt would get very angry."

That had them. They were uncertain now. They must have had some experience of Barratt's viciousness and it wasn't a risk they were willing to take. They were as confused as anyone with two brain cells between them could be. They looked at each other for inspiration, and eventually the one on the left walked to the reception desk and picked up a telephone. I followed him over in case I could hear anything of interest. He repeated what I said, then said: 'yes, Mr Barratt', about four times. Then he paused, then said: "On a scale of one to ten, how severe?" I didn't hear the answer but two seconds later both guys had me by the arms, lifted me off my feet and waltzed me out of the front door and round to the side of the building. There, out of sight of the bright lights and the public gaze, I was given a short sharp and expert working over which came out as a six on my scale of one to ten. I was left slumped at the side of the building, my ribs on fire from a pounding, a pain in my groin from a boot and a busted lip that was spilling blood down my shirt front. I had got away lightly. I think only two of my ribs were cracked.

On almost any other occasion, in similar circumstances, I would have gone home to half a bottle of single malt and some tender loving care from whatever girl I was seeing at the time. But at this time I wasn't seeing anyone, and though I did have a good stock of malt whisky I also had a cheque for £25,000 in my pocket and, like a punch-drunk boxer trying to stagger to his feet when he knows it's all over, I knew I was going to have to go back in there and make a second try. It was the least I could do. I wasn't nearly badly enough beaten up to earn twenty five grand. Yet.

But hold on. Max Slater is not stupid, and is not an ex-SAS hero, so this time I thought I'd try the back door. I shuffled along the side of the building trying to gently explore just how flat my balls were after the kicking, and trying to mop up the blood off my chin with a handkerchief. It was quite dark at the rear of the building but there was a bit of a downlight from the orange street lamps along the side road. I could see a couple of fire exit double doors, and both of them were tightly shut. Now I know a thing or two about fire doors. If you are on the inside, you push a down bar to force them open when the place catches fire. If you are on the outside, and you can get something thin enough to force its way between the crack, you can sometimes flip the bar down and spring them open. But don't tell everybody otherwise the cinemas will be full of people who haven't paid for their ticket.

I started to scuffle around the waste ground kicking my feet in the hope of clanging against a strip of metal or, rather optimistically, an abandoned jemmy. I'm getting nowhere but then I heard the clatter of one of the doors opening and I dropped down behind a parked car. A guy came out and lit up a cigarette and stood there looking at the stars. I got one of my bright ideas, one of the kind I always see working in the movies. My own car was over on the left-hand side of the waste ground behind the club, and the remote central locking had a panic button on the key fob. The question is, was I out of range? I plipped the button, and the klaxon wailed and all the lights start to flash. The guy smoking the cigarette went over to have a look and while he's doing that I just strolled in the back door.

I found myself at the foot of an iron staircase with breeze-block walls painted dirty cream. I headed up the stairs before the guy on the car park came back in, and when I got to the top I was in a corridor with fluorescent strip lighting and a few closed doors. Coming through the walls is that rhythmic-thump dance music that makes you want to go and redesign the sound system using a lump hammer. I was just wondering whether to try one of the doors, and if so which one, when one of the doors opened and another man in a tuxedo came out. He was in his mid-twenties, slim built, and wore a surprised expression. But then he was confronted by a dishevelled looking character with blood down his shirt.

"What are you doing up here?" he snapped.

"Carl sent me," I said.

One of the bouncers who had thrown me out was wearing one of those corporate lapel badges which announced he was Carl, security officer.

"Why would he send you up here?"

"I got hurt in a bit of a fight and he sent me to clean up."

"Right." He seemed satisfied. "Come this way. I'll take you to the washroom."

He led me to the third door and nodded for me to go in. I opened the door, felt a violent push in my back and went crashing across and hit the opposite wall. The door shut behind me. I heard the harsh scrape of a bolt. I made a mental note to include the incident in my rewrite of the Private Detective's Operational Handbook. Never walk into a room first.

My right hand was still hurting from when I smacked against the wall, and I felt around a bit in the darkness to find a light switch. The room was small and windowless and empty except for a few small cardboard boxes, a mop and a galvanised metal bucket. Oh yes. There was also a big twelve pack of toilet rolls.

No doubt about it. Mr Barratt had his security tight. I was not looking forward to what was coming next. Anytime soon I was expecting a couple of guys who could double as wildebeests to come barging into the room and give me a nose job and some other facial reconstruction, and very generously not charge me a surgeon's fee. Suddenly, my £25,000 cheque stopped giving me a warm glow of protection.

I was wrong about two guys looking like wildebeests bursting in the door. There were three of them, one of them Carl, who appeared to have been brought along purely for identification purposes.

"That's him," he said, and left the room. The other two didn't go with him. The smaller one of the two was about the size of Lennox Lewis and he came to the door and stood in front of it while the really big guy walked over to me and did his best to stand face to face, except that his face was two feet above mine. I gave his shirt buttons a nasty stare. He was another shaven-headed character with three silver earrings in each ear, and one of those straggly goatee beards that looked like it had been taken off a regimental goat. He looked down at me. I looked up. I could see his nostrils were neatly trimmed.

"Mr Barratt has asked me to find out what you really want," he said, so softly, so gently that it was ultra-menacing. "So I suggest you start talking."

"First, I think we should establish the rules for the discussion," I said. I had no idea what I was talking about. I thought it might delay me feeling some pain. It didn't. He hit me once, hard, just above the stomach, whooshing the breathe out of me and sending me slumping down among the cardboard boxes and the mop and bucket.

"Agreed," he said. "First rule is no lip."

He waited for me to get up, which was nice of him. He could have kicked me while I was down. I'm still wheezing, trying to get enough breath back to get to my feet, when the door opens and another tuxedo walks in.

"Gary, you're needed at the front right away," he says and goes out.

Gary, the one who was standing by the door, goes with him. He knows the bonehead remaining can keep me on the floor with just his little finger. Now I don't like pain, and in desperate situations you do what you can to avoid it. As I stumbled to my feet, still bent double, I was partly screening the bucket, one of the old type galvanised steel ones with a special receptacle to squeeze out the mop. Our school caretaker used to have one. As the bonehead got within a yard of me I suddenly straightened up, grabbed the bucket and slammed it in an upward arc against the side of his head. There was a reverberating dong like the sound from Big Ben. He went down on the floor.

I leapt past him and out of the door, heading back down the corridor the way I came in. At the top of the stairs I collided with someone coming out of a door. At first, I thought it was Charlotte Rampling but it was the Earl's daughter, Destry. She was wearing a fitted light grey suit with a short skirt, and had great legs from what I could take in just half-a-second. She was startled by my speed and I grabbed her arm and spun her around, pulling her down the stairs, still moving fast and clattering the metal steps.

"Get out of the building," I yelled. "It's about to explode." Stupid, I know, but it was all I could think of.

"What?" she said, running alongside me.

"It's about to blow!"

We burst out of a fire exit and I noticed she was clutching a briefcase.

"Here, carry this," she said, handing it to me. "And don't lose it." You could tell she was an Earl's daughter. She probably couldn't even wipe her own nose.

I stopped at my car and plipped it open. Then I realised I had no idea why I've got her with me, and there's no way she was going to get in the car and drive off with me anyway. Before I could think of anything to say that might persuade her, she opened the passenger door, looked across at me and said: "What are you waiting for? Let's get the hell out of here." Life's full of surprises.

I jumped in, started up and accelerate hard away, leaving as much rubber on the tarmac as you can manage in a Ford Mondeo. It isn't much. Out of the rear fire door I see three or four giant penguins racing for their car as I crash through the gears, racing up the side of the building towards the main road. Parked vehicles and meandering teenagers heading for the club make it a tricky exit and I sheer the door-mirror off one car. It was that or knock down some kid in a baseball cap who veered into view.

I'm heading back into Birmingham and you can tell I'm not used to being in a car chase. There is a gaggle of heavyweight psychos on my trail, and I'm still trying to stick to the speed limit. Big headlights are coming up fast in the rear view mirror, too fast to be anything else except prime beef in dinner suits. Even though it was a hundred yards behind I could still pick out the unmistakable grille of an S-Class Mercedes in the harshness of the sodium street lamps. I knew it had an awesome V8 engine, and a size twelve boot on the accelerator. It's gaining on me as if I'm in reverse.

"Mind if I ask why you're with me?" I ask the girl as I slew hard right into a side street, a tree-lined avenue with less lighting and lots of parked cars.

"I was leaving anyway," she says.

"But you've no idea who I am."

"What's it matter? By the look of it, you're no friend of Lonsdale Barratt and that's fine by me. The more distance I can put between him and me the better. Especially as I've just stolen fifty thousand pounds from his safe."

Now I'm not easily shocked. You never are in my business. But believe me, I was shocked.

"But you're his girlfriend!"

"Ex-girlfriend," she said. "It's served its purpose now."

While we're talking I'm taking lefts and rights at random through a housing estate, and each time I leave one road I see searchlight headlamps curving into the one I'm just leaving.

"He's going to be really mad with you," I said.

"Madder than you think," she said. "I've also hacked into his bank account and just transferred three million pounds to my account in South America."

I take my eyes off the road just long enough to give her a hard look. This is one of those crazy babes who belongs in a Raymond Chandler novel. The type Marlowe always meets up with.

There is a big orange glow of street lamps in the distance and I try to cut towards it, still left-and-righting. The headlamps are getting closer.

"As you can see, I'm rather busy right now," I said. "So I've only got time for the very short version of what the hell is going on with you and Barratt. Give it to me in twenty words or less."

I glance across and she's smiling. In the minimal glow from the instrument lights she looks less plain and more interesting. That's like thinking a waitress looks pretty. Always a bad sign.

"I had my own reasons for latching on to Lonsdale. We were only together long enough for me to find my way around his finances. A means to an end. That short enough for you?"

"Ten words too many, but thanks for trying."

She was looking back over her shoulder and I didn't need her to tell me where the Mercedes was. It's lights were so bright it was probably on my boot lid. I swung a hard right at a junction, then spun another ninety-degree turn onto the pavement, looped around a tree and back the way we came. It was not the sort of neat manoeuvre a sixteen-foot-long Mercedes could do with a deal of grace. The driver had to back up for a three-point turn and we gained a few seconds.

"Anyway, who are you?" she said. "Ten words or less."

"Max Slater. Private detective. Hired by your father."

She looked impressed. "Daddy?" she said. "He sent you for me?"

"No, he sent me to see Barratt with a view to getting several of my bones broken and my face rearranged. Look, do you mind if we discuss this some other time. I need to concentrate on my driving."

"Your driving isn't the problem. It's the car. Damon Hill couldn't lose them in this."

I hit the brakes hard as we came to a T-junction and I'd no idea whether to go left or right. You know how it is in TV car chases. Whatever turn you make, it's the wrong one. I went right. It was the wrong one. If there was a cul-de-sac sign I hadn't seen it. At the end of the avenue was a horse-shoe shaped turning circle with a fringe of houses and nowhere to go. There was no point in even opening the doors and making a run for it. The Mercedes was alongside us, and another pair of headlights were right behind. It was bonehead who hauled me out of the car. His ear was bloody and inflated to three times its size. He was remarkably gentle with me.

"Mr Barratt doesn't want you damaged any further until he has spoken to you personally," he said, in the kind of soft growl you get from a cautious bulldog. "But don't you worry. Severe damage is on the agenda for later." In a way, I liked him. He chose his words well.

They shoved me on to the back seat of the Mercedes with a minder either side like human bookends. Bonehead was driving and Destry was allowed to sit in the front. No one had laid a hand on her, and it suddenly occurred to me that maybe Barratt didn't yet know that she had robbed him.

"I take it I now have Mr Barratt's attention," I asked. "At least he has agreed to see me."

"I wouldn't be too pleased about that, pal," said one of the minders next to me. "He's as mad as hell with you for busting into his club, and then you abduct his girlfriend."

I was right. So far, they hadn't caught on to what had really happened. Destry looked over her shoulder, looking at the minder, but speaking to me.

"I was just going into the office, when he grabbed hold of me and forced me outside into his car," she said.

Neat. In fact she was just coming out of the office having electronically transferred Barratt's money. At least when he found out he couldn't blame that one on me, but whichever way this was all going to end I knew it was going to be messy.

We came out of Birmingham, up the Aston Expressway, onto the M6, off at the next junction and headed into one of the less salubrious areas of the industrial West Midlands, Wednesbury. The Mercedes went through this tattered urban patchwork as if it was out of its class and not wanting to stop or be seen. After a few minutes we lurched off the main road down an unmade track to a large scrap yard with twelve-foot high corrugated steel fencing topped with double strands of barbed wire. In this kind of territory, there were obviously people prepared to risk vertigo and severe cuts to the hand just to steal the carburettor of a 1975

Datsun. The Mercedes stopped and behind it a 5-Series BMW pulled up with Barratts' security consultants on board. Behind, one of them was driving my Mondeo and he took it right up to the gates of the scrap yard. There, a West Indian guy with a bright torch and a large Alsatian dog with more teeth than an animal could reasonably require, were waiting. The gates were opened and we all went in, my Mondeo leading the way. The situation was very unpleasant. I was far too scared to be scared and in any case I was depending on my utterly reliable number one rule of life: something always turns up.

We waited about ten minutes and nobody spoke to me. Scrap yards always remind me of the aftermath of a nuclear war. Cars are stacked on top of each other as high as houses, all eyeless headlights and chrome grins, and there is a burnt and oily smell heavy in the air. Discarded tyres, cannibalised engines, abandoned seats and pools of black muddy water catching a glint of reflection from the security light by the cabin. It looked a desolate metallic hell, the leftovers of consumerist gluttony. I decided I was getting too poetic about the place, and started to map out some well chosen words with which to greet Lonsdale Barratt when he arrived. I wasn't afraid of him. I was terrified. Yet I was also coldly angry that one man could rule so comprehensively merely by fear.

The gates were opened again and in glided a Bentley Mulsanne Turbo, burgundy red with white-wall tyres and a painted radiator grille. It was the only motorised way to understate your wealth. Someone opened a door and Barratt got out. I had seen his photograph but I had never seen the man. He wasn't as big nor as heavy as I had thought, in fact he looked like a diminutive George C. Scott complete with the cropped greyish hair. He had spent a lot of money on a blue pin-stripe suit, without anyone telling him pin-stripes were passe. He wore a pale blue shirt with a button down collar and a blue silk tie with tiny polka dots. Stripes and polka dots! Come on, Barratt. Appearance is important. He walked up to me and looked curiously. He spoke in a soft emotionless voice, like an accountant reading a balance sheet. "I do not know you, Mr Slater, and private detectives are an irritant at the best of times. I shall want the truth from you, but it is my sad experience in life that people do not tell me the truth, at least not at first. I have better things to do than to be here, so in order to minimise my presence at this rather inhospitable venue I intend to place you in a situation which will ensure you tell the truth immediately." He nodded to two of his men, who fastened on to each of my arms and twisted me away from him.

"Hold on, Barratt," I shouted. "I'll tell you anyway. I'm a coward."

He wasn't interested. I was led to a clearing among the stacks of scrap cars, a path lit by my Mondeo which was being driven behind us. Ahead of me was a piece of machinery which I identified as an hydraulic car crusher. I'd seen them on TV. You drive a car in, pull a lever, the sides close in and the car is crushed to a cube the size of a coffee table and spat out the other end. I was put in the passenger seat of my car and bound into it with bright blue nylon rope. My arms were pinned to my sides. The Mondeo was driven into the crusher and the minder got out.

"Don't worry," he told me. "When we're finished, we're going to take you back home. You'll be so flat we'll post you through the letter box." I bet he'd been working on that quip for three or four hours.

Barratt ambled up to the side of the crusher. I suppose he wanted to see my face. Destry was at his side and I heard her say: "There's no need to do this. He told me my father sent him." Barratt put his arm around her. He obviously hadn't yet discovered he'd lost three million pounds. Either that or he was taking it remarkably well. He waved his hand and somebody somewhere pushed a button and there were hisses like the air brakes on lorries, lots of grinding and whirring, and for half a minute or so nothing much happened. Then the slack between the side walls of the machine and the car were taken up, and enormous forces started to attempt to reduce the Ford to the size of a toy. The back window popped out like a cork. The left side back window shattered then the two on the right. Then the windscreen let go and leaped away from the car. The driver's door was relentlessly moving towards me in the front passenger seat. The car was almost half its original width and still closing in. I found myself shouting: "All right Barratt, all right, I'll tell you."

Barratt was enjoying the spectacle, and I don't think he thought I was quite scared enough just yet. Then the roof buckled, and my face was against the one remaining piece of glass. I could feel the floor forcing my feet up. I hadn't felt so cramped since the last time I was on the tube. I could feel the side window glass beginning to bow and I tried to turn my head away and close my eyes. There was a shattering crack and my hair was showered with glass fragments. It was time to play my ace card. There had been no point in playing it sooner. If I'd traded it too quickly, Barratt would have been suspicious. He was a yard away from me, stern and impassive as one of those statues on Easter Island. His track record suggested he liked to watch people in pain, and I had a feeling I wasn't the first person he had encased in a cube of crushed metal. I looked up at him and said: "Stop this right now Barratt or Marjorie is going to be very upset."

His dead fish eyes blinked once and I knew I had his attention. "Marjorie? Marjorie who?"

"Your mother Marjorie."

This time Barratt blinked twice. He waved a hand to shut off the crusher, made a half turn and barked at everyone to clear the area, instructing them to go back to the Portakabin and wait there. They strode off and Barratt turned back to me. He put one hand on the car door and stooped down and leaned in towards me. "What do you know of my mother?" he asked in a voice from a horror film.

"Reach into my inside pocket," I instructed. Unquestioningly, he did so. He pulled out something I'd put there precisely for this moment, a photograph of me and Marjorie having tea at the old people's home, taken when I'd delivered the hamper.

"I know you haven't seen her in ten years," I said. "But I see her every week and if I'm not there at the old folks home in Southport next Thursday, and every Thursday after that, pouring her tea and feeding her Mr Kipling cakes, she is going to be very upset. You see Barratt, I'm her only friend. And she needs a friend seeing as how her only son abandoned her."

I was chancing it a bit there because I saw his arm stiffen and I thought I was going to get a hard knuckle punch. The remark had hit home for it seemed to me that the tar spots that were Barratt's eyes were watering up a little. Here was a man who could blast somebody with a shotgun and not even think about it, yet cry with the burden of terrible guilt over the mother he loved but couldn't face.

"I could never deal with it. Never stand seeing her like that," he said. "I've always seen she's never wanted for anything."

He was just looking at the picture, saying nothing, with tears seeping from his eyes.

"You're right." I said. "She wants for nothing. Except for

friends. So am I going to be there next week having tea with her? Or am I going to be in a Ford Mondeo sandwich?"

Funny isn't it, whenever you've told a lie the next one is easier, and two or three lies later you usually begin to think you might even be telling the truth. I must admit I felt a little bit bad about saying how much of a friend I was to Marjorie. But then, unlike Barratt, I knew she was a happy enough soul in that house. Maybe next week I would send another hamper just to ease my conscience. Barratt summoned a couple of his men to get me out of the car and Destry came running over, the relief evident on her face.

"We're leaving," he told her, "We're leaving now."

"You go ahead," she said. "I'll see you at the club. I'd better square things with Mr Slater about daddy." Barratt nodded and walked back towards his car. He got into the Bentley and it made a swift and silent arc as it turned and went out of the gate. The minders followed in the BMW. Destry was looking at me with a certain admiration. "What on earth did you say to him? He looked quite upset."

"He wasn't holding all the aces," I said. "I kept one back." She looked puzzled but she didn't pursue it. Instead, she took out a mobile phone.

"Excuse me a moment," she said. "I just have to make a call."

While she was talking I moved out of earshot and went over to the Mondeo. I started to get together a few personal effects and wondered how I'd explain it to the insurance company. As I leaned in through the window I noticed that down on the buckled floor was Destry's briefcase. The one with fifty grand in it. I yanked it free and started walking back towards her. She switched off the phone and then hurled it in a high curve and I heard it thump along the scrap cars. "It wasn't my phone, it was one of the spare ones from the club," she explained. She saw I wanted more and added: "I suppose I might as well tell you. I've just given an anonymous tip off to the police. I've given them the make, registration number and route of Barratt's car. I've also told them what they will find under the back seat."

"And what will they find?"

"A large quantity of counterfeit notes."

"He'll say they were planted. I bet he's got a smart lawyer."

She shrugged. "Maybe. But I've also given them the combination of his safe back at the club. In there are the printing plates and details of all his bank accounts. Well, all except the

Swiss one. I've emptied that and destroyed the records. The money is now in my account in a bank in Rio."

"Not you and Ronnie Biggs?"

She laughed. "He's too old for me. But there are a lot of muscled young men in Copocabana who are not. I'm sure they are going to be very very nice to a rich if plain European millionairess."

"You underestimate yourself," I said.

She shook her head: "I don't think so. I've always known I'm not much to look at. Men have never shown much interest in me. Or at least not men you'd want to. I suppose that's why I was so determined to get even with Barratt."

"What do you mean, get even?"

She glanced at her watch. "Long story and I've got to go. This is the short version. When I was eighteen I was absolutely in love with a boy called James Meredith. We were students together. He was pretty stuck on me too. He was my first and only serious boyfriend. First sex too. But it wasn't to be."

The name James Meredith suddenly rang a bell. I'd seen it mentioned when I was trawling through the press cuttings on Barratt. "Don't tell me," I said, excited at making the connection. "He was the have-a-go hero Barratt shot during the bank raid."

She swept her hair back from her eyes, and was nodding. They were nice eyes. I hadn't really noticed them before.

"And you've been plotting revenge all these years?"

"No. I got over it after a while. I was able to put it all behind me and get on with life. But quite by chance, a few months ago, I came to a friend's birthday party at Romanski's. Someone happened to mention it was owned by Lonsdale Barratt, and suddenly it all came back to me. I'd almost forgotten how much he had hurt me. I'm almost thirty five and there has never been another man who mattered, apart from James. He may have been the only one for me. Suddenly I became obsessed with my need to get back at Barratt. I made a point of seeking him out. I made sure he got to know I was someone with an aristocratic background. One thing I'd learned is that it can be something of a turn-on for some men, and Barratt was one of them. He had a choice of women at the club but they were all tarts and hookers. None of them was class. I played it aloof, a little hard to get, that made Barratt all the more keen. It all started to move so fast, even I was surprised. Only a couple of months after we started going out, some girl who ran the legitimate side of his business had to leave and I volunteered. I'd done business studies, computer courses, even had some legal training. Barratt was impressed. He kept going around telling people he had an Earl's daughter working as his personal assistant."

She looked at her watch again. "Look, I'd better go. My luggage is already at the airport." We walked over towards the Portakabin where the lone nightwatchman still stood eyeing us curiously. "OK," I said. "You can lock up now, and keep your wits about you. Mr Barratt doesn't want any more problems."

I used my mobile to call a taxi and we waited together on the main road for it to arrive.

"How did you get hold of his Swiss bank account number?" I asked.

"Just lucky. I had access to his safe, as I did his banking. I was so rich I was trusted. In a book in the safe, I found the account number and the password. They were supposed to be disguised among a list of telephone numbers but I could recognise a Swiss account number. Daddy has one. Initially I'd planned to get evidence to put Barratt away, but when I found the access details I realised I could empty his account. It seemed a more satisfying thing to do."

"You're quite a girl," I said. I realised I was still hanging on to the briefcase so I handed it to her.

"Keep it." she said. "I don't need it. I only took it out of spite. Call it a bonus for all the extra lies you'll have to tell."

"What lies are those?"

"Well, you're going to have to report back to Daddy. Tell him you've broken up the relationship. Tell him I'm upset and I've gone away on a long holiday but that I'll be in touch."

I didn't argue. Freak pay days are rare, and when they come along you should grab them with both hands. She dropped me off in the city centre, and carried on to the airport. I thought it might be a good idea to take a little holiday myself, once I'd reported back to the Earl. Somewhere hot, colourful, exciting. Like Rio.

making me irritable, or controlling myself.

Weekend with Pepe

Sunday June 7

4.30pm. She passes my window again. Always with small ruffle-coated dog on leash. Odd sort of dog. Tail curls almost full-circle. Ears erect and pointy. (Must check what breed). She must live close by as I see her almost every day. Veronica would be a perfect name for her.

Wonder if she has boyfriend. Mostly, wonder how she gets into those tight jeans. Shape defined so clearly, she could be naked. She walks in absolutely upright fashion. Rapid steps as if there is an urgency to her journey.

Monday June 8

The library. Ask plump and strangely eager assistant to direct me to the section on dogs. Surprised at how many books there are on this subject. Dozens. In an illustrated A-Z of world breeds, quickly identify Veronica's dog as a Chihuahua, small breed originating in Mexico. Then notice All You Need To Know About The Chihuahua by Harriet M. Stoneley. Excellent.

Back at the counter, getting the book stamped, the plump assistant looks up at me with interest. "I have a Westie myself," she says. My puzzled look prompts her to add

"West Highland White." Sounds like breed of pig. I nod and try to appear pleasant without actually smiling.

Evening. Am on my way to becoming an expert on Chihuahuas. Ms Stoneley's style staid and humourless, but informative. A half-bottle of Estola helps me through.

Discover the Chihuahua is "fussy about the company it keeps" and is "unafraid of other dogs, whatever their size." And I learn an excellent conversation-stopper: the Aztecs used Chihuahua hair to weave cloth!

All in all, a day well spent.

Tuesday June 9

Tremendous slatting rainstorm. All my pelargoniums flattened. No Veronica. Perhaps she doesn't want to risk getting those tight jeans wet. Needless worry - they couldn't shrink to any tighter a fit!

Wednesday June 10

4.36pm. Veronica walks past. I am (by design) conveniently in the front garden, near the gate, clipping at a rosebush with my new secateurs.

"Excuse me," I call. "Am I right in thinking that is a Chihuahua?" She stops, pulling the dog close to her.

She has a nice smile. We talk about the dog. His name is Pepe. I discover her name is Helen. (Not as fetching as Veronica). I explain I am thinking of getting a small dog. I had read about the many endearing qualities of the Chihuahua. Could she, as an owner, recommend the breed? I stoop down to pat Pepe. There is an explosion of fur, a 'grrrr' of great savagery, and I am viciously bitten. The thumb and forefinger of my left hand are bleeding from deep perforations. Helen shrieks and tugs the dog away. "Naughty Pepe," she cries. She is very upset. Her dark hairs swishes across her face like a curtain as she shakes her head in disbelief. Apology after apology. I make light of the incident, though the pain is growing, pulsating stabs on cue with every racing heartbeat. I say goodbye and go indoors.

6.15pm. Hospital. Finally seen by woman doctor in casualty. Scottish. Unsympathetic. Anti-tetanus injection, light bandage. Back home, allow myself large whisky. Hand still throbbing.

Thursday June 11

4.25 pm. Doorbell. It's Helen - with Pepe! Says she has called to see how I am. And Pepe has come to say sorry.

I glower at the excited brown bundle and keep my distance. We have coffee. She continues to apologise. Twice she casually squeezes my hand (my good hand) when explaining that Pepe reacted "quite out of character".

The creature seems more agreeable today. At her insistence (only my bravado in trying to impress her induces me) I stroke his back. Pepe wags his tail. He licks me. "Now you are friends," says Helen.

Again she squeezes my hand, adding "And so are we."

Saturday June 13

Helen has accepted my invitation to come round for dinner. My penne riggatonne is exceptional, I tell her.

She arrives precisely on time (and without Pepe) looking very sexy in a short simple blue dress.

The evening goes well. We discover many shared interests. She even adores Leonard Cohen! Briefly, we talk about Chihuahuas. Am I still thinking of getting one?

Most certainly, I assure her. Especially now I know how adorable Pepe is. She is delighted.

Midnight. Helen says she must go home. "Pepe will be fretting for me," she smiles. On the doorstep, we kiss once (but quite passionately). She says she is so glad we have met. When I close the door I involuntarily give a sharp, ecstatic yelp of joy.

Wednesday June 17

9.30pm. Surprise telephone call from Helen. Her sister is seriously ill in hospital in Durham after car crash. Could I possibly look after Pepe until the weekend while she visits. "You don't know how grateful I will be," she says. There is no one else she can ask.

I agree, of course.

Thursday June 18

2.30pm. Helen arrives with Pepe, a small circular fleecy basket, three tins of dog food and a tiny pink soft-toy mouse. "He never goes anywhere without Mousey."

I reassure her there is no need to worry about Pepe.

He will be fine.

At her car, she pulls me against her and kisses me with lingering fervour. She will be back Sunday afternoon. We must have dinner. Would I book a table somewhere special? I decide immediately it should be at Mantini's.

Friday June 19

3.10am. Woken by persistent, high-pitched barking from the kitchen. (Pepe has been shut in there overnight).

I open the door and he leaps at me, fastening onto the leg of my boxer-shorts and nipping my thigh. I shout with surprise (and pain) and knock him off me.

The kitchen is wrecked. Waste bin overturned, contents strewn all over the floor. Wallpaper scratched off along one wall, to a height of eighteen inches, hanging limply in ragged strips. One limed-oak cupboard door is open, its corner chewed off. Two inches of wood missing. The oval Turkish rug - a present from my mother - is decimated, fragments of coloured wool peppered all around it. There are several pools of water on the tiles. Yellow water. Smelly yellow water. I stand there silent for I don't know how long.

Keep a watchful eye on Pepe all day. He seems tired and inactive. When, later, he perks up, I immediately take him for 90-minute walk on the common. Tonight, he will sleep! As a precaution, when placing him his basket before going up to bed, I clip on his lead and tie the other end to the radiator.

Saturday June 20

1.18am. Woken by crash from kitchen. Hurtle downstairs, banging elbow hard on newel post. Pepe has chewed through his lead and is standing on the work-surface eating biscuits from an overturned jar. Damage is minimal (I had placed virtually everything out of reach). Almost everything. He has shredded my wallet, cheque book and credit cards, left on the table overlooked.

Afternoon. Pepe has become docile and doting. Even rubs against my legs like purring cat. I take him for (even longer) walk. On return, I have a cup of tea and (tired myself) slip into short sleep on the sofa. Wake to find Pepe has ripped open one of the cushions and spread its feathery contents over half the living-room. My unread copy of Car magazine is confetti. He looks exceedingly pleased with the result of his endeavours, panting quietly and (absurd, I know) appearing to grin.

Sunday June 21

Unidentifiable noises from kitchen during night. Ignore them. Everything it is possible to destroy has been removed.

9 am. Enter kitchen. Curtains are on the floor. So too my Beardsley print, glass broken. Plug socket gnawed away, bare wires sprouting out from the cavity. Trip-switch has shut off power. Fridge and freezer have defrosted. Pepe is sadly unelectrocuted.

5 pm. While taking Pepe for a walk, decide to call at Helen's house (which had turned out to be on the other side of the estate) on the off-chance she was back from Durham. No one in. Glance through bay-window. No furniture, just carpet. At the house next door, neighbour tells me Helen has gone to Canada to start new job.

"She told me she was so pleased to have found a new home for Pepe," she says. "She didn't think she could persuade anyone to have him. He can be a right little terror, you know..."

Cherry Cake

"Would you like a piece of cherry cake?" he asked, pointing to the white paper bag between us on the bench.

Even after more than 60 years I still felt a single missed heartbeat as I heard those words, and the shock forced a graphic still-picture before my eyes like a predatory warning. It flashed, then was gone in just a sliver of a second and, as always, I immediately felt calm and untroubled. I had become used to such happenings.

"No," I said. "No, thank you."

The next sentence should have been left unuttered, but somehow I always said it, almost as if I wanted to provoke a response.

"I just cannot eat cherry cake."

The young man smiled understandingly.

"An allergy, perhaps," he said.

"A lost career," I said, knowing that he would require an explanation.

He had joined me while I was sitting on my usual bench in Holland Park, admittedly not the best known in London but one I liked because of it's smallness of scale. It had a certain intimacy, a cosiness. Besides, it was close to where I lived.

Invariably I sat in the centre of the wooden-slatted bench, a position I felt would deter anyone from joining me. On the whole I preferred to be alone, for idle chatter distracted me from taking in the slow-changing detail of the vista as the sun moved around, though I was always prepared to be sociable to those who intruded.

Today was my 80th birthday, an honourable milestone in any man's life. But then no one knew who I was. Had it not been for the incident with the cherry cake all those years ago then today I would have been famous, respected, revered. Today, The Times would be carrying a well-crafted eulogy celebrating my glittering career. In some of the better glossy magazines there would be 'at home' features, with photographs of me distinguished and at ease in my spacious apartment surrounded by my French furniture, and perhaps with my bronze sculpture of St. Cecilia discreetly on display. But it was not to be.

So today, I chose to sit quietly in the park and study the shadow-play on the glorious frontage of the Heppleton Court Hotel directly opposite. Its pale grey Georgian stonework was almost silver in the forceful down light of the midday sun, and sharp black shadows cut vertically from the jutting pediments in neat deep triangles of matching perfection.

The young man had disturbed my exercise in predicting the progress of shadows by crackling the plastic wrapper as he opened his sandwich. I saw he was tall and pale-faced, his hair over-long and floppy. The grey suit, subdued tie and diffident manner indicated that he was a junior executive from one of the nearby office blocks.

"A lost career?," he said in the puzzled tone they all used. "How can cherry cake cost you a career?"

"How long before you have to be back at your desk?"

He looked at me rather doubtfully, then glanced at his watch. "About 20 minutes."

"That will be ample," I told him.

It was August, 1937 and I was indoors reading as heavy, thundery rain had wrecked my plans for tennis with Gerald.

The telephone rang and it was another old pal from Summerford School, Ellis Ward. I hadn't seen Ellis for months, in fact, since the end-of-term party when we had vowed to keep in touch, despite our chosen careers taking us off in different directions, me to London, him to manage his father's estate in Suffolk. His father, Sir Merrill Ward, the former MP, owned vast tracts of the county.

Ellis and I had exchanged a few letters in recent weeks; I learned that he had taken to estate management with aplomb, and he, pleasingly, had read in the newspapers of my burgeoning success. In his last letter he had ventured a date for me to visit. I had readily accepted. It was the coming weekend.

So when Ellis rang to suggest we rearrange it, deeply apologetic of course, I was just a bit put out, particularly as his reason was so lame.

"It's my sister, Alicia, she's come to stay rather unexpectedly," he said. "Well, to be truthful, I wasn't expecting her. Father says he told me ages ago, but I suppose it must have slipped my mind."

"It's going to be damned difficult to rearrange, old chap," I said, not attempting to much disguise my irritation. "I'm so busy over the next few weeks, and summer will be gone. Besides, didn't you once tell me you were all rattling around in some vast hall with umpteen bedrooms?"

I think he realised that I found his excuse a bit hollow, and quickly relented.

"It's not the space, it's.. oh, doesn't matter, I suppose. It's just a damned nuisance her being here, that's all."

He arranged to collect me from Stowmarket station at two-thirty the next day and he was already waiting when I arrived, leaning against a smart red MG two-seater opposite the entrance.

"Bang on time," he said cheerily, strapping my case to the luggage rack.

On the way to Utsmere Hall we exchanged news eagerly in loud voices, over the wind and engine roar, as the MG raced along the narrow lanes. I was glad to see no trace remained of the mild annoyance he had shown on the telephone.

Once I had seen a snapshot of Utsmere Hall when Ellis was showing off the capabilities of his new Rolleiflex. The photograph showed a boxy, rather austere house - a mansion, I suppose you'd say - with much of its unrelenting brickwork softened by swathes of ivy.

As we turned into the drive, gravel clattering the MG's mud-guards, the place looked more welcoming, it's warm red brick vivid against green lawns and a backdrop of shimmering spreading oaks.

Ellis braked unnecessarily hard as we approached the porticoed entrance, showering gravel onto the wide stone steps. As I unfolded myself from the tiny cockpit of the MG Ellis was already at the front door, beckoning me.

"Do get a move on," he called. "Mother is absolutely desperate to meet you. She's read all about you. She just can't wait."

I followed him down a long wide corridor, rooms to the left and right - one of them a small library.

Suddenly veering left, through double mahogany doors, Ellis lead me into a sunlit drawing room, where an attractive woman sat elegantly in an armchair looking out through small-paned French windows to a low-walled terrace beyond.

"Mother, I'd like you to meet Phillip Lavery."

Walking towards her I could at first see only her right profile, high-cheekboned, fair skinned, tumbling dark hair. Then she rose and turned to greet me, and I am ashamed to say I audibly gasped.

Her left eye was missing, just a shallow well of puckered flesh with a white-line scar fleeing from it towards the ear and then lost under the hair.

"I know it looks dreadful," she said, shaking my hand and smiling. "I'm used to it, but I know the effect it can have on others. I had a nasty accident a few years ago. They told me I should wear an eye patch, but I refuse to go around looking like a pirate."

She laughed out loud at her own joke, as I suspected she had done many times before. Thankfully, Ellis cut in on my mumbled response, diverting attention to the garden and suggesting we sit out on the terrace.

"Mother, would you ask Helen to bring us some tea," he called as we went out through the French windows.

Mention of the maid's name prompted me to enquire of Ellis's sister. "Where 's Alicia? I'm so looking forward to meeting her."

"She's unwell at the moment and is staying in her room."

"Sorry to hear that. Perhaps I'll meet her later."

"Perhaps," he said in a clipped tone that really suggested perhaps not. His manner soured for just a moment, but then he smiled brightly and sat down alongside me at a circular weathered-teak table.

A young rather sullen maid, complete with starched white cap, arrived to lay a cloth over the table and then brought out a tray with tea and a substantial cherry cake, which we cut into with some eagerness.

The view across the lawns depicted a perfect English garden with masses of floral colour, zinnias, lobelias, pelargoniums, edged by dense shiny-leafed laurels and splashes of pink and pale blue papery hydrangeas. Over to the far right a gardener in a Panama hat was crouched down, weeding unhurriedly in the sultry breathless heat.

"Later, when it cools down a little, we'll play tennis," said Ellis. "We have a grass court behind the stables."

That started us off bemoaning the fact that Fred Perry had preferred to play an exhibition tour rather than defend his

Wimbledon championship that summer.

"After three consecutive titles, perhaps he's getting bored," I remarked.

"More likely to be money," said Ellis firmly. "I'll bet those exhibitions pay pretty well."

Behind we heard brisk footsteps, and the young maid was back. But instead of clearing the tea things she leaned over and whispered something to Ellis, who looked exasperated - if not quite angry.

"Please excuse me," he said, getting up. "There's something I must attend to. I'll have some fresh tea sent out."

"No hurry. I could laze here all afternoon."

Two or three minutes passed when I heard more footsteps on the terrace flagstones, but as I half turned I found it was not the maid but a tall, very slim girl of perhaps 25, wearing an ankle-length mauve dress with short puffy sleeves. Her face was white as milk, accentuated by a frame of straight fringed dark hair, but she was smiling prettily.

"I'm Alicia," she announced, sitting next to me on one of the cushioned garden chairs.

"And I'm Phillip - delighted to meet you," I said.

"How are you? Ellis told me you were a little unwell."

"I'm much better now," she said. "Much better. And isn't it a lovely afternoon, far too nice to be indoors."

"Absolutely," I said. "There should be a pot of tea here soon. Would you like a slice of cherry cake?"

"Oh, yes please," she said, almost joyfully.

I reached forward to cut her a slice, but she picked up the silver-handled knife herself.

"I'll do it," she said softly.

I leaned back, my right hand still resting on the table. In a single, unhesitating movement she stabbed the knife down viciously hard into the back of my hand, skewering it to the table. For a moment nothing happened, then blood sprayed upwards splashing the crisp white tablecloth. Then came the racking pain and my high-pitched scream of shock.

The handle of the knife was still quivering, flashing gently in the sunlight.

Alicia just sat there, wide eyes transfixed to the gushing red torrent.

"Look at the blood," she said excitedly. "Just look at the blood."

Her face was now flushed, but it was her eyes that seared my mind, the pupils just dark diabolical pebbles still fixed on the spreading crimson patch.

My cry had been heard. There was the clatter of many running feet lead by Ellis, then two male servants, a maid and a uniformed nurse.

It was all over pretty quickly. Ellis pulled out the knife, bound my hand with his handkerchief, all the time apologising over and over. Alicia was lead away quite passively, continuing to look back and repeating in pleasurable amazement: "Did you see the blood?"

Ellis bundled me in to the MG and sped to the local cottage hospital. A doctor said that there was severe tendon damage from the serrated blade, but that the wound should heal well.

Six weeks later, back in London, I went to see a specialist at Charing Cross Hospital for a final check.

"Very good news, in the circumstances," he said reassuringly after the examination.

"Could have been much worse. As it is, you have regained use of all the fingers, though the middle two are always likely to be just a trifle stiff. You'll hardly notice after a while. Just as well you're not a concert pianist, eh?"

The nurse at his side gasped, and her anguished expression transferred to him.

"I say, you're not, are you?"

I nodded.

"What, professionally?"

The nurse intervened: "I saw Mr Lavery play last month at the Langdon Hall, a wonderful recital, quite wonderful."

The critic in The Times had been more generous. "Mr Lavery's technical excellence, allied with such entrancing spirit and verve, hallmark him as our finest young pianist. He is surely destined to grace the concert stages of the world, to be ranked alongside Skryabin and Poulenc in the fullness of time."

I knew the review by heart. I had read it countless times since the incident at Utsmere Hall, knowing even before the doctor confirmed it that it would be my last review.

The moment the blade rasped the bone and I felt the tendons snapping like rotten string, I knew it.

Ellis's family did all they could to help me. They gave me a very generous settlement, acknowledging not only the need for compensation but for my agreeing not to report the matter to the police.

Alicia had been on a supervised home visit from a mental institution, having been committed eight years earlier at the age of fifteen when, for no obvious reason, she had suddenly lunged at her mother with a carving knife, gouging out her eye.

That incident had also been confined to the family.

It was explained as an accident, servants were paid off and Alicia was moved to a private institution.

Occasional home visits could be made only under the close supervision of a nurse.

But on a hot summers day the nurse has dozed in a chair and, although the door of the room was locked, a sash window was open a few inches because of the stifling heat. Alicia opened the window and slipped out into the garden...

I used the money to buy property, and rented it out. It provided a good income, which I used by buy more property.

Now, I am a rich man. I even own the splendid Hepple Court Hotel, which gives me so much pleasure to observe.

It is all, of course, little comfort. I had always wanted to be a concert pianist, ever since I had begun playing when I was four years old. There could be no greater exultation than to hear the rising thunder of applause in homage to your talent, in a crowded concert hall.

I looked across at the young man, but he had slipped away unnoticed. In his haste he had left behind, on the bench, a torn paper bag that had contained his lunch.

A whisper of breeze fluttered the paper, folding it back and unveiling a single slice of deep yellow cherry cake.

There were two exposed cherries in a line, just a little apart, and they seemed to stare at me with the glassy deadness of Alicia's eyes on that hot summer afternoon an entire lifetime ago.

Escaping The Rain

I just happened to be looking in that direction when I saw him put his hand up her skirt. There was a startled stifled cry and she tried to pull away, but he was holding her against him, grinning because he knew she was helpless, cradling the empty glasses in her arms.

In any case he was a customer, and I suppose she didn't want to create too much of a scene. She was trying to make a joke of it. "Hey, come on now. Behave yourself."

But it was obvious she didn't like what was happening.

I didn't know her. I'd never even been in the pub before. She was just one of those pretty but tired-looking barmaids, the type that catches your eye but then turns out to be not quite so good when you get up close.

Still, she was acceptably pretty, and the short skirt was revealing nice, bare legs. She had been collecting glasses. The place was jammed, and when she had reached the table nearest to me those bare legs had just proved too tempting for the bearded biker-type, sprawling there with two other quasi-neanderthals.

I stepped over fast. "That's enough," I said, sharpish. "Let her go."

He looked up at me, unperturbed and amused. "What's it to you?" he asked. The voice had the inevitable looking-for-trouble edge to it.

"Just let her go. I'm not on duty tonight and I don't need the paperwork. But if you're still holding her in five seconds I'm arresting you for indecent assault."

He let her go after four seconds, making an indistinct comment to one of his pals. It was something about "fucking coppers everywhere."

The girl gave a timid nod of thanks and backed away, still holding stacked pint glasses in her arms, hugging them to her chest. Nice chest from what I could see of it.

Time to go. Outside, I hesitated in the doorway. It was raining hard. It had been raining for weeks. It was getting to me, making me irritable, even making me sad.

Occasional rain I can take. Persistent rain day after day erodes the soul.

Tonight's rain was the heavy stuff, big globules slamming vertically like buckshot, hammering onto the parked cars with a harsh monotone drumming. My car was thirty feet away, and I knew that I'd have water hosing down my neck before I'd taken two steps.

Behind me the pub door opened and the barmaid came out, pulling on a short black leather jacket. "Fuck it. Fuck them all," she said vehemently, as if we knew each other. "I've had it. I've quit."

"Good for you."

We were both looking at the sheeting rain and not wanting to step forward from the shelter of the doorway.

"Driving?" I asked.

"Bus."

"Want a lift?"

"Why not. What else can go wrong?"

"I could be an axe murderer."

She laughed at that, and I knew we had kind of clicked.

"You're a copper, aren't you?"

"Made that up," I said. "I'm no hero. He'd have laid me out. I'm just a driver."

The whole scenario struck her as hysterically funny, and she was laughing like girls do, wide-mouthed and unrestrained. Nice even white teeth. I like good teeth. They tell you a lot about a person.

"Ready?" For some reason I took her hand and we ran for it, heads down, her shrieking, me trying not to fall over. I should have got the key out first. While I fumbled for it, the rain was bouncing off us like pebbles. We fell into the car, laughing and cursing and shaking ourselves like big dogs. Her dark hair danced and glittered with rain-stars.

"Bastard rain," I snarled, starting the car. "I'm beginning to rust. When was the last time we saw the sun?"

"This morning."

"Come on! It's been pissing down all day long!"

"I cheat. I have a massive poster in my room, facing the bed. It's one of the islands in the Seychelles, and at the top of it is a big golden sun. First thing I see when I wake up."

"You'd better lend it to me," I said. "I need the therapy."

Her name was Angie, and she had a third-floor flat in a council block in Brent Cross. I pulled the car in as close as I could to the flat concrete canopy over the entrance and waited for her to get out. That was what I expected her to do. I had other things on my mind, and in any case she probably lived with some shaven-headed plumber with an attitude as hard as a lead pipe.

"Want to come in and see my poster?" she said, eyes showing a diamante shine. I knew what she meant, and she meant me to know what she meant. Clinical as that.

The flat was okay. Colourful. Vibrant I think they say in magazines. Travel posters covered the walls, mostly white sand beaches, palms and indigo skies. There were lots of African and Indian touches, rugs, tapestries, carvings, pottery.

"In my mind, I live somewhere else," she explained, watching me as I weighed it all up. "This is my place in the sun." Already, she was unbuttoning her top.

Great sex. Always is when you both want it and you don't know each other. No emotional clutter. You do it because you want to do it.

We didn't talk at all. She kissed a lot, liked to be on top. Energetic but always controlled, smooth and unhurried. Sex with certainty. We both knew it was working, so nothing needed to be said.

Slim body, small firm tits. Peach of a bottom, though I didn't get to see much of it until later when she got off me and walked to the bathroom. She knew I was looking. She walked very slowly.

"Thanks," she said softly when she came back and slid alongside me again. "You don't know how much I needed that kind of end to the day."

It was about eight when I woke. I could hear the rain still scrabbling at the window behind the bed, like something nasty trying to get at you. Already, I was getting depressed. Angie was still asleep, half curled around me, breathing gently onto my chest. The light that filtered through the thin cotton curtains seemed grey, dead light, any brightness screened out by the driving rain. I stared at the Seychelles poster opposite, and even the big yellow sun high in the paper sky seemed to be shining through fog. For ten minutes I fixed my eyes on it, trying to draw out its radiance, feel its warmth.

I was still looking at it when Angie stirred.

Slipping on just a T-shirt she went to fill the kettle. Leaning over the sink, the T-shirt rode up and I didn't want her to ever move away.

There was half an hour of small talk, kind of cosy, with coffee and toast and honey, which I hadn't spread on toast since I was a kid.

"Travelled much?" I asked, pointing at posters of the French Riviera, India and Morocco.

"Majorca. Ibiza. Rome once. Package tours. Not really travel is it? You?"

"Went to California a couple of years ago. Loved it. I'd like to live in San Diego. Fantastic Spanish-Mexican feel to it. And you know what's best of all. It never rains!"

"I'd like to go there," she said. Well, I think that's what she said. She was holding a triangle of honeyed toast in her mouth while pouring more coffee.

"In fact, I'd like to live anywhere away from this dump. But only after I've been to the Seychelles."

"Why the Seychelles?"

"Fell for the place after I saw a TV documentary. Lifetime ambition to go there. I'm saving up."

There was a brief self-mockingly wry smile. "At the present rate, another ten years should do it!"

Gathering up the plates she went over to the sink and I followed her, reaching for her from behind, pressing hard against her, and feeling her breasts under her T-shirt.

"I have to go," I said. "Got to be somewhere."

It was true enough. I had.

"Is this it then?"

"Do you want it to be?"

"Do you?"

"I'll see you tonight. Okay?"

She kissed her finger and placed it firmly on my lips.

I left her peeking out from behind the door, open just six inches. A couple of shuffling pensioners were crabbing along the walkway, and that T-shirt didn't cover much.

A hard-faced wind was battering the block, deflecting javelin rain under the canopy edge and spraying it against the far wall. I was getting soaked just getting to the stairs, when a gust of extra spitefulness blasted gushing water from a broken downpipe all over my trousers. I was so despondent I couldn't be bothered to swear.

The day was already mapped out. Go home, get changed, couple of phone calls. Start work at two. Collection in Bracknell. For a while I thought the skies were brightening, but the rain was relentless, and I was drowned again putting my old Ford in the lock-up and getting out the Mercedes. Always has to be a Mercedes when I pick up McAllister and Vaughan. They are fanatical about quality.

"Best car on the planet," says Vaughan. "Like a luxury tank."

So I was using a year-old Mercedes E-class, twin-headlight model, metallic silver with grey leather. I knew they'd like it. And what do you know! As I pull away the rain stops!

I got them to Bracknell with time to spare. They called themselves specialists in financial transport, and today they were planning to transport a factory payroll.

Without permission.

I'd worked with McAllister and Vaughan five times previously. They were serious professionals, blaggers with sawn-offs who - so far - had never needed to use them. Their technique was noise. They shouted like maniacs, smashed plenty of glass, created instant terror.

I'd heard they were slick, but I'd never actually seen them in action. I was just the driver.

McAllister was short, wide, goatee beard, and from Tyneside. That's about all I knew about him. You never got close or met socially. You meet once before the job, then at the job, then you were out of it until the next time. Vaughan was odd. Hardly ever spoke. Looked vacant. Cold eyes. I thought he could be vicious given the chance.

They worked from tip-offs, usually generated by bribery. This time it was a security guard at the factory. Big place, payroll around a hundred grand.

They'd been told the system and reckoned it would be, as McAllister put it: "just walk-in, walk-out."

Estimated in-and-out time was three minutes. The Merc was ticking over in virtual silence. I had to keep watching the rev-counter to check it hadn't stalled. The car was stolen two nights ago, re-plated and fuelled up. It had 220 horse-power under the bonnet, and 140 mph on tap. Yet I'd never once squealed a tyre or broken a speed limit on any getaway. Bad practice. Speed draws attention. Just drift along with the traffic and no one notices.

A few spots hit the windscreen, then it starts coming down heavy and I flick on the wiper. The tarmac in front of the wages office is awash, and even though I'm in the car I start to feel chilled and damp. How much more rain can there be? I watch the doorway, squinting through the slashing deluge, convinced mildew is forming on my skin like a creeping, contagious rash.

Out of the door comes McAllister, running hard, his slabby feet bombing through the puddles. He's always out first, carrying the moneybag. Vaughan always holds back a few seconds, waving his shotgun, bellowing like a bull.

Now I see him twenty yards behind, moving fast, knees high, arms flailing, shotgun gripped in his right hand.

Behind them a shrill alarm bell starts up.

I have the rear door already open, as usual. McAllister follows a set procedure. Two paces from the car, he throws the moneybag and his shotgun onto the back seat, then leaps in with Vaughan right behind.

Not today. As I heard the bag thud onto the seat I floored the pedal, and the Merc blasted off like a two-ton bullet. In the door mirror I had a millisecond view of McAllister bouncing off the rear wing and spinning across the tarmac. Vaughan is just a diminishing figure frozen in shock. Had to do it. Only way to escape this fucking rain.

The rear door was still open and I did a hard left to force it shut. On the main road I settled into the traffic, and a mile along turned into the Tesco car park. On the other carriageway a pair of police cars streaked past with sirens blaring.

Smoothly I slotted the Merc into a row of parked cars. There were a few people around, but their heads were down or they're under umbrellas, and there was nothing for them to notice anyway. The money was in a linen sack and I shoved it under my coat and got out. At the car alongside, a woman was trying to load shopping and hold onto a small child. I help her hoist the bags into the boot. She said thanks, and made a comment about the rain. "It'll stop soon," I told her, and I knew I was right.

From the payphone in the store, I called a taxi that dropped me half a mile from my flat. There I line a suitcase with the cash, pack some clothes and call another taxi. I'm at Heathrow in less than an hour.

At the meeting point I see Angie, white jeans, black leather jacket, sports holdall at her feet. She has no idea what's gone on.

Might tell her later. I have a feeling she can handle it. Can probably handle living in San Diego afterwards too.

I'd phoned her before setting out on the job. I knew then what I was going to do. Told her I'd booked a surprise holiday, and to meet me at the airport.

"Where are we going?" she'd asked, very excited.

"Seychelles," I said. "Where else?"

When she saw me, she ran forward and planted a hard-lipped kiss. "I can't believe we're going. It'll be scorching out there."

"It had better be," I said, picking up her bag. "Because if it's raining, I shall want my fucking money back!"

The Recognition Shift

It doesn't happen too often these days but it happened again last night. I work the nightshift at the petrol station. It suits me. It leaves the days free, and I don't sleep too well anyway. My shift starts at 10pm, and it must have been around midnight when it happened. This woman - about 50 I'd say - was paying for her fuel.

"That's £15.80 please," I say. She looks at me in that odd kind of way. They always do. I've got used to it.

"I know you," she said. She was staring at me, squinty and hard.

I said nothing. That's how I always deal with it, at least at the start. The woman was still scrutinizing me, tilting her head from side to side so as to get a little of my profile. "Say something else," she said as a curt order rather than a polite request.

"Like what?" There was no need to make it easy for her.

But the two words were enough.

"Jonathan Cayne!" she exclaimed, pointing her finger at me. "Jonathan Cayne. It's the voice. You never forget the voice."

I knew what was coming next. It seldom varied.

"I'd never have recognised you from your face. You've really changed."

I'd like to have told her that she too had probably changed in the last fifteen years, like gaining those three chins. But it's best to be polite.

"I wondered what had happened to you. Wait till I tell Derek when I get home."

She signed her credit card slip and left. Ironical. I have to ask for her signature, yet twenty years ago she would have wanted mine. You see, I used to be famous.

Remember Cooper's Court, the TV soap in the seventies and eighties? I played Bernie, the deputy manager of the hotel. Fifteen million viewers. I was in it for 12 years, big money contract, the full star treatment. I had a chauffeured car, even my own hairdresser.

You know what happened - it was in all the papers.

New producer, radical ideas. Half the cast sacked, even Jane. She had played Amanda Cooper for 20 years, right from the start. They named the series after her, for God's sake. How can you axe someone like that? Doesn't make sense.

Mind you, not much in TV these days does make sense.

Now, there are just three criteria. Ratings, ratings and ratings. So the quality is shit, believe me.

I was okay for about five years after. There were a few guest appearances on daytime TV and game shows, but that doesn't last long when you're not current. Then there were the touring plays. Now don't get me wrong. A play in the West End is good money and plenty of kudos, but rep in brain-dead towns like Northampton or Halifax is soul-destroying. And the money's shit.

You know the rest, I suppose. The tabloid pack gave it pages for weeks. I was stitched up. The girl had told me she was 17. Then she sold the story: 'My schoolgirl romps with TV's Bernie'. That sort of trash.

Karen left me of course. Well, things hadn't been too hot between us for a while. I think she was looking for an out, and I gave it to her on a plate. Then, somehow, she gets none other than Clemson Holroyd as her lawyer. I think that bitch Davina put her up to it. She and Karen were always a bit to girlie-close for my liking. And Davina didn't like me anyway, ever since I made that pass at her at the BAFTA party. Well, I'd had a lot of champagne. I'd never really fancied her, and she knew it. That's what turned her against me.

So Holroyd screws every last penny out of me for the settlement. Karen got the kids, our house in Stratford, and the villa in Marbella. Even my AC Cobra ended up in her garage, somehow.

There was more publicity, of course. Karen sold a 'My Living Hell With Sex-Mad Bernie" to the News of the World, and a couple of one-night-stands came out of the woodwork to cash in.

Then producers started to give me a wide berth. Time was I just walked into parts, now I had to audition. And the audition was usually as far as I got. Producers who had been pals for years didn't return my calls. Even Harry, who was always telling everyone I was like a son to him, backed away. When I heard he was casting that new crime series, I knew I was perfect for the pushy inspector, but Harry blew me out. Cleverly, mind you. He told me he was worried about me still being type-cast. Crap. I'd shaved off my Bernie moustache years ago, cropped my hair, and dyed it. What the hell did he want - plastic surgery?

So now I'm on the nightshift at the motorway services.

I've been out of the business almost three years now. I say out of it but I'm still in the casting directories and Eric is still my agent, but 15 per cent of nothing means he doesn't try too hard. And if he calls me dear boy once more I'm going to break his nose.

The one good thing about Eric is that he's always optimistic. Something is always about to come up, he assures me. "There's a part for you in a new medical drama," he told me last month. "I've put your name up to Brendan. He's assistant director, and he and I go back years. I was godfather to his first child."

Nothing came of it. Nothing ever comes of anything.

Now, I'm too far back, forgotten. TV's gone young. Girls fresh out of media studies courses are made producers. Crazy. What do they know? They aren't even old enough to know who I am. Only time I've been in the papers lately was when I rated six paragraphs in a Where Are They Now? feature in one of the Sunday papers. Some slimy hack spent half an hour on the phone recapping my life and promising this feature could help put me back on the map. I told him I was planning a comeback, but when the piece appeared it just finished by saying: "Jonathan is no longer in show business. He now works at a service station."

Bastard. I was going to ring him up but in the end I didn't bother. I might need him someday, when I'm back.

And for a while I thought it still might lead to something. You know, someone casting a play or a series. They see my name, remember me and decide to give me a chance. Didn't happen though.

Most days I sit around my flat. I rent it from the council. It's too quiet now, after Denise left at Christmas. She called me a loser. Me, who once had fifteen million viewers. Fifteen million. How many can say that?

I spend hours writing down all my ideas. I've even sent off a few scripts. Nothing so far. They come back with printed rejection letters. I don't think anyone even reads them. They won't take risks anymore. Everything is written by established names, with proven track records. Even Fools and Horses wasn't a hit right away but they stuck with it, built up the audience. Now they say its the greatest sitcom in the history of television. So why won't they build anything up anymore?

Ratings. That's why. They can't risk a dip in the ratings.

I had this idea for a new sitcom, a real winner. It's about a dodgy car dealer, you know, all mouth and scams. He sets up in business right next door to a very posh car showroom run by a real snob. One has a dimwit son, the other a flirty daughter and they fall for each other. You can see the potential. I thought Nigel Havers would be perfect for the posh one, and maybe John Altman - used to be Nick Cotton in EastEnders, remember - for the dodgy one. It has all the makings. I called it Car Wars. It came back from the BBC in less than a week with a letter saying they were inundated with scripts, and the standard of comedy writing was very high. I bet they never even looked at it. Anyway, I've decided maybe writing isn't the way back. I don't think Eric is either. I'm going to have to do it myself.

The other night - well, it was about two months ago, I suppose - it happened again. This salesman-type, mid-forties, low-key suit and vivid tie, picks up on my voice when paying for petrol. It happens on average about every six or eight weeks. The recognition shift, I call it.

So I'm giving him his change and saying thank-you-sir and have-a-nice-night, as I've been trained to do. That's a joke in itself, with me being an actor. Anyway, I tell him thank you and he looks at me in that strange way. But then straight off he says "Bernie - Cooper's Court. Right?"

I nod and smile thinly. I like it better when they know me straight away.

"You were great," he says. "You were my favourite character. The way you used to sort out the problems caused by that dippy receptionist. What was her name?"

"Gloria."

"That's it - Gloria. You were great. Why you're not on TV now beats me."

"Beats me too," I said. Best not to converse with them too much. They can stay there for hours, asking if you knew Bruce Forsyth and stuff. Painful.

Still, it's good to know the fans miss me and want me back. It keeps me going. Because, believe me, there are times when you feel like topping yourself. All I have to do is look around the pit I live in. Not quite like a timbered manor-house in Stratford, is it? And my clothes used to be Acquascutum. Now they're Burtons. But at least I can make the best of them. It's how you wear something that counts, and actors have a way of walking, even just standing, that makes what they wear look better than it is. You'd never know my suit was £40 in a sale.

Often, when I'm watching TV, I see someone making a real hash of a part, a part I could sleepwalk, and it really starts to get to me. In the early days I used to hit the vodka when I saw that sort of thing. You probably read about that in the papers too. The brawl outside the TV studios wasn't my fault anyway. It was the photographer who was being aggressive.

I spent a few years on and off the bottle but I had to quit eventually. Couldn't afford it for one thing. Now I've been back on track for a while I can deal with seeing these young actors fresh out of RADA becoming stars in some new series, despite the fact that their acting is so wooden they could grow branches. It's just the way they look. They don't want actors any more, just models. It's always been like that with women, now its men too.

Still, it helps make me determined not to give up. You just need the time and the break. I keep thinking about the advice Roger Moore once gave me. Yes, I knew him quite well at one time. He said: "People don't realise it's such a tough profession. Sometimes it can take 50 years to become an overnight star."

I'm going to give it another shot. I know it's all changed, but there's no point in living in the past. I've done too much of that. I can get back, I know it. People still want to see me. They still recognise me after all this time. Star quality, that's why.

I've got it all planned out. I've heard on the grapevine - the forecourt grapevine, that is - that there is a nightshift vacancy coming up at a petrol station in Manchester, not far from Granada Studios. A sales rep I was talking to a couple of weeks ago tells me he sees no end of Coronation Street stars there, filling up their flash cars. He was behind William Roache in the pay-queue the other night. I met Bill a few times back in the old days. A nicer man you couldn't meet.

So what I'm going to do is this. I'm going to see if I can get the new job, then get a flat up in Manchester. All right, perhaps not a flat, just a bedsit to start with. Then I'll start auditioning again. A small regular part in Coronation Street would suit me.

I've got all the experience they need. I can play any character they like, barman, mechanic, postman, even a neighbour from hell like that Les Battersby. Small part, regular work. That's the way to start. Build myself up again. I know I can do it. You never lose the talent. Never.

Observing The Pool

Monday

Here I am. First morning of my two-week stay at the Hotel Vista, and already I have a perfect vantage point to suit my objective. I have taken prime position on the sun terrace, a corner location shaded by a tall spreading spruce tree. Almost all the sunbeds are in front of me. It provides the exact setting for my observational holiday.

There. I knew you would smile. So do my friends. But that is the way I always describe my holiday. The only reason I go away on holiday is to observe the swimming pool or, to be precise, to observe those who gather around it. There are those who would find this a strange way to spend a holiday. They are the people who spend little time around the pool but go off on excursions to markets and monasteries, take boat trips, browse the shops. It is I who find these people strange.

Watching people is just so fascinating, it is a complete entertainment. I have no need to visit the tourist traps, make new friends, socialise. All I require is a nice location - this summer I am in Majorca - and I am happy. I am enjoying my holiday. I have no need to mix or socialise. My own company is enough.

While I am not a psychologist, I think it is fair to say that it is while on the terrace that people become less guarded, less structured in their behaviour. I think it is because among so many others also relaxing and seeking a tan they feel they become almost invisible. They think there could be no one specifically observing them. It is I, of course, who have thus become invisible!

Today, my first day, I start with gentle perusal, ascertaining if there are any obvious prey. You must understand, of course, that the immediately obvious can in itself be misleading. More often it is within the subtlety of detail that the key players in my exquisite observation drama begin to emerge. But you have to begin somewhere.

Tuesday

Hotel Vista is perched at the centre of a small C-shaped bay, a few kilometres west of Pegeura. Its box-like glass and concrete structure would easily have escaped short-listing for any architectural merit award. But it does have the most perfect setting. Its large sun terrace is elevated several metres above the beach, and fringed by a waist-high aluminium rail. The view is splendid, with the thickly-wooded hills either side closing pincer-like around the turquoise bay, giving the location a certain sense of intimacy.

Pale grey square tiles surface the terrace, with a scattering of darker grey tiles laid down by someone who cared little about geometric symmetry. The central pool is an odd angular shape, but I can view its entirety from my shady observation-post. I am unconcerned about acquiring a tan, though I enjoy the warmth.

On only the second day a pattern is beginning to become established. Those I noted yesterday have mostly secured the same positions. They will continue to do so for the remainder of their stay. Already I have identified a number of prospects. One is a very fat girl, quite young, probably still in her twenties. She is the size of a small rhino, too enormous really to be inflicted on public view. She is embarrassingly obese.

Worse, she is wearing a bikini. I did not know they made a bikini that size. It is dark blue with flecked white markings, and its dark contrast as it struggles to stretch across the acres of pale pinkish flesh serves only to emphasise her epic size.

Wednesday

My small coterie is becoming established! Can I call this group a coterie? I think so, for while they are unknown to each other, and have no known common interests, they are collectively of interest to me!

There is the fat girl, as you would expect. And the Italian Woman, as I have titled her. She is, I guess, about 35. She dresses not for the pool but for a cocktail party. She arrives at the pool in a long, elegant dress and stiletto shoes which click-click on the hot tiles. And she feels the need to display much gold jewellery, several bracelets clink on each wrist, plus a watch. She also wears at least two necklaces, and an uncountable number of rings. And large drooping earrings. Exhibiting so much gold in such an inappropriate place suggests a certain lack of self-esteem, I feel. Yet she has no need to feel inadequate about her figure. When she eventually discards the dress she reveals a slim, lissom figure, already deeply tanned. A tiny bright yellow bikini is vivid against her dark skin. Though her dress has come off, her jewellery stays indolently on.

Then there is the German couple. I cannot confirm they are German, but they look it. At least she does. Attractive girl, but her face has just a hint of masculinity. They are deeply in love, oblivious to all around them. That assists me, of course.

And the English girl. After due deliberation I conclude she is the prettiest girl at the pool. Exceptionally pretty, though not in an obvious way. There are other girls who initially are more eye-catching, but this one is quite demure, even a little unsure, which is most engaging. I do not know her name, so I shall call her Chloe.

Thursday

Fat Girl reverberates across the terrace towards her lounger, rolls of flesh slapping with each thumping step. As she pauses I see her shoulders are viciously burnt red. The skin appears to have been blow-torched raw, yet she stays stubbornly in the sun. Is there no limit to the pain people will endure to acquire a tan? It is not as if, in her case, it will enhance her appearance in the slightest.

The handsome young hotel sports instructor, a boyish Spaniard, announces over the tannoy that the aerobics class will begin in five minutes, at the the rear of the poolside bar. Fat Girl pays no attention.

It is 2pm. The sun's blaze presses dead weight on the blistering tiles. It is too hot to lift even an eyelid.

No breeze, and the air seems too heavy to pull into the lungs. It has a faintly oily pungency. Many have been driven inside to air-conditioned chill, a lazy lunch, a siesta. Or perhaps the particular delight of hot, sticky afternoon sex.

A few poolside inhabitants remain, and my attention is drawn to the German couple. The girl is tall and slim, with long permed hair brashly streaked with blonde. Oddly, I find it quite appealing. She wears a one-piece lime green costume. Her boyfriend, also in his mid-twenties, is muscled and athletic, and wears skimpy black Speedo trunks. They sit on plastic chairs facing each other in the centre of the terrace, in the full scorch of the sun. No hats, not even sunglasses. They are even drinking hot coffee! They chat and laugh, especially when he massages sun cream on to her upper thighs.

How can they take so much heat? Do they have metallic skin? I conclude it is because they are German.

Four o'clock. The young English girl appears. I know that she is English as I heard her speaking to her parents. She is about 17 or 18, tallish, long legs, taut figure. Superbly shaped breasts. Indeed, they are slightly larger than her overall build would dictate, making her profile quite riveting. She has dark hair, with just a hint of applied reddishness. It is cut to just touch her shoulders. Her bikini is simple black. I like it.

I think she is at the point in her life when she is becoming more aware of her visual powers. She has a slow, minutely exaggerated walk designed, I surmise, to draw attention. Even when doing something routine, such as adjusting the back-rest on her lounger, she does it in a time-slowed manner which keeps her on view that little longer. I appreciate her efforts.

Friday

8am. Already all the towels are out, a colourful fabric army guarding sunbeds until their "owners" require them. Large poolside notices - in four languages - forbid such a practice, but the rule is not enforced. It is rare to actually see someone place a towel, however early one is up and about. Perhaps they steal out in the middle of the night, tip-toeing in the moonlight to stake their claim. Happily, there is little competition for my position under the tree, though I must still rise earlier than I would like in order to be sure.

Were I in charge of the pool area I would employ someone to come early, gather up the towels and fling them into the pool. I, as the inventor of the scheme, would of course be exempt.

This morning I just caught a glimpse of the Italian woman throwing down her pale pink towel and scampering away like a naughty child. It was a little after 6.30am, and she was wearing a decidedly unglamorous, crumpled dressing gown and no jewellery! I laugh almost aloud at this minor triumph.

At last Chloe arrives. I spot her immediately. She walks along the terrace edge, close to the rail, unhurried feline gait, head high, looking straight in front. When she reaches her sunbed, she pauses and slowly glances around. I think she is checking if anyone - any men - are watching her. She cannot be aware of me, for my watching technique always feigns reading or sleep.

She puts down her bag and then turns in my direction,

passing within a few feet. For the first time I see her face closely. I am shocked to discover that she is clearly only about 17 years old. Her body may appear older, but there is no mistaking the youthfulness of her face.

I turn to see her go into the mini-club games room. It is for the under-16s! She starts to play table tennis with some of the younger children. The innocent scene deepens my shock. And my shame.

I try to focus my gaze elsewhere. But now, more compellingly, my eyes are drawn to Chloe. I cannot prevent it. She has become even more entrancing than before. This is not so much in a sexual sense, more in a sort of devoted admiration. That is what I tell myself, anyway.

Saturday

Fat Girl struggles up from her lounger and flat-footedly stomps towards the pool. Then, a surprise. Another girl of identical junior-rhino size comes to join her. There are distinct facial similarities, which indicate they are sisters. I am stunned. It is bad enough that there should be one of these vast, lumbering creatures. But two?

They chat briefly at the pool's edge, preparing I think to plunge in. I estimate that even at some eight metres distance from the pool I may not be safe from the tidal wave.

I add to the coterie - an extraordinary English family of father, mother and son. Each is almost polar white and very thin. The father is about six feet tall with dangling knee-length arms and long pointed feet. The mother is so thin the breeze seems to flap her skin against her bones.

The child, about 12 I would say, has a disturbing gauntness and a chiselled face devoid of expression. The temperature is some 34 degrees and he wears a quilted jacket. A name immediately comes to mind for this bizarre assemblage - the Puny Family.

Sunday

Italian Woman arrives in statuesque style, imperiously wafting along in a red satiny ankle-length dress, a clingy off-the-shoulder number, held up by almost non-existant straps. As she passes to my right her gold bullion clanks sonorously. Her left arm is fully extended to carry a loop-handled beach bag, and on the hand is a glittery intricate gold bracelet in the form of a scorpion, its body a shiny black stone. I seem to recall once reading that after love-making the female scorpion stings its mate to death. I look at the woman's lean, sensuous body and easy smile. But above are hard, glassy eyes always looking through you to the middle distance.

One of the men who twice daily sweep the terrace says something to me in Spanish. He is quite young, and keen to be over-respectful. I do not understand him, but it is obvious he wants permission to clear pine needles from under my sunbed. I nod approval, and with a few flicks of his red-handled broom this tiny part of his job is done. The rest stretches out never-endingly as the light sea breeze brings the needles tumbling down with stoic regularity.

It seems to me that he is not well organised. For one thing his broom is too small, the size you might use in your kitchen. It takes an age for him to clear what must be at least 200 square metres of terrace. His method is also ill thought out. He sweeps in small forward-push movements, just a few inches at a time, instead of long lunges of three or four feet. He also congregates the needles in small heaps at spaced intervals, but as he abandons one heap to begin creating another the prowling breeze dances by, skittering some of the needles back across the smooth tiles. He then has to regroup each heap before fetching a black plastic bin, on a wheeled base, to load them in.

As I am thinking: "That is not the most efficient way to gather up pine needles, you stupid man," one of his colleagues, a sort of foreman I surmise, walks up and jabbers forcefully at him. Again, I do not understand what is being said, but I like to think he is being told: "That is not the most efficient way to gather up pine needles, you stupid man."

Chloe seems more fidgety than ever today. She is up and down, rummaging in her bag, adjusting her lounger, applying sun oil, changing tapes on her Walkman, sipping Coca-Cola from a plastic litre-bottle. Today's bikini is palest blue.

She disappears for a few minutes, soon to return clutching a camera and takes a snap of her father, slumped asleep in what I assume is some comical pose. Always she walks with that heightened natural grace, her body movement transmitting latent sexual energy. I remind myself that I am still in shock.

Monday

Fat Sisters try to make a new fashion statement. One has on a bright green bikini bottom, and an orange bikini top. The other is wearing a bright green top, but with an orange bikini bottom.

This has the effect of doubling the visual migraine already triggered by the gargantuan size, and is so offensive an act that I decide it must be deliberate. Perhaps it is their way of hitting back.

Chloe has struck up acquaintance with another English girl, also attractive but not in the same mesmeric way. Together they have the confidence to talk to a group of three boys of about 16 years, who are noisily splashing around in the pool. Chloe and friend sit on the edge, feet dangling in the water. Chloe is wearing a low-cut white top and a short wraparound indigo cotton skirt, split up the thigh. She pulls the skirt further apart so that her legs are more exposed to the late afternoon sun. As she leans forward her breasts are beautifully showcased.

She chats to the boys, and a searing frisson of jealousy rips through me. I feel an intense sense of personal possession. I ache for her, not for a long and fevered night, not even to touch her. Just to be with her. I truly think I would forgo the fevered night for just minutes of quiet conversation. I do not know what I would say.

I try to quell the savage twists of pain in my stomach. Again I sternly tell myself she is too young for this kind of attention. I force myself not to look in her direction. For at least ten seconds.

Tuesday

A wind-chime sound signals Italian Woman turning over on her lounger. She faces me, eyes closed. Her make-up appears perfect. No smudge of mascara of lipstick, no glisten on her powdered skin. Does this woman not sweat? Perhaps her gold booty draws all the heat, leaving her body chilled like a supine corpse.

Demand for the large blue and white parasols is ferocious. The problem arises because there are too few available. I have seen several arguments develop over alleged parasol "rights", with much pointing of fingers and vehemence of tone.

The parasols are essential for some to protect from the searing midday heat. The parasol poles fit into moveable circular concrete bases, each weighing at least 50 kilograms. These bases cannot be lifted easily unless by fit, rippling young men, who scorn their use anyway. Most of those who do crave a parasol find the bases almost impossible to move. It is pitiful to see this shuffling geriatric gaggle straining and panting, attempting to drag these recalcitrant lumps of concrete a few metres across the terrace to their sunbed residence.

Then one man, perhaps 60-ish and with white chest hair stark against his teak finish, decides to roll a base like a wheel. Within minutes the method has spread. The terrace drones dully with the trundle of concrete wheels. Several potential coronary attacks have been averted. The roll-along inventor is hailed a hero. An absurd hero, but a hero nonetheless.

The Puny Family arrive at the poolside late today. They have to search for vacant sunbeds, pulling them scratchily across the tiles to a sector shaded by the building. Despite Mr Puny sporting a jacket and long trousers and his wife a calf-length dress and woollen cardigan, they are for some unaccountable reason barefoot. They hop and skip on the sizzling surface as if demonstrating some crazy tribal dance.

Behind them, out in the bay, a bright white catamaran powers effortlessly in a wide arc, its wake like piped cream. The Punies are unaware of its graceful progress. They never look out to sea.

Almost 5pm, and only now does Chloe visit the poolside. Perhaps she has been out with her parents today, maybe visiting the market at Andraitx. Her hair is tucked behind her ears, a style less pleasing to me. Standing by the rail she pulls her T-shirt over her head exposing those teasing breasts, today held in situ by a purple top. I prefer her black bikini.

In slow-motion she adjusts her towel, takes her Walkman from her bag, locates the headphones and then settles back. She is lost to my view as my line of vision is directly behind the raised back of her lounger. Half a minute passes. I have not dared look away. Then I see, rising above the top edge of her sunbed, her right foot, the toenails painted a dark purple colour. Her hand appears briefly, squirting cream from a pump-action dispenser onto the foot. For a few moments her hand languorously massages the cream, then slides out of sight. Yet the foot remains high in the air, the only part of her delectable form visible. It waves gently from side to side as if secretly beckoning to me.

Wednesday

After more than two hours prone in the worst heat of the day the German duo stir on their loungers. There are brief words, and he gets up and heads towards the poolside bar. Even the Germans cannot avoid dehydration.

The route takes him past me, and just as he gets alongside he drops his sunglasses and bends quickly to retrieve them. I see a most extraordinary sight.

His back is to me, and as he bends the upper edge of his trunks pulls down a fraction and into view comes a small tattoo. It is exactly at the base of his spine.

I see it for only a split second but time enough to see that it is in the form of an eagle, wings outstretched, above a circular wreath enclosing a swastika. It was the symbol used by the Schultz-Staffen, the notorious SS.

Why should this handsome, personable young man, distanced from the war by two generations, feel the need to pay this hidden tribute to an elite squadron of brutal torturers and killers? I cannot guess.

As he walks back, cold drinks in hand, I find myself looking hard at his fixed, unsmiling face, as if seeking evidence that he is growing a small moustache.

Mr and Mrs Puny finally acknowledge that a blinding yellow ball in a cloudless silvery blue sky may indicate that it is hot and sunny.

Mr Puny is attired in sharply-creased charcoal-grey trousers and white shirt, but is rolling up the sleeves to the elbow with careful precision. His wife wears a below-the-knee floral dress, dark blue background with large scattered pink roses, and a lightweight woollen cardigan. She sits down and takes out some knitting from a gaudy-patterned supermarket plastic bag.

I push back my baseball cap to a jaunty angle and order a Perrier from the waiter. It is a forlorn but necessary gesture to try to appear not to be British.

No Chloe today. Perhaps another excursion. I believe there is a trip up to the monastery at Valdemossa, and to the scenic railway at Soller. Without Chloe's vibrant presence the terrace seems a lifeless wasteland of slumped and slumbering bodies, devoid of interest. Her absence actually hurts.

Thursday

An incongruous trilling sound, persistent and increasingly loud, causes heads to turn. It is a mobile phone belonging to Fat Girl One. She dives a pudgy hand into her green canvas holdall and pulls out the warbling instrument, embarrassed by the attention it has drawn.

I hear a vague drift of conversation, involving staccato stabs of "Oui" and "Non", and then, explosively: "L'imbecile!"

So it appears she is French. I did not know the French got that fat. Or that they were churlish enough to bring their mobile phones with them on holiday.

No. No. This cannot be. After days of being so unquestionably, elegantly and expensively Italian I hear the Italian woman speak to someone on the adjoining sunbed. With a Welsh accent!

I learn from the small talk that she is from a Cardiff suburb, and is complaining about a mountain of washing she knows will be waiting for her when she returns. With the dolce vita image, faintly imperious manner, and admittedly overblown symbols of wealth, I had her down as perhaps an Italian countess. With a maid - several maids - to take care of her washing. I am crushed.

Welsh! I just cannot comprehend how someone who appears so chic can be Welsh.

This evening the hotel restaurant is more crowded than usual. The tables have been edged closer together, some now barely two feet apart.

And Chloe is seated at the table next to mine!

She is dining with her parents. I am pleased at her proximity, yet strangely unsettled. She looks taller, older, in a short tight blue skirt and clinging white sleeveless top. I can see her hair is newly washed, fresh and shiny. Eye make-up is evident, so too lip-gloss. She looks achingly pretty. I may be forced to eat without ever looking at my plate.

Her parents are facing me, Chloe seated slightly at an angle so I do not look directly at her. She made momentary and doubtless unintentional eye contact as I walked to my table and sat down. She has not looked in my direction since. She has no reason to, of course.

I push salad around my plate. I am not at all hungry. I sip self-consciously at a San Miguel.

Chloe chats with her parents. She eats little, drinks Coca-Cola, declines dessert. Then she gets up, tells her parents she will see them later and leaves. Perhaps she is off into town with her new friends.

I find I am starting to worry about her safety.

Friday

Puny Boy slyly shifts away from his oppressors who are squeezed together under a parasol. They are reading and do not notice. He is wearing a black over-large T-shirt, the sleeves flopping down to below his elbows. His shorts are very long, to mid-calf, and his white sports socks are stretched up to virtually where the shorts stop. Only a couple of centimetres of flesh are exposed. Even so, the risk of him being mercilessly fried to a small heap of smoking ash is evidently still too great. His father, looking up and seeing the child has wandered, summons him back to the protection of the parasol. It would seem you cannot be too careful if you are a Puny.

Another scorching day in the cauldron, not even a wisp of cloud. The sky is eerily pale, the sun so strong it bleaches colour from the landscape. A flustery wind darts in from the sea, lightly cooling the terrace to tolerance level.

I look around, checking positions. Fat Sisters sleep face down like basking hippos. The clustered Punies I have noted. Italian Woman - I shall still call her by that title - lies face up to the sun, and for the first time I notice an extra item of adornment, a slim gold chain around her left ankle. The German couple fondle each other, sunbeds barely an inch apart. The pool attendant glides discreetly around chasing errant pine needles, broom barely whispering on the sleek surface. Everyone is present.

Except Chloe.

Surging anxiety, heart-rate up. I scan the terrace, hearing my own silent scream of panic from within. Then I see her, emerging from the sliding glass doors and onto the terrace. She follows her familiar route along the perimeter to her sunbed, which is facing out to sea. She walks that walk. She wears my favourite black bikini. My world around the pool is complete.

Saturday

For several days now my observation of Chloe has been mostly at a discreet distance. We occupy different territories on the terrace, and her route back to her room does not bring her in my direction. I do not venture close to her by the rail. It would contravene my rule that observations must mostly go unobserved. Also, to be so near would further cloud my disturbed emotions.

Today my emotions are more fraught than ever. Today should have been my last opportunity to view Chloe for tomorrow I go home. But Chloe has not appeared at all, though her parents sunbathed for an hour or so in the afternoon.

The level of my anxiety has surprised me. I find it difficult to accept that she will no longer be a part of my daily routine. This is not the normal feeling I experience at the end of my holidays. I can always leave my coterie, for there will always be others.

Somehow, I know there will never be another Chloe.

It is almost 7pm and there are just a few people left around the pool catching the final minutes of the fast sliding sun. I start to gather up my towel and my books.

And then she comes out of the hotel, heading for the pool!

She strides across the terrace, stops at the first abandoned sunbed, and dumps down her blue shoulder-bag and a folded towel. Pulling her T-shirt over her head, she shakes her hair back into place while deftly unfastening her skirt and letting it fall at her feet. She is wearing a bright magenta bikini.

This is odd. It is too late to sunbathe. Perhaps she is going to swim.

But no. She turns in my direction, walking purposefully. I am the only person left in the corner by the tree, yet I am convinced that I am not the reason she comes this way. She has no reason to approach me. I exist only as a smudge on the pool backcloth.

For three seconds I indulge in speculation about what I would do if she spoke to me, started a casual conversation, maybe. What would I say? Comment on the good weather, the nice hotel? I do not know if I could have a conversation with her.

She is 20 metres away, now ten, striding directly towards me, long legs lengthened by the high cut of her bikini bottom. Despite almost two weeks in the sun, it registers with me for the first time that she is not very tanned, nor even pinkly sunburned. But her skin is not the fresh white of a newcomer on holiday but more a smooth ivory paleness which heightens her beauty, giving it an almost spiritual quality.

Five metres away and I see the absolute tautness of teenage skin. Two metres, I see the divine pucker of her belly button.

She passes me by, no word, of course.

Turning, I see her stop at the edge of the poolside jacuzzi, just five feet from me. She slips sleekly in, sitting so that the burbling water stops exactly under the cups of her breasts. Her arms are fully extended either side, resting on the edge of the jacuzzi and gently supporting her.

I am transfixed, paralysed in position. Unable to look away.

She is facing me, looking up, making direct deliberate eye contact. No smile.

Her expression is unreadable. There is not a hint of friendliness, but not any sign of resentment. It is just a cool, challenging look. I am glad I am wearing sunglasses. They mask my unease.

Her eyes are wide and vivid, and cannot ever be forgotten.

They are, I think, eyes that know.

We maintain an unbroken, unblinking stare for maybe two minutes. Then, unhurriedly, she eases herself out of the water, first sitting on the edge of the jacuzzi then standing upright.

Snaking streams of water run down from her stomach and thighs, puddling at her feet, and then trickling back into the jacuzzi. Her painted toes are neatly lined up with the edge.

Straight-legged, with shoulders high and head inclined towards me, she stands perfectly still. Her unrelenting gaze seemed to pierce the shield of my sunglasses.

She holds the pose - for that was what it undeniably was - for perhaps 15 or 20 seconds, controlled and at ease with herself, the stand almost defiant.

It was as if she was wordlessly saying: "I know you want to look at me. So there - look at me."

The seconds unfreeze too soon. She walks away, gathering up her bag, wrapping herself in a towel, and the sliding doors of the hotel steal her.

There was no backward glance.

I look unseeing across the stilling, silent water in the azure pool as long-fingered shadows edge in. The feeling of utter emptiness is so final, the air around me takes on a cold, unnerving touch.

Girl With A Gun

The girl sat naked in front of the dressing table and reached forward for her make-up, being careful not to touch the sawn-off Purdey shotgun. Among the mascara, lipsticks, combs and brushes the gun seemed strangely impotent, early morning sunlight sheening the short brutal barrels. At the side of the shotgun lay a pair of transparent surgical gloves.

Staring hard at her reflection in the oval mirror, the girl realised that her hair, still damp from the shower, was drying quickly and she scraped it back and clipped it down before it became too unmanageable. With casual ease she began to apply her make up. Behind her the alarm clock went off signalling it was 6am, but she had already beaten it, awake and preparing herself.

Her clothes were laid out on a chair, and she dressed quickly in light blue jeans and white tee-shirt, then slipped on a bright red cotton bolero jacket. There was a neat duffel-style black shoulder bag on the floor, alongside a small wicker hamper with leather-strap fasteners. Picking up the bag, she opened the top and then placed it on the bed while she pulled on the tight, clinging surgical gloves, and only then did she pick up the shotgun. In cut-down form the Purdey was exactly 24 inches long, and it slid neatly into the bag, the draw-cord pulling it closed over the polished walnut stock. Removing the gloves she rolled them into a ball and tucked them into her jacket pocket.

Finally, from the drawer, she took a short straight-cut ash-blonde wig, pulled it firmly down over her pinned dark hair, tweaked it a couple of times and then turned to look at herself full-length in the mirror of the wardrobe door.

It was just a precaution for, although she didn't feel at all nervous, she wanted to confirm that she didn't betray any signs.

With the bag over her left shoulder, and the hamper in her left hand, she used her right hand to close the door quietly as she stepped out into the hotel corridor. It was too early for anyone to be on reception and she lifted the night-latch and walked confidently out into the deserted street. The hotel was one of a rank of several in a gridwork of streets in London's Earl's Court, and it took only a three-minute walk for her to junction with Cromwell Road and just two minutes more to flag down a passing taxi, giving an address four streets away from her destination in South Kensington.

A year ago it would not have been something she would have thought of doing, but then a year ago she wouldn't have needed to do it anyway. Since then she had read a lot of books and watched a few carefully selected videos as background research.

It was 6.38am when the taxi dropped her off at the corner of Stanford Road and Kelso Place, and she began to make her way by an indirect route to the Harper Court Hotel. Breezing in through the revolving glass door the girl was a welcome sight to the night-porter, who had already read his morning tabloid paper twice and was finding it tedious filling the last 20 minutes before he went off duty and the day-staff came on.

The girl was a flash of colour in her red jacket, white-blonde hair and the bouncy stride. As she came up to the desk her smile showed glossy red pouting lips and white even teeth, like the page 3 model he had been looking at only minutes earlier in his paper.

The blonde fringe of hair emphasised just how vivid blue her eyes were. Before he could speak the girl put down the wicker hamper on the desk in front of him, then leaned forward on her elbows so that she was nearer to his face. He caught the faint drift of her perfume, and the close contact gave the moment a sudden sensuousness. Softly, slowly, with the pink tip of her tongue tantalisingly on view, she said: "I do hope you'll be able to help me."

Again, before he could respond, she was speaking softly but quickly, telling him how her fiance, Mr James, was staying there, that it was his birthday, and that they were meeting later for lunch at their favourite restaurant in Chelsea, but that she wanted to surprise him now with a special treat. The words tumbled out with no pause for breath, and as she spoke she opened the hamper and pushed back the lid, showing a bottle of champagne, two glasses and a single red rose.

"Don't you think he'll just love it," she said, her enthusiasm rippled with excitement. "I just can't wait to see his face."

Again the night porter was poised to speak, if only to tell her that really he should ring Mr James first. But almost as if the wide blue eyes could read his thoughts the girl said: "I expect you have to telephone a guest when there is a visitor but that would spoil the surprise, wouldn't it?"

Leaning further forward, so that her face was only inches from his, she blinked her long lashes and said: "Be an absolute angel and use a pass key to let me in to his room. Now I know you shouldn't, and I'm asking you to be very naughty, but I can tell just from looking at you that you're a man who understands all about romance... I'm right, aren't I?"

Vaguely, the night porter, who was 55 and divorced, could remember romance but it was long long ago. Yet somehow this girl had started to remind him of a girl he'd known when he was 20. A girl not as pretty of course, but still capable of making the pulse race just on sight.

What did it matter, he thought. He was off duty in a minute and, anyway, he was certain that later he would get a good tip from Mr James, who was a regular client at the hotel. For he rather suspected Mr James was going to get a much more pleasurable early birthday treat than just the champagne, and suddenly he felt envious almost to the point of pain.

He walked round from behind the desk with the key to room 1108 already in his hand.

"Come with me," he said with the merest trace of self-importance. "Never let it be said that George Adams stands in the way of true love."

As they stepped into the lift she leaned over and kissed him briefly on the cheek. "An angel, that's what you are. An absolute angel."

George Adams didn't know what to say, but he was compellingly aware of his pulse racing, just like it did that first time with Edna all those years ago.

"Quietly," the girl whispered as they approached room 1108. "I want to wake him myself. It must be a big surprise".

George nodded and slipped the key noiselessly into the lock and turned it slowly. There wasn't even a faint click as the door opened. Turning, the girl kissed the index finger of her right hand and then placed it fleetingly on the lips of George Adams. Mouthing the word thanks she closed the door with slow-motion movement.

It was curious that the idea came after she had discovered the gun rather than before. Indeed the gun had given her the complete plan in just an instant. It all came flowing into her mind and clicked into place, as if the discovery of the gun had been the last piece of a complex puzzle which had just become clear and obvious. She had been visiting Uncle Clive, who was near to death and being nursed at his home. Depressed as she was at another death in the family, she forced herself to drive to Broadway in the Cotswolds where the old man lived alone, except for his nurse, in a large almost mansion-size house of honeyed stone and ivy leaves. When she was a child she had visited often, and had many happy memories of the place.

Back then Uncle Clive was a vibrant man, a renowned womaniser with a history of four wives and at least a dozen mistresses. But in the past there years cancer had settled the score, and now he had become a gaunt and almost unrecognisable figure slipping in and out of consciousness. Having allowed the nurse a couple of hours off to do some shopping, she spent some time talking uselessly but fondly to the drugged uncomprehending figure made smaller by the largeness of the double bed. Then she began to wander through the bedrooms, eight in all, recalling with nostalgia the family visits and parties at the imposing old house. She had even held her 21st birthday ball here, with Uncle Clive, then in his sixties, still trying to pull one of her girlfriends only a third his age.

In a bedroom used for storage, among the scatter of books, trunks, redundant furniture and even a massive brass parrot cage, she noticed a long shallow brown leather case resting on top of a tea chest full of old farming magazines.

Just a couple of inches deep, and maybe six inches wide, it was about three feet long and she knew instantly what it should contain. But was it there? Undoing the stiff cracked buckles, and noting Uncle Clive's gold-tooled initials on the lid, she opened the case to reveal a Purdey double-barrelled shotgun with beautiful chased engraving. Just under the case, recessed in the tea chest, were two boxes of cartridges. She knew then that if this wasn't Divine Intervention then it was as close as you could get.

It came back to her that Uncle Clive had, until his illness started taking its toll three years earlier, been a keen grouse shooter. Now, in and out of a coma and expected to live only a few more days, he would have no need of the gun, and it would be unlikely than anyone afterwards would even miss it. If anyone did recall it they would assume he had disposed of it when he gave up shooting.

Putting the gun and cartridges in the boot of her car before the nurse returned, she drove back that evening knowing exactly what she was going to do. All she needed to find out was how to use a shotgun.

An hour of intense concentration and note-taking in a reference library, with Hadleigh's Practical Shotgun Techniques, gave her the theory. The practice took the form of a few quick-succession test shots at dusk, on a summers evening, deep in Forestry Commission woodland. The noise and vehemence of the weapon's kickback startled her, but she was thrilled at actually being able to load and fire.

The remaining problem was it's size, too long for easy transport. She had frequently heard of sawn-off shotguns being used in bank raids, so she assumed that in cut down form the gun would still work. Laboriously and exhaustingly she cut a foot off the barrels, after first strapping the gun to the kitchen table, using belts and tape to keep it rigid while she used the hacksaw. It took quite a time but eventually, when the surplus barrel clanged to the tiled floor, she was sweaty and headachey but pleased.

In the semi-darkness, with just seepings of diluted grey light from around the curtains, she could hear gentle rhythmic breathing. Slipping on the surgical gloves she placed the duffel bag on the thick carpet, pulled the draw-cord and extracted the Purdey, it's barrels cool even through the thin rubber of the gloves. Releasing the safety-catch she walked forward towards the bed.

The man lay asleep on his right side, and his left profile showed a tanned complexion, loosely-cut black hair and the sort of angular chiselled face that was popular in 1940's movies. He was a man who was very good looking, and no doubt knew it.

Breathing quite audibly, but not snoring, he was covered only by a single white sheet, which came up just above his waist. One arm was out over the sheet, fingers outstretched and relaxed. After watching him for a full minute the girl reached over and switched on the bedside light. Either the sudden splash of light or the click of the switch caused the man to stir. His eyes had narrowed against the harshness of the light, and as he focussed he found himself looking at the black unforgiving stare of the shotgun, just six feet from his face. Beyond the barrels he saw slim but steady hands curled around the gun, but it was the sight of the rubber gloves which unnerved him. Very slowly, he looked upwards and saw the face of a girl he was certain he had never met.

The absolute precision of her manner and the total self-control were impressive but, really, it was the sight of those surgical gloves which were chilling. It seemed a logical conclusion that someone intent on not leaving fingerprints was hardly playing a prank.

She delivered a single sentence that was so terse, so economic, it must have been carefully rehearsed.

"This shotgun is loaded, and if you move or speak I'll shoot."

Her voice was steady, matter-of-fact, emotionless and utterly convincing.

"You don't know me, you know nothing about me. I am therefore an unknown quantity," she told him, and the flat mechanical tone, bereft of feeling, did as much to disturb him as the presence and proximity of the shotgun. "The one thing that is certain about unknown quantities is that they are highly unpredictable."

Shifting position slightly, and moving back from him, she raised the gun marginally so that it pointed directly at his chest.

"Were I to pull both triggers, at this range you would redecorate most of the room."

She was proud of that line, which she had stolen from one of the many crime videos she had watched in preparation, maybe an Eastwood or Bronson. If it sounded any less threatening from a girl, Barrie James didn't notice. He believed her.

Moving back a little further, almost to the foot of the bed, the girl gave a clipped, concise instruction.

"Throw back the sheet," she said. "Very slowly."

He did so and revealed himself, as she had thought, to be naked. His body was tanned and hairy with a distinct white outline in the shape of shorts. His penis was limp, and against the muscular tones of his stomach and thighs seemed intensely vulnerable, like a small newborn creature huddled for warmth. Swiftly, she jammed the black-eyed barrels onto his genitalia, pinning him down, and in the same fluent movement sat on the edge of the bed. She held downward pressure on the gun as his eyes widened in both disbelief and wincing pain.

"Now you know exactly what will happen if you move," she told him, as if she were explaining to a child who might not have grasped the full significance of the action.

Barrie James knew the situation well enough. A good clay-pigeon marksman, he was familiar with shotguns and saw immediately that the safety catch was off. And the skin on her trigger finger was taut and whitened at the apex of the joint, visible even through the semi-transparent glove.

"I suppose you want to know who I am and why I am here," she said. "I've been wanting to tell you for quite some time. In fact, I've been wanting to tell you for exactly one year and nine days."

The tip of her tongue ran lightly across her lower lip and in the brief pause he sensed a change in her, a ripple of inner electricity suddenly sparking life into her eyes, and when she spoke again there was the first detectable edge of emotion, raw and cold as a polar wind.

Nicola was dead in the bath, with both wrists razored open and the blood around her almost an inch deep as, for some reason, the plug had been left in. She was as pale as the ivory bath, eyes closed, forever asleep. The sight of her sister, so obviously dead, hit the girl with a physical impact. She spun to the side, crashing against the wall, mewing with pain and horror and sinking to the floor. When sometime later she was able to bring herself to tenderly touch the body it was eerily cold, and so tragically lifeless that there and then she decided retribution was the only way to even slightly ease the savage screaming pain.

Nicola had told her all about Barrie James. She had met him at a party a couple of weeks before and he had taken her home. Then there was no hassle, no groping, no pressure to come in for coffee. The next day she recalled how Nicola had excitedly told her it wasn't often you met a guy who didn't want to maul you on a first date, especially one who was a property developer with a red 911.

"He's absolutely gorgeous. I just can't believe how I almost didn't go to the party," Nicola had said. The two girls spent a long lunch of giggling gossip, and it was good to see Nicky so happy. At 19, doing so well at university and now with a terrific boyfriend, her life was really mapping out.

But a week later Nicola wasn't excited, nor giggling. She had been crying for two days, afraid to phone, ashamed to phone.

On the third date Barrie James had raped her.

The sisters talked it through. They were going to deal with it together. No point in calling the police. The my-word-against-his would would mean a tortuous trial, harrowing cross-examination and Nicola, always a fragile personality, just couldn't take it. They talked on and off for three days, sleeping curled tight together at night, like they had as children, and it appeared Nicola was coming through it.

Then, when she seemed quite calm, she said she wanted a few hours on her own to "get my head straight".

That's when she did it, let her precious life ebb into a cold and crimson lake. Her note just read "I'm so, so sorry."

The grip on the gun had tightened at the memory, and Barrie James was trying to breath almost imperceptibly lest the movement of his chest provoke a reflex action.

"I am going to be brief - I have to leave in just a few minutes." She spoke as casually as if announcing she was going shopping.

"I've been following you for the last few days. I'd not done anything like that before, but like so many things you try for the first time it turns out to be surprisingly easy. Once I knew you were staying here it gave me the opportunity to put this into effect. If it hadn't been here, it would have been somewhere else quite soon."

There was now an almost lyrical flow to her voice, a distinct and obvious pleasure at the telling of the story.

"It has taken me a year. In fact one year and nine days. And if you don't know what happened then, I'll remind you. One year and nine days ago my sister took her own life."

A certain shocking realisation flickered across his face.

"No..." he said, forgetting the warning not to speak. She leaned harder on the gun and pain choked further efforts.

"I see you knew her, but not well enough it seems. Otherwise there would have been no need to rape her."

He looked for some slight sign of emotion, a lunging straw of vulnerability, but she remained a detached empty android. Her hand was still steady, the knuckles were still white.

"I won't go into details. You were there. You know what happened."

Somehow he had managed to faintly pale beneath his tan, and on his neck beads of sweat glistened and trickled, meandering through the hairs on his chest.

"At first I wanted revenge immediately," she told him, her voice rather retrospective as if she was talking aloud to herself and there was no one else present. "But I work in an architects' office and on the wall we have a silly notice which says 'The Plan Is Everything'. Suddenly, for the first time, I really knew what it meant. So I spent the last year planning this event. It has taken time to get everything right, to get myself right to do it. I started to look for you about a week ago. You are an easy man to find. Red Porsche, personal number plate. And while being well known at certain hotels and restaurants may have its up side when getting a room or a table at short notice, you are now experiencing one of the down sides."

After pausing for a few moments, she suddenly smiled and her voice took on a noticeably lighter tone. "It was important I tell you all this," she said. "I couldn't leave without knowing that you knew."

He relaxed slightly. This had been a scare. And it had worked. It had been five minutes of genuine fear but it had been a show, and a good one. He had never been certain whether or not she would pull that trigger. She was so calm, so clinical, that you couldn't tell whether she was controlled or maybe psychotic.

Taking a deep breath he tried to close his mind to the stabbing, pulsating pain from his penis, pinned with unremittingly pressure.

The girl smiled the open, friendly, winning smile that had won George Adams and his pass key. "That's it. I just wanted to tell you, show you fear and pain. It was necessary. You deserved it."

Rising slowly off the edge of the bed, she kept the pressure on the gun, still pinning him, as she leaned over him. "Actually, you deserve more."

For just a second before she fired, he knew she was going to do it. There was a sudden iciness to her eyes, a tightening of face muscles. Then there was the blast, the shocking blinding pain, and the fleeting, utterly unredeemable knowledge of what she had done to him.

In a deft single movement she had flicked a pillow over the gun, closed her eyes and squeezed both triggers. The boom was only slightly muffled but was over in what seemed like a blink.

As soon as she felt the kick of the gun she turned from the bed and walked towards the door. There was no need to look back. If the shock hadn't killed him outright, the gushing loss of blood soon would. Pulling off the wig, she snatched out the clips and shook down the long dark hair. Taking off the red bolero, she took out a crumpled cream linen jacket from the duffle bag, and slipped it on. The whole process took no more than 20 seconds. Sliding the gun into the bag, she paused to pick up the hamper before opening the door.

The shotgun had made a single boom, the sort of sound someone asleep in adjoining rooms might think they had heard, but when they listened further and heard nothing more might think they had been mistaken or had been dreaming. And if there was anyone in the corridor, someone peering out to see what was happening, then she too was going to look mystified and concerned.

But there was no one in the corridor.

Rather than use the lift, the obvious way for someone to come up, she walked unhurriedly down the stairs. At the bottom, instead of walking towards reception, she pushed open the locking bars of a fire exit and stepped into a side alley. Looking back there was no one, and so she walked unhurriedly to the junction with Old Brompton Road and started to walk east, towards Christie's.

Within a minute she saw a taxi coming towards her, and at a wave of her arm it neatly U-turned and pulled alongside.

"Where to, miss?"

Giving an address a few streets away from her hotel she perched on the edge of the seat and reflected on how easy it had been.

The taxi driver half-looked over his shoulder. "You're an early bird, " he said.

"Late night party went on too long," she told him in simple explanation.

"Birthday, was it? "

Closing her eyes, she leaned further back and her face took on the total serenity of an Eastern goddess.

"No," she said. "It was just an anniversary."

Deceptions of Truth

Long before I saw the car I heard the faint drone of its engine drifting across the valley stillness, sounding at first like the hum of a persistent insect. When I finally realised it was a car I looked up, irritated by its presence. For the past nine days I had enjoyed being the only guest at what seemed an unviably small hotel in the remotest of locations, and I didn't want company now.

"You'll love it," my friend Steve had insisted, back in London. "It's the perfect hotel for finishing your book. "I discovered it myself when I was writing my Hikers Guide To Spain. It's so far off the beaten track that if you don't find it by chance, you don't find it at all."

Two days later I caught a flight to Malaga, hired a VW Polo and headed for the foothills of the Sierra Nevada mountains, aided by a scribbled sketch map from Steve with footnoted instructions which seemed to make no sense at all.

"Follow the valley road on the north side of Las Alpurjarras. Just before you get to Orjiva, at a tiny village called Veya Cata, turn left at the fork, but not the first left fork but the second."

How many left forks can a fork have?

After much doubling back, and a heat-haze headache which seemed to be pounding my brain to pulp, I at last reached the Hotel Arnendez, set elevated on the lip of a sparing plateau, where the long dust bowl valley had given up the struggle to stretch onward, beaten by the rising rock face.

Today, the day the car came, I was spread languidly in the cushioned comfort of a deep rattan armchair on the terrace. My feet were resting on the rail of the decorative cast-iron balustrade. My manuscript had long fallen to the floor as I slipped gently into a heat-induced stupor.

The late-afternoon September sun was blazing down like a solar blow-torch, scorching the juice of life from anything it could reach. Even the vivid purple bougainvillea, draping heavily over the glaring white outer walls of the courtyard opposite, hung drained and jaded as if longing for the cool of evening to revive its vibrant beauty.

The drone of the car grew louder as I watched its unhurried progress along the valley road, twisted like discarded apple-peel. There were occasional blinding starbursts of light as the sun caught the windshield, and turned it into a fiercely piercing mirror, signalling it's presence lest I was unaware of it.

I sat up in my chair and took a sip of warm water, which had been ice cold when brought to me just ten minutes earlier. Now all my attention was focussed on the car. My initial irritation at it violating my almost secret world had given way to unexpectedly deep curiosity. Who else could be coming here on this baking dusty road to nowhere?

The car made the acute turn into the white-pillared gateway of the hotel with a slight slew of tyres sending clouds of lifeless beige dust upwards, trailing behind like a giant chiffon scarf. It was a Mercedes-Benz convertible of the palest gold. The roof was down, and I could see it had cream leather upholstery and a lone woman driver of instantly riveting presence.

My first glimpse was as she got out of the car, her movements quick and precise. She had the confidence to not be bothered to check her hair or make-up in the rear view mirror. Barely had the wheels come to rest than she was out of the door and hauling a small suitcase from behind the seats. It was an unmistakable Louis Vuitton, and already I was expecting no less.

She was late twenties, tall and poised enough to be a model, but not, I thought, displaying any signs of the required self-obsession. Her hair was dark with sun-highlights, and cut sharp and short to the base of the neck. It swirled with precise rhythm as she turned.

Her legs were bare and tanned beneath a very short linen skirt, and unpainted toe-nails peeked out from dark leather mules with a modest high heel. She wore a clinging sleeveless top of almost iridescent lime green. Large sunglasses, maybe Klein or Armani, partially masked her face.

In the heavy, honeyed light of late afternoon the pale gold car was changing colour to a deeper more lustrous finish, a rich thick gold. Caught in this almost heavenly luminosity she had the ethereal and immediate erotic mystique of a haughty princess alighting from a golden carriage.

Without a backward glance at the car she walked towards the open door of the hotel, intent and purposeful, looking directly ahead. I was disappointed that she did not glance in my direction, though if she had what would I have done? Waved? Smiled? I was annoyed to realise that I didn't know. It was just the fact that she hadn't looked that bothered me...

From the lobby I could just hear the drift of voices as, presumably, she was being booked in by Azul, the owner. Or, as he put it with immense pride: "the owner AND manager."

I sat transfixed, frantically, fervently trying to recall every detail of the mesmerising arrival. Reaching for my drink, I noticed with slight shock that my hand was trembling, and also that my heart was thumping against my ribs.

Leaning back in my chair, breathing deeply, I tried to fathom what was happening. It wasn't that she was so beautiful. There were lots like her, and they didn't force me back to that desperate life-or-death adolescent longing that scarred the teenage years. It was just the way she arrived, so compellingly enigmatic, and with such disdain, as if nothing and no one mattered or could affect her. She had more than just the self-assurance and mild arrogance that money brings. Somehow, I just knew that even without the Mercedes-Benz, and the other evident hallmarks of wealth, she would be just the same. Had I seen her standing at a bus-stop I was convinced she would still exude the same aura of absolute assurance and irresistible allure.

I stared blankly at the faded blistering terrace ironwork. By now the sun had fallen to the jagged mountain skyline, its dazzling glow of deep orange spread over the frazzled landscape like spray-on honey.

Dark shadows were beginning to slide along the terrace, and the vivid red and peachy-white hibiscus flowers in large terracotta pots began to take on subdued hues for nightfall. A sudden tingle of anticipation ran through me with disturbingly violent intensity.

Glancing at my watch I saw that it was two hours until dinner, and the chances of being able to refocus on my work seemed not just remote but impossible. The fact that I had lost interest in the project didn't help. I suppose my enthusiasm had faded before I had come to Spain, and I should never have accepted the publisher's offer but the occasional book was as close to fame, or at least local recognition, as I was likely to get. At the age of 38 I had long accepted that writing the great novel was just a fireflash of hope that had lured me onward during those early optimistic years. I never started the novel, like I never travelled to the Great Barrier Reef, or achieved other youthful ambitions. Instead, I settled for the comfortable existence of college history lecturer, and occasional author of niche-market county history books.

It was a reassuringly predictable life, but not one, as it turned out, that Lucy found agreeable. Hard to say why such a tiny insignificant event should provoke her into leaving. I can still see her standing, hands on hips, by the fireplace, her face reddened and her eyes wet and glittery. She was wearing that long, shapeless green dress, the one I said was too long, the one that started the row. It all came out then, venom spitting around the room like sparks in a steel works. How I always eroded her self-worth, was never satisfied with how she looked. How she could never measure up to some fantasy image I obviously kept in a dark file in my mind.

She was just being stupid I told her. I just didn't like the green dress because it made her look too old, I added, knowing as I spoke that the sentence should never have been said.

In one single sweep of her hand she cleared the mantel piece of china figures, framed photographs, even the Edwardian clock her parents had given us as a present. They hit the polished board floor with a reverberating crash, and then a nothing-more-to-be-said silence lingered like a savage winter, unwilling to break.

In less than five minutes she left the house with an overnight bag. A couple of days later two of her friends came around, shuffling uncomfortably. Their mask of concern was no more concealing than frosted glass. They said they had been sent to collect the rest of Lucy's things, and I said nothing, just waved an open invitation to come in.

Fifteen minutes was all they took to collect her bits of our life, and that was that.

There were no kids, not even the modest thrill of a divorce; we had never married, so the split was at least uncluttered by lawyers. The first couple of years afterwards I spent ricocheting around the girl students at the college, like a human pinball, and didn't have to make too much effort.

Girls always want to sleep with their lecturers, and offered firm bodies and frantic screaming enthusiasm with the kind of casualness they gave away cigarettes.

Then, during the past year, I noticed a certain futility edging in, pervading my emotionless state when I least expected it. I started to lead life more alone and then, to my surprise, I found myself thinking more about Lucy, recalling our wine-drenched conversations in the embers of an evening. In those early days, soon after we met, she was addictive, her casual, effortless beauty and haunting cachet made me feel she was a visiting classical goddess.

Term had just ended, the summer stretched out ahead, and my book on the history of Shropshire was crowding its deadline with the same finality as a tax demand. With the house evoking too many wistful memories of Lucy it seemed right to get away, find some sun and solitude.

Steve had taken me to the airport, prattling on about how much work he had on, how he wished he could flee to a beach, how lucky I was, how, if he were me, he would be taking one of the latest batch of first year students. When we stopped outside the terminal I hauled out my suitcase, slammed the door and just walked away. I didn't even say thanks.

She didn't come in for dinner, and my disappointment was profound. I don't know why it should have mattered that much, but I felt I had fallen from a roof and was flattened, gasping for breath. All though dinner I expected her to come into the room, but she didn't. For half an hour or so I had been moving a small piece of cheese and a few black grapes around my plate, playing a strange sort of solitaire until Azul came in and asked if he could get me anything else. Moodily I requested a Cointreau and then, trying to sound as if I didn't really care, I said: "I thought I would see our new guest this evening." But if I was expecting any clue from him it didn't come. He just raised his eyebrows and sloped off towards the bar.

Convinced I would have trouble sleeping, that the divine memory of her would keep intruding, I allowed five or six Cointreaus to settle shifting thoughts, and slept surprisingly well. When I woke I felt a little less concerned, less tense, though it might just have been the hangover. Even so, on opening the shutters I looked down into the courtyard hoping that the golden carriage would still be there. It was parked in the same spot, the roof still down. On its bonnet there were four or five Swallowtail butterflies basking in the early warmth, their large black-patched wings perfectly still in the rising morning heat. Against the gold they looked like they were sipping at a pool of nectar.

I quickly showered, pulled on some dark blue shorts, a light blue soft-cotton Californian shirt and went down for breakfast. The room contained just eight tables, and could be scanned in a sliver of a second. It was completely empty. By now I was cooling on the whole thing. Her arrival in my tranquil retreat had sent my imagination soaring, made her an object of utter fascination. But now I was getting angry, with her, but more with myself.

Sitting at a table by the window I looked out across the courtyard. The diluted blue of the early morning sky stopped abruptly at the high, sharp edge of the glaring white courtyard wall, like an architect-drawn line. Below, still shadowed, were straggles of poinsettia, scattering scarlet flecks. The intensity of the colours was uplifting. Half closing my eyes, I leaned back in my chair, and let the heat sooth over me.

Then, she was just there. I don't know how long she had been there, but when I opened my eyes she was just leaning in the doorway looking at me. She was wearing a bright yellow sleeveless top, held together at the front by just one button.

It wasn't revealing, just promised that it might be.

Around her waist she had loosely tied what looked like a large flimsy, multi-coloured scarf, knotted on the hip, exposing the left leg almost completely, and virtually hiding the right, apart from the ankle. She wore soft slip-on sandals, with a slightly raised heel, in contrasting red and yellow pattern.

Even when it became clear that I was staring at her, she didn't move, didn't speak. Yet she never looked away, returning my stare with either interest or indifference, I just couldn't tell. Getting up, I walked over, smiling, and said: " Hello. I'm Ben.... Ben Carey. Seems like we're the only guests here at the moment..."

I left the sentence hanging, waiting for her to pick up on it. She continued to appraise me, but said nothing. Still smiling, I hoped not inanely, I indicated the table by the window. "Would you like to join me for breakfast?"

"Thank you, but no," she said. Her voice was soft and firm, and had the trace of an accent that I couldn't quite place. It was

English with a faint blurring of something else, maybe Canadian. Taken aback by the brevity of the rebuttal I must have shown my obvious disappointment. There was much she could have said to cover my flustered embarrassment, but some seconds passed while she looked at me, curiously, studiously.

Her eyes were the palest grey, and not once did they blink.

"I prefer to eat alone," she said rather clinically. "You know how it is - small talk can be so tedious."

She smiled rather mechanically, walked past me, and sat at a table on the other side of the room, as far from me as it was possible to get. Pouring herself a glass of orange juice from the tall jug on the table, she sat gazing out across the gardens. I felt as if I had been dismissed, discarded, of no further interest.

An hour or so later, from my vantage point on the terrace, I saw her walk into the garden and settle down on a lounger. She wore a clinging dark blue top with thin shoulder straps and white shorts, which accentuated the slimness of her legs and their light touchable tan. She never glanced towards the terrace, or at least I never saw her do so. She wore small round-framed sunglasses, and she kept them on while flicking idly though a glossy magazine.

Trying to get her out of my mind, and concentrate on my manuscript proved beyond me. I could never get to the end of a single sentence before the words blurred and my mind started to speculate about her. Each time I glanced in her direction, she was sleeping or reading but never once looking my way. Her confidence, her poise, her elegance had all the hallmarks of a model. She was certainly tall enough. Or maybe she was an actress, but then I dismissed that thought. She was just too cool, too aloof, too downright unsocial to be part of such a narcissistic trade. With the obvious signs of wealth and her rather haughty demeanour it occurred to me that she might even be the daughter of an ambassador, even an aristocrat. Or worse, his wife.

My mind turned over the possibilities, the permutations, but I started to get angry with myself. Anyone so indifferent to me did not deserve my attention. I slapped shut the manuscript, gathered up my pens and sunglasses and strode back to my room.

Sharp slits of light from the tall shuttered windows split the darkness in narrow fans, and I paused for a few seconds, allowing my eyes to adjust and breathing deeply the cool, stilled air. My folder and pens I threw rather carelessly onto the low oak table in the centre of the room.

"Mr Carey.... do you have a little time to spare?"

I turned, startled, to see her standing in the doorway. I had left the door partly open, intending to go out again, and she had pushed it wider yet not stepping into the room.

Leaning casually against the frame of the door, looking directly at me, holding unwavering eye contact, her face was a mask of non-expression.

"Or do you have other things to do?"

She finished the sentence leaving several seconds between it's two halves, time in which I said nothing because I just couldn't say anything.

Stepping forward, she closed the door behind her and then, to my total stupification, she pushed across the bolt with a sharp click, sealing us in.

As she came forward she stepped into a slim shaft of half-light, it's condensed intensity bleaching her skin tones and emphasising the unrelenting gaze of her large and mesmeric eyes.

"No," I said. "No... I... I don't have anything to do."

The corners of her mouth moved minutely on the way to a smile, but I saw no smile in her eyes. "Good," she said softly. "That's good".

"What ..."

She stepped quickly forward and put a long cool finger to my lips. I could feel the edge of a polished nail against my nostril.

"Don't say anything," she said, and the brittle urgency of her voice seemed to tear at the torpid atmosphere. "Don't say anything at all."

"But.."

For just a fragment of a second I thought I saw a distant flash of anger, a reflex tensing of the muscles around the cheekbones. She pressed her finger harder against my lips, the errant nail digging into the soft flesh at the base of my nose with pin sharpness.

"Say nothing," she told me. Audibly, it was no more than a request. Visually, it was no less than an order. "There is no need to talk. We have nothing to talk about."

In a smooth, deft movement she lowered her hand and began to unfasten the buttons on my shirt. As it fell open, she slid it off my shoulders and left it fall to the ochre stone floor. I stood oddly immobile and utterly uncertain.

Outside the window I heard the staccato hoarse, hissing call of a hoopoe perched in the shrubs below my balcony, the sudden sound stirring my trance. We stood a metre apart in the centre of the room, lit palely by sunlight squeezed and washed out as it forced its way through the cracks in the shutters. In the air I could see magnified specks of dust hanging in the stillness like stars in space.

In a swift swirl of arms she pulled the tiny blue top over her head, threw it aside and ran both hands through her hair, fingers outstretched wide. The movement caused her breasts to dance lightly. They were fuller that I expected of someone tall, and there was absolutely no trace of whiteness from a bikini top. At once the smooth promise of her skin became my only reason for being.

We both removed the rest of our clothes, unhurriedly, each carefully watching the effect on the other. Then she looked towards the bed, it's white sheets a landmark and it's black ornate ironwork already lost as the day faded.

It would be good to say that we made love, but it wouldn't be the truth. We just had sex. There was no love there, though there was some tenderness. Neither of us spoke, no words at all, only the grunts the whimpers the cries that come with two people wanting each other so supremely.

Sometimes she closed her eyes for a few moments, but mostly she looked at me steadily and unflinching, even as our bodies moved in a slow rhythmic unison. We rested, and then started over. We rested again, and started over again.

During the first interval, as our bodies cooled in the sudden damp chill of the sheets, I wanted to say something, wanted to ask, wanted even to know her name. I don't know if my mouth was forming silent words but again her hand slid across it, and I saw her eyes were as forlorn as those of an abandoned child. She shook her head, and the damp tangled strands of her hair swished from side to side as if in double emphasis. Perhaps realising I had to have some sort of explanation she lifted herself higher, onto one elbow, and spoke with ruthless economy.

"If we talk, then one of us might have to lie," she said. "And even if we did not, then sometimes the truth itself can be a deception."

Pressing her head into my shoulder, and folding her body against mine, she looked upwards, her eyes widening, imploring. "Just hold me," she said, her voice softening for the first time.

During the following intervals I said nothing. Inevitably, I slipped eventually into sleep, with her clinging to me. When I awoke I was alone, and I knew it was much later for the slats of light had moved around the room and had lost their intensity.

I don't know what caused me to wake, maybe a noise somewhere. Then I knew what the noise was - the sound of the engine of the Mercedes being fired up.

Striding towards the window, I pushed open the shutters. By now light and darkness were beginning to merge, but in the gloom I could see the Mercedes making the acute turn out of the arched gateway. The hood was still down, and I could see a fleeting flutter of dark hair through the rising dust as the tyres left the cobbled courtyard and bit into the crumbling track outside.

A corner stole the car from sight, and in just seconds I had dived into my shorts and shirt and was running down the stairs to the lobby where Azul was reading a newspaper.

"Where did she go," I demanded, my voice louder than I realised. "The senorita - where did she go?"

Azul shrugged, unruffled by my agitation.

"No quieres saber, Senor Ben. No quieres saber."

Seeing my blank look, he added: "You don't want to know."

"Of course I want to know," I snapped, leaning forward on the reception desk. "Where did she go?"

Azul shook his head again. Suddenly, I got it - he wanted money. Racing back to my room I grabbed a handful of peseta notes, at least fifty pounds in sterling.

Back at reception, breathless from the sprint, I thrust the notes towards him. "Tell me," I pleaded, my tone less demanding. "Where did she go?"

Azul looked startled at the dramatic production of the money, and he paused for several seconds before reaching for it. He smoothed out the notes, lined them up neatly, tapped them on the counter, and then handed them back.

"Senor Ben, let her go..."

" Who is she? Where has she gone?"

He shook his head very slowly. "It is best you not know. Go back to your work. Forget her".

"I can't forget her. Tell me, please..."

It must have been the undisguised anguish in my eyes, the

sheer compulsion in my manner, but Azul curtly nodded, and expelled a long, resigned sigh.

"OK, OK. You must know, then I tell. First we have drink."

I shook my head my head violently to stress my exasperation.

" I don't want a drink. Just tell me."

" It is I want drink," he said unhurriedly, and from under the counter he produced a bottle of Rioja, two-thirds full, and two glasses. He had barely finished filling the second glass when I snatched it up and sank it in one.

"I've had my drink," I said, crashing down the small, thick glass.

Picking up the bottle and glasses Azul walked over to a table and sat down, nodding for me to join him. He appeared to be weighing up what to say, or perhaps how to say it.

"Do you know her?" I prompted.

"Si senor. I know her. She stay here before, two times, maybe three."

"Alone?".

"Si, always".

"Why .. why does she come here?"

Azul sat deeper in the chair and took a long drink. He rested his elbows on his knees and clasped his hands in front of him. Leaning forward, he seemed almost conspiratorial.

"Senor Ben, girl stay here because she break long journey. She go much further journey."

"But there's nothing beyond here, is there? It's just mountains."

"Just one place. It long drive north, maybe four hours. It is castle owned by famous man. Very famous man. Rick Canata, estrella de la musica. You say I think, rock star. Maybe you hear of him in England?"

I hadn't heard of him, but to save time I nodded, unable to make any sense so far.

"Many years ago he very famous in Spain, and in America. Many big records, many tours, much money. Now, he old man, retired. Un recluso. Maybe bit crazy, who can say..."

I was still looking bewildered.

"Every month, Senor Canata telephones Malaga, special number in Malaga. They send him girl."

He looked at me. "You understand," he said "Very beautiful girl. Very expensive girl."

I knew I had to be misunderstanding him, but he read my face like that of a child.

"Si, senor. Un prostituta..."

He was nodding constantly, determined I accepted what he told me.

"Sometimes there are others, but she has been back few times. Two, three times. Long drive from Malaga. She stay here one night, to rest. Then she have to go to him."

Azul stopped, and drank the last of the Rioja. He sat back in his chair, opened his hands expansively, and shrugged.

There were sudden, stinging tears at the back of my eyes, but I couldn't let them out.

Over at the reception desk Azul was getting another bottle. He handed it to me, and pointed upstairs. "Take it. Go. You feel better later."

I walked slowly back to my room. By now it was almost dark, and as I switched on the lights, mellow pools of soft diluted amber provided a welcoming intimate glow. A big shaded table lamp spilled brighter light across the creased and crumpled sheets. I stared at the sheets, shaking and crying. Raising the bottle I had been gripping with intense ferocity I hurled it high against the wall over the bed. It shattered like a grenade, streaking red wine down the wall and splashing, spitting bloodstains onto the sheets.

Outside the window, I heard a lone hoopoe pierce the cooling night air with a wounding whiplash scream of betrayal.

The Man Who Loved Dogs

Hardy had left his dog Joe tied up outside the shop as usual while he went inside to buy his morning newspaper. He was just coming out of the shop when he saw the most extraordinary incident. Someone hit Joe.

The assailant was a tall thin severe man, wearing a grey double-breasted suit and carrying a tightly rolled umbrella. And it was with the umbrella that he hit Joe. Admittedly it was not a hard blow, but it was hard enough for Joe to leap back with surprise and give a short startled yelp. It was an entirely new and unsettling experience, for Joe had never previously been hit.

Hardy had acquired Joe as a six-week old puppy. A cross-bred Pointer - crossed with just what Hardy didn't know - Joe was a tall handsome dog with a narrow body, big chest, and was mostly white with black patches and lightly speckled gangly legs. His high curled tail was all white and greatly expressive, more so than most dogs Hardy thought.

Joe's tail was not wagging now, it was down, trailing, looking as if it was no longer connected with his body. His dark brown eyes were hurt, uneasy, and mystified. He didn't know what he had done wrong. Hardy didn't know either. He had witnessed the incident. The pavement outside the shop was fairly narrow but then Joe had been fastened on a quite short lead, and there was still more than enough room for someone to walk by.

There was no need for the man in the suit to have stepped aside, so there was certainly no need to lash out at Joe with his umbrella, clearing the way in a rather imperious fashion. Immediately, Hardy knew that Joe's assailant had to be taught a lesson. The man was striding purposefully down the street, not looking back, utterly unaware that his action had been observed. Fussing Joe to reassure him, Hardy kept the man in sight. Gently massaging Joe between his ears, just where he liked it, Hardy murmured: "Good boy, good boy," in expected reassurance and then smoothed his hand along the dog's sleek side, as if to soothe away the shock of the smack from the umbrella, even though he knew that the blow would have caused no real pain. It was the sheer unnecessity of it that rankled, the spitefulness it betrayed.

Crossing the road Hardy began to follow The Suit from the other side, so as to minimise the likelihood of being seen. After about a quarter of a mile The Suit turned into a pleasant side street of 1930's detached houses, many of them faced with some token black and white boarding redolent of mock Tudor.

At the fifth house on the left The Suit stopped, opened a dark green painted wooden gate that gap-toothed beneath a trimmed privet hedge and walked up the pathway. Back at the corner Hardy was partly screened by shrubbery from neighbouring gardens, and he paused for a couple of minutes after the front door had closed before striding by. A single glance from the opposite side of the road revealed it to be an immaculately maintained property, the lawn and flower beds neat and precise, and even a collection of vases visible through the bay window symmetrically arranged on the sill to give perfect balanced appearance.

Noting the house name - Craig-Lea - and the name of the avenue, Hardy made his way back to where he had left his car and went home.

He considered the time of the incident to have been significant. It was just around the time when the commuter train from London deposited passengers at the station near the newsagents shop.

Next day, at exactly the same time, and for the three consecutive days, Hardy kept a discreet watch near the station. His vigilance was rewarded with just what he expected - a complete record of The Suit's movements, which rather predictably followed a distinct pattern. Each week day he arrived on the 6.10, and made the five-minute walk home. Most evenings, at around 9.00pm, The Suit went out for a stroll, first down the road and then around the edge of a golf course, eventually forming a circle to return home. The Suit was named Richard Corbett, and he lived alone. It had been very easy to find out.

Hardy had visited the house next door to Corbett's, clipboard in hand, supposedly carrying out a survey into newspaper choices. It had taken just a couple of minutes with an over-blonde very gregarious woman who lived there to learn that Corbett was an insurance company branch manager, a rather aloof character, and not very neighbourly. "He complained about my hedge hanging over his side of the fence", she said.

Another useful snippet Hardy gleaned was that Corbett's wife had left him some ten years ago, preferring, it seemed, the company of a double-glazing contractor who had fitted new windows at the house. "She left while he was at work - just took her suitcases and her budgerigar in a cage." It was all useful material for Hardy who was building up a picture of The Suit, and already beginning to form a plan which that evening he carefully explained to Joe as they sat having tea and chocolate biscuits. Joe, of course, had his own mug, a wide bright yellow pottery mug that allowed room for his long slender pointed nose to slip in and give his big pink tongue access to the very bottom.

The memory of first acquiring Joe was still very vivid in Hardy's mind, although the dog was now seven years old. In the pub one night he had heard a man asking if anyone wanted a pup, the last of the litter. Hardy knew there and then it was fate, for his own dog Bess had that very day been put to sleep, aged sixteen, the vet unable to do any more for her failing heart. For a dog to be so immediately available to fill that huge vacuum of love and companionship that the loss of Bess had created seemed something approaching divine intervention to Hardy, and he arranged to go to see the pup that evening.

As soon as he saw the thin, wriggling bundle of fur he picked it up and put it inside his coat, gave the owner £5 and walked away. Joe, as he decided to call him immediately, was squirming under his jacket, frantically trying to lick Hardy's chin, and furiously trying to wag his tiny tail under the folds of the coat. Joe was so tiny Hardy thought that he was probably crossed with a Jack Russell, even though there was much evidence of the Pointer connection. The dog's paws seemed as tiny as mustard spoons, and his tail little thicker than a piece of string. His ears mostly drooped floppily, but when slightly erect gave Joe a rather quizzical expression. The thing which moved Hardy most were Joe's eyes. Unlike many pups that he had known, Joe's eyes were not bright and frantic and eager. They were quiet, reflective, and utterly expressive.

In the seven years since, Hardy had built up a bond with Joe that only dog lovers can totally appreciate. He regarded Joe as not an animal, but as a small person inside a furry suit. And while a dog communicates in wholly different ways, and on different levels, there was still an immense level of mutual understanding between the two, each capable of reading each others moods.

Hardy had lived alone for more than ten years following the death of his wife, who had been struck down and killed by a car while using a pedestrian crossing. She too had been a great dog lover, and they had bought Bess together as a pup and shared her life for the whole of their marriage. They had not had children, but Bess was their child.

Hardy's view that dogs were special creatures with a distinct affinity to humans, making them more deeply devoted than any other animal, had been forged in boyhood. Already closely bonded to the family pet, an old collie called Judy, he had come across a quotation from Jerome K. Jerome which seemed to underline all he already perceived about dogs.

Jerome had noted: "A dog never asks whether you are rich or poor, silly or wise, sinner or saint. Come luck or misfortune, honour or shame, he is going to stick with you, to comfort you, guard you and give his life for you if need be. You are his pal, and that is good enough for him."

The bond forged between Joe and Hardy over the seven years they had been together was as strong and powerful and unbreakable as many that might exist between brothers, between father and son, between husband and wife. They were the greater part of each others lives, and it was unfortunate for Mr Richard Corbett that he should unwittingly choose to strike the soul mate of a man who loved dogs.

The plan to exact revenge came to Hardy from nowhere. It just seemed to fall into his mind and seem so right. It would show The Suit the true worth of a dog, and in a way which he would not forget.

Five days later when Richard Corbett was taking his evening stroll, along against the golf course, he felt for just a fraction of a second a single blow struck with perfectly judged, ex-marine force at the base of his skull. He blacked out instantly and slumped forward. Hardy caught him, quickly draping one of Corbett's inert arms around his shoulders to spread the weight, and semi-dragging him a few yards into the edge of the road where his car was parked. Had Hardy met anyone he was going to say that his friend wasn't feeling well, that he had fainted and he was helping him home, but he doubted that he would meet anyone and he was right. The car was parked close to the shrubbery which fringed the road, acting as a buffer between it and the edge of the golf course. It was the same shrubbery in which Hardy had hidden, waiting for Corbett to walk by. It had taken just a few seconds to push Corbett onto the rear seat and drive off. The spot had been chosen carefully. No houses fronted the course at that point.

After a few minutes Hardy turned his old Volvo estate car off the main road and up a single track lane. He then stopped long enough to take out a pre-prepared chloroform pad from a sealed air-tight tin and taped it across Corbett's mouth and nose. He knew that would keep him out for the remainder of the journey.

When Corbett eventually regained consciousness he was first aware of how cold he was. Very, very, cold. In still-confused state, he tried to pull his clothes more tightly around him, then found that he was not wearing clothes. He was naked. This realisation seemed to sharpen his senses, pulling him from the depths. It was completely dark and he started to get up. Immediately he cracked his head on an exceptionally low, hard ceiling and fell back to the floor. Then as his mind struggled to overcome his bewilderment, he was suddenly shockingly aware that as he had moved there had been an accompanying scraping, grating metallic sound. And then he became aware of something else too, something more frightening.

There was a tight clamping device around his neck.

His fingers scrabbled about trying to gain some mental map of his surroundings. His sense of touch told him there was a heavy studded leather collar around his neck, with a dangling padlock fastened beneath his chin. From the padlock was a chain stretching back several feet to a heavy steel ring set in a concrete floor.

Corbett realised he was chained up like a dog.

He shouted and then screamed for help continually for maybe half an hour, until his throat began to sting with the hoarseness of the effort. Between bouts of yelling he listened, but the silence stalked around him like a watchful witness. He had fallen into an exhausted silence for maybe fifteen minutes, when coming towards him he saw a golden yellow tunnel of torchlight and as it neared, a gentle pad of unhurried footfall.

"Help me," Corbett gasped, his throat cracked and his voice splintered.

"Help me, please."

The end of the torchlight jerked upwards and shone full in his face forcing him to lower his eyes and look away.

"I can't help you," said a voice from beyond the torch. A soft toned, unthreatening voice, yet somehow seeming distant, uninvolved.

"Why .... why not? ".

"Because it was I who bought you here."

Corbett was stunned. Stupidly it had just not occurred to him that his finder might also be his keeper. Now, it seemed obvious. Until then, the appearance of the light had seemed a salvation. Corbett had no idea of what had happened. His last clear memory was of going out for his walk.

Now, despite his puzzlement, he was feeling stronger, and with regaining strength came a certain frisson of anger that was beginning to rise above the initial fear and self pity.

"I demand you release me," he said, his managerial authority beginning to flow back.

"It doesn't seem to me that you are in a position to demand anything," said Hardy, with almost indifferent casualness. "But do correct me if I'm wrong."

The real significance of the situation still hadn't completely dawned on Corbett. "You can't do this," he insisted. "Abduction is illegal. I shall report you to the police. You'll go to prison."

Switching off the torch, Hardy sat down on the edge of the wall of the old pig sty in which Corbett was chained. When illuminated by the torch Corbett had been crouched just inside the roof section of the sty, his skin almost alien in its whiteness, and seeming starkly artificial. He crouched on hands and knees, the flabby folds of flesh of his stomach lined up in a neat rank. He had big feet with long finger-like toes, and a lot of black and silvery hair on his shoulders and back. He looked such a pathetic sight, Hardy felt compelled to turn off the torch and blot out the hunched and bony figure.

"So you'll report me, will you," said Hardy. "You don't know who I am, where you are, or why you are here, yet you'll report me."

His voice was still level, unconcerned, just as relaxed as if he was discussing the weather with a friend. He had paused deliberately to allow the significance of his words to sink in. "You are chained up and, you may be assured, you cannot free yourself," he continued. "But you can go on making demands if you like - I'll be back in an hour or so."

"No, no, wait," said Corbett. "Just tell me what you want. Tell me why I'm here."

"You hit Joe," said Hardy, simply. "That was not a very nice thing to do. It really upset him."

Corbett had no idea what this madman was talking about. "You must have the wrong man," he told Hardy. "I've never hit anybody in my life. I'm not a violent person. I just don't hit people."

"You did, I saw you."

"I didn't, I didn't," insisted Corbett. "I just don't go around hitting people."

"Joe is a dog," said Hardy, keeping the sentence brief so that its impact would not be diluted.

"A dog?", said Corbett, the incredulity in his voice so intense it raised the tone a half an octave. "You've bought me here because I hit a dog?"

"It upset him," said Hardy. "He didn't understand. He wasn't himself for the rest of the day."

"When was this?" said Corbett. "I can't recall it."

"Ten days ago, just outside the newsagents by the station. You hit out at him with your umbrella."

The incident came back to Corbett as insignificant to him now as it was then. "You can't keep me here just because of that," he said sharply. "It was just a dog. It was in the way. You just don't kidnap someone for that."

"I do," said Hardy dryly.

By now Corbett was getting angry again. He was a man not used to being in an uncontrolled situation. All his instincts rose against it, and now he knew what it was all about, he felt better, more positive. It was just a small incident, and one he knew could be sorted out. This situation, he was certain, came down to a simple question of bargaining. He could tell from Hardy's voice he was dealing with an educated man, articulate, professional and therefore open to reasoned negotiation.

"How much?" he asked. "How much do you want?"

"You mean money?" inquired Hardy, intending to cause further exasperation.

"Of course I mean money. What else could I mean? How much do you want to release me, forget about the whole thing? Settle the matter."

"It's not a question of money," said Hardy. "It's a question of fairness. What you did to Joe was unfair. He just didn't deserve it. So what I want you to do is apologise."

By now Corbett had edged out from the pig pen, his chain rattling behind him and he stood up in the walled section, his eyes becoming accustomed to the minimal light available from the few stars in the cloud washed sky.

He felt foolish and he felt vulnerable, but despite that his natural ire rose like a surfacing whale.

"Apologise! Are you mad? I am not going to apologise to you for something as preposterous as that."

"You miss the point," said Hardy. "It's not me that you have to apologise to. It is Joe. He has very sensitive feelings."

Corbett could not see the figure in front of him, just a dark shape against a darker background and he lunged forward clawing at the air. The chain jerked tight, the collar cut deep into his windpipe and he jerked back and fell on to the rough concrete floor. From there, he screamed abuse at Hardy, the night sky and at the very ground he pounded with his fists.

Hardy let him blow himself out knowing that sense or exhaustion would bring the tantrum to a close. The night was beginning to turn chilly, Joe would be waiting for his tea and biscuits, and it seemed that Corbett would need more time before he was ready to face reconciliation. "You can shout all you like," he told him. "There isn't a building within two miles. I'll come back when you're feeling more agreeable." Corbett made some snarling unintelligible response.

Hardy looked up at the star-filled sky. "It's getting a bit cool to be out here, so I'll bring you a blanket. And I suppose you want some supper."

Corbett realised that he was intensely hungry, the pangs suppressed by his rebellion and fury. Restraining himself from hurling more abuse, he made a greater effort to moderate his voice and rather resignedly, said: "Yes."

Within five minutes Hardy was back at the sty, putting down a bowl of tinned dog food into the pool of torchlight and throwing an old blanket alongside. "The blanket is one of Joe's," said Hardy helpfully. "He's prepared to lend it to you. He is not a vindictive dog. And he is prepared to share his food too, though not of course his chocolate biscuits." The torch beam snapped out, and the footsteps faded.

Rage had blocked Corbett's throat, clamped his tongue, frozen his mind. His heart was bursting with the need to generate energy to quell the anger.

He sat motionless, unaware of the numbingly cold concrete until the chill night air cooled his fire to the point where he reached for the blanket and draped it around his shoulders. He refused the dog food, though his hunger was overwhelming. From behind the slowly shifting cloud clusters a thin new crescent moon emerged. Corbett stared up at it and then slowly at first, but then with quickening pace and screaming crescendo, began to shrill abuse and obscenities upwards in a rising parabola, piercing cries, peaking and then dying away.

Then he realised with dark sobering shock that like a dog, he was howling at the moon.

It was not until 3am that Hardy returned. In the intervening period Corbett had undergone a series of changes of mood. His anger had disintegrated, crushed into tiny valueless pieces by the cold discomfort and hopelessness of his situation. He had carefully examined the collar, chain and steel ring embedded into the pigsty floor, and it all seemed unbreakable, unslippable. He kept reminding himself that he was dealing with a mad man, and that he must be acquiescent. Must control his temper. But he knew that controlling his temper was not a thing he found easy. Margaret found that too, which was why she had fallen for that mild mannered, easy-going double-glazing salesman which she found so appealing and so charming. Corbett found that however much he resented having to give in, he knew the best course would be to go along with the madman's notion. So he rehearsed a suitable level of subservience and contrition, and then waited.

When Hardy returned at 3am precisely, he shone his torch into the sty and saw Corbett sitting in a corner with the blanket swathed around him.

Corbett, shading his eyes from the light said: "You're right. I should apologise. It was a stupid thing and I shouldn't have done it."

"No use saying it to me," said Hardy. "I'll go fetch Joe."

The dog walked into the sty without eagerness but with a certain curiosity. Corbett saw that Joe was a languid looking creature with lazy eyes and an apparent reticent manner. Oddly, the dog didn't sniff around him, or show any excitement, just steadily gazed into his face which, with Corbett seated on the floor, put them almost at eye level.

"Tell him what you told me," instructed Hardy.

Corbett swallowed hard. He could not really believe that he was about to offer an apology to a dog. "I'm sorry," he said, the words struggling to climb over his teeth. Joe stared back at him.

"Is that all?" said Hardy, his voice making it clear that it wasn't.

"I'm sorry I hit you. I shouldn't have done it. I apologise."

Joe turned around and ambled out of the spotlight thrown by the torch, and disappeared into the blackness beyond.

"All right," said Corbett. "I've done it. I've done exactly what you asked. Now you can let me go."

"It's not that simple," said Hardy. "You see, Joe doesn't believe you."

"What?"

"He doesn't believe you. He doesn't think you really mean it."

Corbett struggled to kerb a crescendo of rising hysteria, the raw frustration boiling like volcanic lava. Somehow he managed to level his voice.

"How do you know?"

"It was obvious by the way he reacted. He wasn't convinced. You'll have to try again with more feeling, more contrition. We'll be back in an hour."

The arc of torchlight began to turn, then swung back to shine on Corbett.

"You see, you really need to appreciate just how special dogs are, how their love and respect for us runs as deep as the soul itself."

Hardy leaned against the pigsty wall, switched off the torch, and decided Corbett might benefit from a few illustrative examples of dogs unquestioning service to humanity.

"In both the first and second world wars, dogs were used for a variety of work with troops - carrying messages and ammunition, detecting enemy patrols, leading men through mine fields, that sort of thing. Now you might argue that all that was just the result of training, and up to a point you'd be right. But dogs often went far beyond what they were trained for, saving lives, often giving their own lives, yet doing it for love of their masters, not just because they'd been taught.

"Dogs were shelled, shot, gassed, but kept at their tasks, even when wounded. There was more to it than just training - they could easily run away from the noise and mayhem of battle. But they didn't because of their devotion to us, their need to serve.

"I read about one dog, Ricky his name was, a Welsh collie, who detected mines in the last war. Even when a mine went off near him, blowing away part of his face, he wouldn't give up. He carried on locating all the other mines until the area was clear. Didn't have to - he wanted to."

Hardy rotated to a less uncomfortable position on the wall, and sifted the many tales he could tell.

"There was one dog, Rob I think he was called, who made more than 20 parachute jumps with the SAS. They didn't have to throw him out of the plane - he jumped out of his own accord. He was determined to be part of the team.

"But it was a dog in the first war who best shows what devotion to man a dog can have. The town of Verdun was under siege, being flattened by heavy shell fire. The French troops were outnumbered, and nearly out of ammunition. One of them, a dog handler called Duvalle, had sent his dog back across the lines carrying a message pleading for help, and was awaiting the dogs return. Crouched in a trench Duvalle saw his dog running through a hail of bullets and shell fire when, suddenly, it was hit and fell to the ground. Duvalle leapt out of the trench, shouting to the dog, and was immediately killed. But the dog had picked out Duvalle's voice and incredibly, struggled to its feet. Badly injured, with one of its back legs shattered, it dragged itself more than 200 yards to reach Duvalle.

"It got there, and in a container on its back was a message saying reinforcements were about to arrive, and they hung on until the town was saved."

The tone of Hardy's voice had briefly faltered with emotion as the story ended.

"Why do you think it went through all that?" The question was rhetorical, for Hardy gave no time for an answer.

"I'll tell you why," he said. "It was because once a dog takes you as its friend, it bonds itself to you for life. You become its reason for being. Even if you ill-treat it, it will usually remain faithful. It takes its pleasure from pleasing you. So even in a terrifying situation, like war, a dog's need to serve you can override its fear of explosions, gunfire, the screams of the dying.

"I don't know what sort of man Duvalle was, but his dog did. He had set it a task and it wanted to complete it, despite its terror and its pain. Duvalle was its life and it would give that life for him.

"All dogs have this vast capacity to give unlimited love and loyalty. It's just that people like you don't see it, can't appreciate it. So you don't treat them with respect. To you, they're just animals. Of course, there are those who would argue this is a simplistic view, with all logic eroded by emotion."

The disdain in his voice razored through the still night air, and the next sentence was totally dismissive. "They just don't understand dogs, and that's their loss."

Clicking on the torch he saw Corbett still sitting on the ground, slit-eyed against the light, face tightly expressionless.

"Did you know there was an animal version of the Victoria Cross," Hardy asked, but Corbett didn't acknowledge the question.

"There is - it's called the Dickin Medal, and it was first presented in the second world war. On it is engraved 'For Gallantry. We Also Serve'. It was awarded only for exceptional gallantry. Know how many dogs won it during the last war? Sixteen, that's how many, sixteen.

"God knows, many more deserved one. Thousands lost their lives, shot, blown up. The bastard Russians even had a squad of suicide dogs. With a bomb strapped to their back, they went and lay down in the path of advancing Panzer tanks, and blew themselves and the tank up when it crushed them. You might say they didn't know what they were doing. I say they did, at least after the first few. They learn. They saw their pals going out, and would realise that they didn't come back. Yet they still kept doing their job. It is unquestioning loyalty and devotion. You can only get a dog - or anybody for that matter - to do something like that for love. Fear just wouldn't be enough."

There were a few seconds of contemplative silence, and then fading footfalls as Hardy returned to his cottage.

Corbett stayed huddled, unmoved by the stories, but knowing that when his captor returned at the allotted time of 4am his contrition would have to be convincing. Yet as the long minutes passed, he realised with some slight surprise that he had started to feel rather sorry for hitting Joe. Or was it that he was just starting to nudge against the perimeters of insanity himself?

Yes, he felt he now recognised that a dog could be sensitive, have injured feelings. Yes, a dog might, through some superior interpretation of vocal tones, be capable of understanding an apology, and yes - No! He WAS going insane!

Corbett was past caring. He just knew he wanted to be away

from here, back to his neat secure home, his bowls club, and the comfort of his music. How soothing it would be right now to hear the theraputic flow of Prokofiev.

So when 4am came and Hardy returned with Joe, Corbett decided to give it his best unstinting effort. In the pale yellowy white light of the torch, Joe's brown eyes took on a deep interior tint of reflective phosphorous green. They returned Corbett's gaze evenly, unblinkingly, searchingly, their ghostly intensity seeming to examine his very soul.

"I really am sorry Joe. I should not have hit you. It was a very thoughtless unnecessary act. I am truly, truly sorry."

Joe continued to stare at Corbett for several stretched seconds and the gaze of the dog's eyes exuded a palpable mesmeric power. Corbett had never paid a great deal of attention to dogs in the past. His family had not had one as a child, and he had not had one as an adult. He knew little or nothing about dogs. Yet now he was aware, quite unmistakably that behind Joe's eyes was some distinct form of intelligence, admittedly in its own parallel, but capable of taking in far more of the human world that he had ever suspected. Slowly, Corbett reached forward and gently touched Joe's head, the short sleek fur cool and silky on his fingertips. "I'm sorry Joe, really."

Joe stepped forward, his long nose shining like fresh wet gloss paint.

Then his wide pink tongue flashed out in a single swipe left to right across Corbett's cheek and nose. Then, Joe turned and was gone.

"He believes you," said Hardy, pleased and not the least surprised.

The bizarre penance was completed when Hardy brought out a mug of not quite hot coffee. Corbett was able to drink it quickly and gratefully without realising it was not hot, precisely so that it could be consumed rapidly. Inevitably, it was drugged.

At just after 9pm Corbett came around, at first muggy, but within a few minutes, fairly focussed. He realised that he was fully dressed and back in his own living room on the sofa. He felt grubby and incredibly weary. For just a second or so, he thought he had suddenly come awake at the end of a bad dream, but the chafed soreness around his throat indicated reality could be crazier than a dream. Corbett found he could not really assess just how he felt about the whole thing. Certainly serrated anger still cut at him, stinging and searing. Yet he also felt strangely unresentful.

As he recalled the events he kept seeing Joe's large gentle forgiving brown eyes as if they had been indelibly stencilled into his consciousness. He sat up and then noticed on the coffee table in front of him a small cream coloured piece of paper bearing a few handwritten lines in brown ink.

He picked it up and tilted it to a better light. It said: "The following observation by a little-known Belgian poet called Maurice Maeterlinck may serve you well in future: 'We are alone on this planet, and amid all forms of life not one, except the dog, has made an alliance with us. We have not had to gain his confidence or friendship - he is born our friend. While his eyes are still closed, already he believes in us. Even before his birth, he has given himself to man.'

Corbett stood still for several seconds, the letter gripped so tightly, the paper had puckered and creased. He became aware that his hand was shaking quite uncontrollably.

Cafe Conquistador

Fifteen years ago she would have been a real heartbreaker. Even now, in her late thirties, she still created a mesmeric trail as she threaded through the clustered pavement tables of the Cafe Conquistador with swaying small-step grace.

The night air was cooling now but there remained a fevered heat, which seemed to stir an undercurrent of repressed Latin passions. Certainly, as she sat alone at a reserved table near the bar, the minds of the three waiters who sped to serve her could not have been focussed entirely on the prospect of a tip. I was near enough to hear her order a margarita, in a voice as soft as the slide of a satin sheet.

Her legs were long and bare. As she settled back in the curved cane chair she crossed them, with an ease so measured I was certain it had been carefully rehearsed. Her shoes were delicate strappy high heels, and I knew they were Gucci. Her black dress was off-the-shoulder and just small enough to make you care. Harsh down-lighting burnished the blondness of her hair, an expensive classic-Sixties cut redolent of Doris Day in her glittery golden years. Her only jewellery was worn on the right wrist, a slim arc of diamonds which rippled and flashed its unique, unmistakable Morse code for wealth to even the furthest transfixed observers.

Cafe Conquistador was the largest building fronting the main square. Although single storey it stretched above the palms because of its spiralled monument of neon, lofting its name up into the night sky like the lilac flame-trail of an ascending rocket. The vivid flash could be seen for at least a kilometre in either direction along Avenida del Santiago. It was an alluring beacon of promise, and they came in convoys, spilling out of cream-and-black Mercedes taxis as if arriving at a movie premiere.

Already every table was full, and on the outer fringes those who couldn't find seats were jostling for even an additional centimetre of standing space.

The crowding created a scuffle just in front of the towering chromium-domed cappuccino machine at the end of the bar. Two men, one wearing a white suit, faced each other, posturing absurdly for their women, and each refusing to concede a fraction more ground to the other.

The raised voices caught the attention of Leon, the head waiter. Six feet six, thin rather than slim, and with the lithe agility of a dancer, he seemed to twist and glide through the packed mass of human tissue bearing two of his famous Blue Marendo cocktails in tall frosted glasses.

His thick, dark moustache moved visibly upwards as he smiled, with a flash of white enamel and a glinting gold front tooth.

"For the beautiful ladies," he said, handing them the cocktails with exaggerated flourish. "Compliments of the management. It is an honour that you join us tonight."

The girls giggled, the men stiffly nodded acceptance and the incident was quelled.

I had let it distract me. Looking around I saw she was still alone at her table, casually reading a note delivered by a waiter. I knew exactly what would happen next. Without looking up she crumpled the note into a small ball and carefully dropped it with telegraphed disdain into the small metal ashtray. She always did that.

Then, a two-piece keyboards and guitar band started playing a sensual Dire Straits number with more enthusiasm than talent. She tapped her foot and gently rocked her shoulders to the music, and looked around with languid, feigned disinterest.

Two tables away from where she sat was Jules Demetrini, big in real estate, big in organised crime, and just big.

His bearded, bloated figure was in no way improved by the best tuxedo laundered money could buy. He was trying not to watch her, and to the casual onlooker it would appear his attention was diverse. But I was no casual onlooker, and I calculated that he looked left - towards her - far more often than he looked right. A ratio of five to one, in fact. The note she had rejected may even have been from him. Demetrini was one of several men whose arrogant presumption she had coolly crushed at one time or another.

Earlier I was by the entrance when he arrived, his chauffeured white Cadillac almost yacht-sized, gliding an effortless course through the swarming traffic as if it were docking. Almost before it had stopped his bodyguard, scowl enhanced by lizardish dark-green wrap-around sunglasses, was out of the car and opening the rear door with a theatrical flourish.

Demetrini emerged smiling and waving like a B-list movie actor. He had none of the style, yet all of the ego.

Sliding out behind him, reaching for his arm as no doubt instructed, was a girl of about 20, dark-skinned with boyish short-cropped dark hair and a Bardotesque pout.

She was an appendage to help Demetrini make a statement - that he possessed, or could acquire, anything he wanted.

Not quite everything. I had something he wanted and she still sat alone at her table, temptingly within reach, but as unattainable to him as immortality.

Her solitary beauty and huge inherited wealth had fuelled the ambition and desire of several notable men in this close, naked community, creating a raw, rampant urge for possession by Demetrini and his rivals. Their efforts were entertainingly absurd.

I knew more about her than anyone. It was known that I was her confidante, and this privileged position had resulted in my becoming more popular, more courted, than my natural social talents would justify. I admit that I enjoyed the modest power play this engendered. Especially when it involved dealing with Demetrini.

"You must come to stay at my villa at La Plata," he says. "The views are beyond words." He pauses and adds carelessly: "Bring someone with you."

"Maybe," I say encouragingly. "I will certainly mention your offer."

The next week, he targets me at the Kiseto Beach Club.

"When you come to stay?" He places a hand on my shoulder as though we are old friends. "My villa is magnificent at this time of the year. It is yours. Just say when."

I nod, but then add: "Unfortunately, my plans are uncertain at present. It is most annoying."

The words are well-chosen, for it would be inappropriate for him to ask why my plans are uncertain, so he widens his smile. It does not entirely mask the sting of disappointment. Politely, I smile too.

I could be more brutal, just pointedly refuse the offer. But I enjoy keeping Demetrini on a taut line, able to reel him in when I choose. Few in this town have something that this gross and odious man needs.

The band hammer into a rough but pulsating version of the Stones's Brown Sugar and she edges forward in her seat, dress intentionally riding a little higher. Her feet tap alternately with the accentuated bass rhythm.

A charge of vibrant excitement starts to spark and crackle around the crowded tables. The runes of Saturday night promise are being cast. The arc of diamonds flashes briefly as she raises her hand, the signal for another margarita to be served. Around her a dozen men have begun to run the opening sequences of dark and private fantasies.

No doubt about it, I thought, even though I admit I might be accused of just a little bias. When it came to making an impact in the ever-changing microcosm that was the Cafe Conquistador, no one could come even close to mother...

Justifiable Punishment

The subject of revenge came up as one of those jokey conversation-fillers at a rather tedious party. Neither Philip nor I knew anyone, and neither of us would have been there at all had we not been sent to represent the company.

I suppose party wasn't really the right word for the event. It was a reception, a glitzy PR bash at a minor stately home to mark it turning itself into an historical theme park. Our firm had won the marketing contract and Philip and I were there just to make up the numbers, to provide back-up for Jordan. He was running the show, gliding around with his pin-on smile as if he was some sort of celebrity. Admittedly, he had created the campaign which had won the contract, but his overt pomposity was irritating.

"Having a few more bodies around will help create the impression we're a bigger outfit," Jordan told us at the briefing. "Just circulate, make new contacts and - most important - ensure your ID badges are on show. We have to let people know who we are."

He was proud of those badges, which featured our new corporate logo. They were dark green ovals with a gold-rim and the company name in bold gold script, and our individual names in neat capitals underneath. "Classy, very classy," murmured Jordan as he handed them out with the same kind of ceremony they probably employ when awarding an MBE.

It wasn't his design at all. It was mine. I had done a virtually identical logo for an antiques company about two years earlier. It was on the files, and that's doubtless where Jordan came across it. Big ideas were not his forte. Being devious was. No point in my taking the matter up with him. He was my boss, and apart from denying this blatant creative theft he would take it out on me in other ways. Like diverting the best clients to other staff. That way he could curtail my performance bonus.

He was like that. You don't become creative director without being creative when it comes to office politics.

Let me give you a for instance: last year we took on a new

guy, sharp, loaded with ideas. Almost immediately he was outshining Jordan, which, let's face it, wasn't that difficult. But this kid was hot, destined for a meteoric rise. We could all see it. Including Jordan. Know what he did? He faked the guy's signature on a sarcastic letter to a client, who of course then complained. Jordan reports the matter to the MD, who then shows the new guy the door. Nasty.

And I know that's what happened because I got it direct from Katie, Jordan's ex. She and I had a thing going for a while - two weeks actually - after she split with him. Seemed he liked to talk about his dirty tricks when they were in bed. Must have been a turn-on for the sad bastard.

Katie enjoyed telling me about it. I think she hoped I would spread it around. Everyone likes a little revenge, don't they?

I think that's what sparked us off at the reception. I'd told Philip about Jordan's bedtime confession and he recounted a couple of incidents he knew of himself, including one where Jordan had stolen from the petty cash drawer and fixed the blame on some teenage girl in accounts who wouldn't sleep with him.

Philip and I were standing together in the large marble-floored entrance hall of a grand Georgian mansion. The hall was circular and so vast it dwarfed a hotel lobby, so the party was being staged there. The house itself was - well, let's just say it was located in the north west of England. It's best to be careful with names and places. The people involved are still around.

There was the usual mailing-list mixture of utterly witless people mingling, dispensing loud cheery greeting, and with enough false sincerity sloshing around to have floated a cruise liner. Jordan - that's not his real name either - was fixedly engaged in sucking up to Lord M—- and his ambitious son. His Lordship was about 70. He looked frail and worn-out, and wishing he was elsewhere. His son was late-thirties, flush-faced and odious even by aristocratic standards. I guessed it was the son's greedy ambition and persistence which had forced the old man down the theme park route. Or perhaps it was just lack of cash. These stately homes are worth a fortune but often have little or no income.

Lord M—- and his son were among the few faces I could put names to. And Lady M—-, of course. I gathered she was the second wife, very much younger than the old boy, probably in her mid-forties. She seemed, at least from a distance, an attractive and energetic woman, flitting busily between guests with the kind of dedication only strict orders to meet everyone could induce.

There were also a few local businessmen I'd encountered through my marketing work, though I didn't know any of them that well. Jordan always took over client-liaison, even if it was someone else's project. He claimed it gave the client reassurance to know that someone senior was taking an interest. We all knew it was so he could take most of the credit.

"Maybe I should concoct a plan to take revenge on Jordan," I said to Philip, not meaning it too seriously. It was just said as conversational lubricant.

"It would have to be a good one," he said, and I could see he was amused. "He certainly deserves some particularly unpleasant retribution."

Then I noticed his eyes darkening momentarily, hooding as his brows closed and he concentrated his thoughts.

"Revenge is most effective when it's not instant and dramatic but spread over time," he remarked, half his thoughts still elsewhere. "That way it's unrelenting. It wears the victim down, destroys their self-belief, completely breaks them. It can be horrific to witness."

"I think I feel one of your stories coming on."

Get Philip onto almost any subject and chances are he's known of someone who had an extreme experience and he then delights telling it as a salutary parable.

"We've got the time," he said, choosing to ignore my jibe. He motioned for us to sit down on a large red-leather Chesterfield, and he plucked two more glasses of champagne from a waiter gliding past.

"I was once involved in a most calculated and ruthless act of revenge," he told me. "It was more than 20 years ago, when I was out in Malta working for a big hotel group. There were a lot of Brits out there even then. I don't mean tourists but people who actually lived and worked there. Quite a strong ex-pat community, as there usually is. I'd been there only a couple of weeks or so when I was introduced to a man called Herbert Gardner. Now you'd expect that with a name like Herbert he would be at least middle-aged. But no. He was, like me, in his mid-twenties. Civil engineer. Pleasant enough in a quiet way. He wasn't at all outgoing, quite a dull personality in fact. But always came over as very genuine."

I nodded agreement. "I know the sort," I said. "Worthy to the point of boredom."

"He wasn't that bad," said Philip. "He was just a nice but unremarkable chap. Our offices were almost adjoining and we often had an end-of-day drink at the same bar just across the street. Lobo's, I think it was called. Something like that anyway. Doesn't matter. So over the weeks I got to know a fair bit about Herbert.

"His parents were typical middle-class. Father was in the civil service, mother was a magistrate. Just the sort of parents to call a kid Herbert and not realise the stick he would get at school. It was the 1960s, for God's sake!"

"There was a boy at my school called Theodore," I said. "He was picked on almost hourly. We drew up a rota and took turns."

Philip seemed to resent the interruption. He liked to get a flow going. "Anyway, the only surprising thing about Herbert was his wife. She was breathtaking. Stunningly beautiful. Turns out he had acquired her - and I use the word advisedly - in Malaysia about two years earlier, when he was out there working on some drainage project. I don't know much about her background but it appeared she was an orphan. She'd been working in a bar when Herbert met her. At least he claimed it was a bar, but I'll bet it was one of those strip-joint places.

"Either way, Herbert fell for her. Not surprising really. He was one of those repressed types, awkward with women. When she played up to him, he was hooked. He asked her to marry him in less than a week. She said yes, of course. Obviously marriage to an Englishman would be a big step up for her, and she went for it. It gave her instant security, an easy life and even the opportunity to travel, as Herbert's job took him all over the world. She was very bright, spoke excellent English, and was able to slot into his lifestyle perfectly. When they moved to Malta they quickly became a popular couple among the ex-pat community, largely due to her social skills. Herbert seemed to gain more self-confidence too. He became more outgoing, and he freely admitted it was all due to her. 'Amelia has changed my life,' he once told me. 'I just don't know how I existed before I met her.'

"Trouble was, Amelia was becoming too popular with other men. It didn't take her long to realise that with her looks she could do much better than Herbert, who was completely unacquainted with the concept of fun.

"First there was a golf pro, then an Italian restaurateur, then a naval officer. After that we began to lose count. Several of Herbert's friends, and even an attache at the embassy, put up no resistance. Anyone who was handsome, athletic or free-spending was a target, married or not. And what made it all the more shocking was that she seemed to make not the slightest effort to hide her activities. Everyone knew in no time at all. It was as if she didn't care whether or not Herbert found out."

I forgot that I was supposed to keep quiet. "I'll bet he wasn't so mild-mannered when he did find out. Those quiet types can really lose it and go berserk."

"Not Herbert. He was very civilised about it. I learned later that initially he just had 'a quiet word' with her, a warning shot so to speak. But she ignored it. She knew how much he idolised her and I think she felt that he was so weak, so doting, that he'd tolerate the affairs because he couldn't face losing her.

"On the surface, in public at least, they still played the devoted couple, even hosting the occasional party, though the guest list was shrinking fast as friends began to shy away from them. Most of us could see that, despite Herbert's apparent tolerance, underneath he was tortured and hurting.

"A time or two, over a drink, I broached the subject, but it was something he found deeply embarrassing and he was reluctant to acknowledge the scale of it. He even tried to make excuses for her behaviour, but he could see I didn't believe a word of it so we left it alone.

"It was obvious the situation couldn't last. Something had to happen. To those of us on the fringe it was like an unexploded bomb ticking away. Often, while Herbert was at work, she was posing around the island in a white Fiat sports coupe he'd bought her, and having afternoon sex romps on secluded beaches, and quiet hotels, with any man who took her fancy. Only the locations weren't always secluded or quiet. She was seen quite frequently, once actually in action, so to speak, in the sand up near Marfa Point. A couple of her friends saw her while looking for a picnic spot. Know what? She even waved to them! That incident may even have been the last straw for soon after that, without any warning, Herbert left."

"Hardly a surprise," I ventured. "Most men would have left her sooner."

Philip was shaking his head. "No, I don't mean he just left

her. He left the island completely. Abandoned her without saying a word or even leaving a note. Turned out he'd been plotting it all for weeks. Without anyone knowing he'd used his contacts to get a new job in Belize. It was the first move in an act of revenge which he later described to me as 'justifiable punishment.'

"The day after he left, and while she was still wondering if he'd merely stayed overnight with friends, his solicitors served divorce papers on her. It was incontestable. He had all the evidence. He'd hired a detective to follow her, get statements, even take some steamy photos of her in action in a hotel room she used regularly. Hidden camera, so she never knew. Copies were enclosed with the divorce papers."

"Neat move," I said, by now hooked into a story which at first had seemed entirely mundane.

"More to come," said Philip. "That was just the beginning. I was able to learn much of what happened when Herbert telephoned me a few months later. He got in touch because he found he'd still got some books I had loaned him and wanted to know if he should send them on. I told him to keep them, but we got chatting and he started to open up. I think he wanted someone to know that he hadn't been taken for a complete fool, that his eyes had been wide open to it all. He'd just opted, in his unassuming, insular way, to go for revenge rather than confrontation. That was when he corrected me when I referred to it as revenge. 'Not at all,' he insisted. 'I was merely metering out justifiable punishment.'

"So what happened to her?" I asked. "What did she do?"

"Well, initially, she was in shock. She just hadn't expected Herbert to react at all, let alone so drastically. She had been carrying on for months and he had seemed tolerant of it, so when he did make his move it was utterly unexpected. She had evidently never heard of the worm turning.

"The day after the divorce papers were served she received notification that the lease was up on their house and that she had just a month to move out.

"She had no money at all. Herbert had always paid the bills and bought her everything she wanted. She had her own bank account, of course, but her only income was a pocket-money allowance transferred from Herbert's account once a month. When she contacted the bank she found that his account had been closed and her allowance cancelled.

"At this stage she wasn't too worried. She knew she could sell the expensive sports car he'd bought her. But when she took it back to the dealer she learned it was only leased and the next payment was overdue.

"Next step was to sell the furniture, but that didn't fetch much, just enough to tide her over for a couple of weeks. She had to move out of their lovely beachside villa up the coast to a cheap apartment in a rough part of Valetta, and was forced to take a job as a waitress. She had no qualifications for anything better.

"There were no friends to help her, not among the women anyway. She had been ostracised for quite a while. A few of them had even told her to her face exactly what they thought of her, but it made no difference. She didn't care what they thought. It was only mens' opinions which mattered to her. Trouble was, she didn't know men as well as she thought she did. She still felt it was only a matter of time before one of her boyfriends set her up in a new apartment, maybe left his wife for her. But Malta is a small place, and the scandal, for that's what it was in those days, took its toll. The married men retreated fast, and those that weren't backed off too. They'd already had her and now she was potential trouble - financial or emotional. Either way, she was bad news."

"Why didn't she go back to Malaysia? There must have been someone who could send her the fare."

"There wasn't. Remember, she was an orphan, a fact Herbert hadn't overlooked. No family, and the friends she had had years earlier were in the same trap she had been in. They were just working girls struggling to survive. How else do you think Herbert was able to get a beautiful young wife so easily?"

"So what did she do? Someone must have come to her rescue. Someone always does when it's a beautiful girl."

Philip slowly drained his champagne glass, unwittingly heightening the tension. I don't mind admitting I was now caught up in it all, and anxious to know the fate of this dazzling but destructively stupid young woman.

"She was marooned in Malta, and it might as well have been the North Pole for all the chance she had of getting off the island," said Philip. "She was barely earning enough to get by, with no chance of saving for an air ticket. So there was only one thing she could do, if you know what I mean."

"Prostitution?"

"Not quite, but as close as you can get. Just months earlier she had the pick of the men on the island, now it was any man who might show his gratitude with a bit of cash. She didn't actually work the streets, but she did target men in hotel bars. In fact, that's when she approached me."

"You?"

Philip was amused at my aghast expression and incredulous tone. "But you had been a close friend of Herbert," I said.

"Exactly. I think that's why she came to see me. She was in tears, sobbing like a child. Said she was in debt, owed three months rent, had been told to get out. It was painful to see her so desperate, so pleading. Then she just came out with it - offered me sex if I'd pay off her back-rent."

"And...?"

"What do you think? She was a very attractive, very vulnerable woman. I had so often envied the men who had been with her that, I have to admit, I dispensed with any moral considerations. It was a great night, believe me."

"I'll bet it was!" I'd just never have believed it of Philip. Not in those circumstances, anyway.

"Next day, I suppose inevitably, I felt very bad about it. Totally ashamed. Couldn't look her in the eye at breakfast. I imagine that's why I then did what I did. I settled her debts and bought her a one-way air ticket to London, which was where she wanted to go. I took her to the airport, waved her off, and that was the last I saw of her."

"So you've no idea what became of her?"

"I do as a matter of fact. A year or so later, when I was back in the UK, I was in a dentist's waiting room and I picked up one of those Hello-type magazines. And there she was on the cover - glamourous society wedding. Lots of pictures of the happy couple."

"That sort invariably manage to land on their feet," I said. "I'll bet she targeted him too."

"Why don't you ask her for yourself," said Philip, grinning. "I think she's on her way over to see us."

I looked up. Our hostess, the entrancing Lady M—- was weaving elegantly between the chatting clusters and coming straight for us. The clingy turquoise dress had been chosen to emphasis her still-perfect shape, and her dark hair was swept up and pinned with a crescent emerald clip.

She appeared to be smiling, but it was just her mouth that

gave that appearance. The corners lifted high, the neat, perfect teeth shone against the dark red lipstick, giving an instant welcoming impression. But I was looking directly into her eyes. There was nothing behind the outward glisten. Nothing at all. They were the deadest eyes I ever saw on anyone still alive.

Stepping between us she took us by the hand and steered us towards the other guests. "I've been watching you two," she said reprovingly. "You haven't moved from that sofa all evening. You must meet some people. I'll introduce you."

She left us with a couple of financial advisors and their meek and silent wives. We extracted ourselves after five polite but frustrating minutes and took refuge behind some tropical shrubbery in huge blue-glazed pots.

"She's quite something, isn't she?" said Philip, well aware of the impact his little bombshell had had on me. "And before you ask, she didn't recognise me. Why should she? It was 20 years ago. I was four stone lighter and had a full head of hair then."

We were both peering through the foliage, watching her on her programmed mission to meet and greet everyone, a darting vision in turquoise, her smile set to maximum radiance, the same few phrases slipping from the full and glossy lips.

I realised, quite suddenly, that I felt very sad, not for her, but for myself and what had seemed so important in my pathetic little world. Like getting even with Jordan.

Any desire for even the most minor revenge had evaporated, become utterly pointless, too small of consequence to even register when compared to the shocking raw reality of someone else's life.

I had just witnessed an empty woman giving a pleasureless mechanical performance. In its own way it was a bizarre form of prostitution, the calculated sale of mind and spirit for status, money, but above all, security. I saw a forlorn and lonely woman, bereft of spirit, devoid of passion, living a captive life with a tired old man, hating it yet terrified of losing it.

Philip, when I confided my theory later, felt I was reading too much into it all. "You're in marketing, not psychology," he cautioned.

But then he hadn't seen her eyes close up, like I had. Those haunting, stone-dead eyes. I knew that years earlier, on that sultry Mediterranean island, Herbert Gardner, in a chillingly clinical act of revenge had not just taken away her home, her car and her confidence. He had also taken her soul.